Henry Brooke

The Poetical Works by Henry Brooke

Vol. III

Henry Brooke

The Poetical Works by Henry Brooke
Vol. III

ISBN/EAN: 9783744680974

Printed in Europe, USA, Canada, Australia, Japan

Cover: Foto ©Andreas Hilbeck / pixelio.de

More available books at **www.hansebooks.com**

THE
POETICAL WORKS

OF

HENRY BROOKE, Esq.

AUTHOR OF GUSTAVUS VASA, FOOL OF QUALITY, &c.

IN FOUR VOLUMES OCTAVO.

Revised and corrected by the

ORIGINAL MANUSCRIPT;

WITH A

PORTRAIT OF THE AUTHOR,

AND HIS

LIFE.

By MISS *BROOKE.*

THE THIRD EDITION.

VOL. III.

DUBLIN;

PRINTED FOR THE *EDITOR.*

1792.

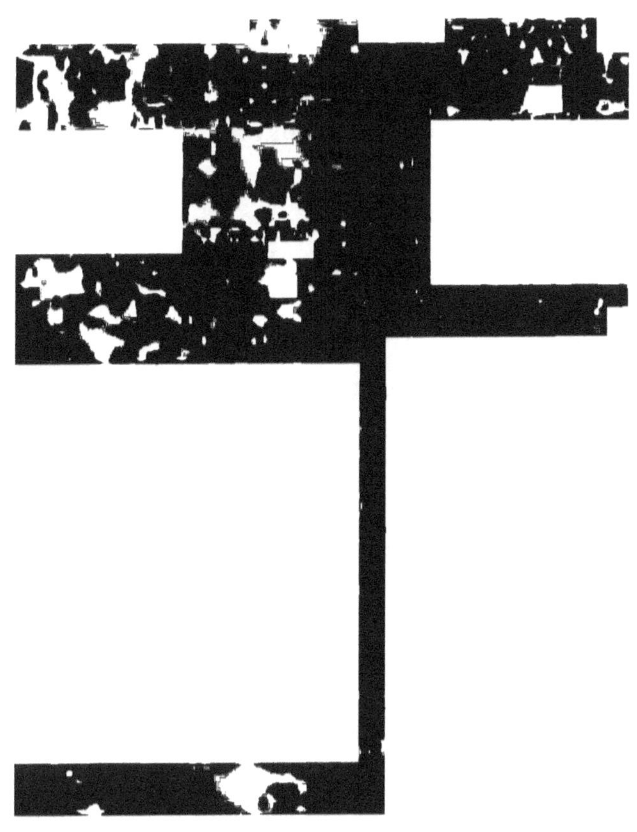

PERSONS.

MAHOMET, the IMPOSTOR.

ZAPHNA,
CAAB,
HERCIDES, } Adherents to MAHOMET.
OMAR,

SOPHEIAN, Prince of MECCA.

CALED, his Friend.

PALMYRA, { Daughter of MAHOMET, and Captive of SOPHEIAN.

SCENE, MECCA.

Í M P O S T O R.

A C T I.

S C E N E I. The Palace.

S OPHEIAN and Caled.

SOPH. NOW, by the foul of our great father
               Ifhmael,
This is not faith, but wonderful conviction.
Soft—let me fum thy reafons in my foul—
" No GODS," thou fayft, " but ONE; One
           Power Supreme,
" Parent of nature! And, from him, one man,
" Parent of human kind, in whom united
" Man grows to man, and ftill the focial eye,
" In every face it meets, falutes a brother!
" And then the fall of that unhappy parent,
" Sunk from his Paradife with all his fons,
" And caft into a world of guilt and pain;
" From whence reftored, this GODHEAD in the
           breaft,
" Supports our frailty through the mortal war,
" That fenfe doth wage with virtue."

B 2

CAL.

CAL. True, my lord—
This argues to the heart.

SOPH. It does, my CALED!
Had man ne'er fallen, he had no sense of evil;
No sense of good, if not redeemed—'tis manifest!
This solves the great ænigma of our natures;
And, through the dusky maze of Providence,
Leads forth to light. By outward revelation,
Heaven answers to the truths revealed within—
I feel their sacred force; and reason comes
But as a second witness to confirm them.

CAL. Nor reason only—universal nature
Hath given authentic credence to her Lord,
And vouch'd the word of our Eternal Prophet.
Bards sung his future day; and ancient seers,
Rapt through succeeding centuries, foretold
The story of his time—To greet his birth,
Angelic choirs made jubilee on earth—
Before him shrunk the powers of hell—The sea
Smooth'd at his bidding, and the storm was hush'd
Attentive to his voice—At his approach,
The lame sprung forward, and the blind man
            gazed
With new-created organs!

SOPH. Yet, my friend,
Even all his mighty works to me import,
But as they greatly serve to authorize
The mightier words he utter'd—As the eye
Bears witness to the light, or the charm'd ear
To tuneful undulation; so my heart
Strikes unison to his great Law of Love,

And

And proves their fource the fame—I own his miffion,
And all my country's gods fall down defore him.
    Cal. Then let thy faith inftruct thee to contemn
This modern fable—this God Mahomet,
Who boafts the attribute of power, yet wars
With wifdom, as with mercy.
    Soph.   O the robber !
The curft impoftor, whofe all fenfual heaven
Is fix'd in luft ; who claims his dire apoftlefhip
By blood and devaftation !—Sayft thou, Caled,
Oppofe him!—yes, the root of our antipathy
Sinks to the center, and its future growth
Muft reach through all eternity.
    Cal.   Alas!
That ftarting tear implies a mournful meaning.
Soph. O Caled, friend, thou feeft a lonely
              man,
Stript like a withering cedar on the hills ;
And fhorn of every branch that once adorn'd him.
Bitter remembrance !—Stranger as thou art
In fair Arabia, haply thou haft heard
Of Ommia's royal houfe.
    Cal. I have, my lord.
    Soph.   I'll tell thee then—Of that thrice noble
              houfe,
We were two brothers, Jofeph and myfelf,
The laft furviving heirs, twinn'd in one womb,
As nature had foreclofed our bond of amity,
Made perfect e'er election. I, the elder ;

B 3

But

But no precedence claiming, in my brother,
As in a dearer felf, I liv'd, we grew,
Link'd through our wanton years, each will and wifh
As a new rivet to our clofing fouls,
That mock'd at feparation.—Doft thou liften ?—

 CAL. Ev'n as the breathlefs night, when tuneful
    Philomel
Doth lift her fong to filence.

 SOPH. Mark me, then—
Ere we attain'd the ripening noon of life,
Two maidens of the princely tribe of Joctan,
Yet in the morn of their unveiling beauty,
Engag'd our love ; Almeydab and Mamuna.
Blefs'd to our wifh, we fued, prevail'd, and
    wedded ;
I to Almeydab, to Mamuna Jofeph ;
Nor hence divided, but as num'rous links,
More ftrong and more enfolded—Do'ft remember ?

 CAL. Not a word fallen.

 SOPH. Almeydab, at the firft,
Promis'd no heir ; but our belov'd Mamuna
Brought forth a fon, the blooming Moawias,
And gave him to our arms, welcome and dear
To me, as to my brother ; dear as though
My own Almeydab's gift. Thus, CALED, thus,
The human feelings, all the charities,
That knit the focial family of man,
Were join'd to make me bleft——to make me
  wretched !
           CAL.

CAL. Alas!

SOPH. Doſt ſay?—I ſee thy nature's touch'd.

CAL. No, my good lord—a ſhort lived weak-
    neſs in me;
I pray, proceed.

SOPH. O CALED, now my tale
Muſt turn to tragic! for our loved Mamuna,
Burſting the circle of that fond ſociety,
Sicken'd and died—around her memory,
As ſtatues for her tomb, ſadly we ſat,
Converſing by our tears.   My Joſeph thence—
Thence mine no more—acquired I know not what
Of diſtant gloom; grew alien to himſelf,
To me, and to the world—then diſappear'd,
Made all ſearch vain, and tore me from myſelf.

CAL. O, moſt unkind!—no doubt, ſome deep
    occaſion—

SOPH. None given by me.

CAL. What, none?

SOPH. So judge me, Heaven!—
No, not in thought—It was ſurmiſed indeed—

CAL. What?

SOPH. No matter what—I would not taſk his
    memory—

CAL. Nay—pray you—

SOPH. 'Twas ſurmiſed, the bile of melancholy
Had ſeiz'd his better man, engendering thoughts
Foreign and crude—tending, I know not how,
To devious luſt, and thirſt of empire.

CAL. Heavens!—
Surmiſed, by whom?

B 4

SOPH.

Soph. A faithful wretch he was—
Hercides !—a kind inmate to us both,
An ancient of our houſe—
    Cal. Said he of luſt ?
    Soph. Even of my wife and ſceptre.
    Cal. O the powers !
    Soph. Thou ſeem'ſt concern'd—
    Cal. O pity, that ſuch brothers—
Pity, that villainy—that two ſuch brothers !—
Pray, to your ſtory.—
    Soph. To me and to Almeydab thus forſaken,
Young Moawias was an only ſolace,
A pleaſant, yet a mournful monitor
Of what his parents were—At length, our ſtorm
Of grief ſubſided ; and my kind Almeydab
Became the mother of a recent happineſs,
Even of a daughter fair : ſo, all again
Was well, as hope might look for in the lots
Of mortal diſpenſation—O, too well !—
For ſo Heaven deem'd—'Twas then that Mahomet
Firſt dared to broach his fable here in public.
With indignation fired, through Mecca's gates
I chaſed the fell impoſtor, who, belike,
Although his godhead then was in its infancy,
Retained his dark abettors even in Mecca :
For, like a wolf, the midnight prowler came,
In my own palace caught my hour of abſence,
Murder'd my babes, and on my nuptial couch
Seiz'd my ſole bliſs, my loved, my loſt Almeydab!
    Cal. Ha ! ſure he durſt not—
    Soph. Thanks to the bleſt protectreſs of my
       honour !—

Yes,

Yes, the infernal fatyr !—but Almeydab
Broke from his grafp ; and where the cafement looks
Upon the flint beneath—a fearful fteep !—
Headlong fhe dafh'd her beauties, and expir'd
A victim to her virtue!
    Cal. O Sopheian !—
Thy cup of forrow hath indeed been bitter,
And thou haft drank it largely.
    Soph. Since that hour,
I walk the world, as in a wildernefs—
No focial face to cheer ! All nature feems
As one unvaried blank, upon whofe leaf
No comfort can be written—fave of vengeance;
And now 'tis in my grafp.
    Cal. On Mahomet ?—what vengeance ?
    Soph. As near to Yathreb's foreft on a day
I led fome troops, a fquadron croft my eye,
Who bore the tyrant's ftandard : we engag'd,
And conqueft crown'd my arms. Among the captives
There was a maid, whofe lovlinefs difgrac'd
The coftly gems fhe wore ; and but that memory
Still holds Almeydab to my fight, this ftranger
Might ftand unrival'd forth. Three waining moons
She lies my pris'ner, tho' in filken bondage ;
But, yefternoon, a flave betray'd her birth,
And fhews her for the daughter of the tyrant.
    Cal. Of Mahomet ?

Soph.

Soph. Of him—Think what should follow!

Cal. In truth I am to seek—

Soph. Just retribution ——
Revenge might follow!—but Sopheian's hand,
Sopheian's heart forbids it!—Yes, my Caled;
Yes, tho' I knew her for the tyrant's offspring,
A kind of soft enchantment stole upon me ;
Some secret power, unweeting, drew my steps,
To gaze upon her with a parent's fondness.
Then, as she look'd and spoke, my tears swell'd up-
　　　　ward—.
And oft with pain I've check'd these aged arms,
That long'd to clasp her with a chaste embrace.
But see, she comes !—observe her near, my Caled.

Cal. To sight she is a wonder.

S C E N E II.

To them Palmyra.

Pal. Fair morning to my lord ! May Heaven,
　　　each day,
With early gratitude expand my heart—
Thus give me to approach, in humble duty,
And pour my thanks before you !

Soph. Why, Palmyra!—
Sit thy chains light ?

Pal. As on a fluttering bird,
Cag'd only to be cherish'd—such kind cares

As suit the hovering goodness of a father,
Have sooth'd my griefs, and made my bonds a
          blessing.
     Soph. Not such the measure, which thy father
          gave
To my unhappy children !—
     Pal. Ha !—my father ?
     Soph. Yes—Mahomet !
     Pal. Nay, then, I am betray'd ;
And mercy shall no longer know Palmyra.
     Soph. Alas, fair innocent ! though I should plant
Thy sufferings thick as grain, what fruits would
          grow ?
My joys must still lie fallow—Will thy blood
Make the cold tomb conceive, the grave to quicken,
And yield Almeydab back—give back my babe,
My young Ayetia to my arms ? O, never !—
My comforts, with my wife and children, lie
Too deep interr'd, and will return no more.—
Dismiss thy fears, thou art guiltless of my griefs—
From other hands than mine, my child, expect
Afflictions when they fall.
     Pal. Thus, grateful, as to Heaven, I bend with
          praises—   [Kneels.
For O, whate'er my different faith may dictate,
My heart informs, that, of that Heaven, you are
The most excelling pattern ! Do not think
Your slave depraved from truth ; truth sits secure
Within my soul, and mocks the reach of bondage !
Hence am I free to tell you, that my heart
Ne'er felt like awful love, like tender reverence,

                                        Not

Not for my proper father—Yet—my lord,
There is a caufe—there is a caufe, my lord!—
   Soph. O, rife, fweet maid! command, nay tafk
        my power—
'Tis thine to its extent.
   Pal. Unhappy I,
Who, now profefs'd the daughter of your foe,
Muft ftir your foul, by my detefted fight,
To grievous recollection; a dire monitor
Of the fad fource from whence your loffes fpring,
Fretting your fmootheft hour!—Ah, royal fir,
There's yet a bafhful caufe—elfe, witnefs Heaven!
No choice of mine to part—Return me, then,
Reftore me to my kindred; take, in lieu,
Cities and fcepter'd nations—Mahomet
Weighs not the ranfom by my little worth,
But by his large affection—then return me,
Reftore me to——O fir!—
   Soph. Unkind Palmyra!—
Thy fire hath ftore of wives and little ones;
Me he bereaved of all—and one for all,
I only covet one from his abundance.
Henceforth be thou my child—that Power, who fees
And winds the fecret fprings of human paffions,
He knows we muft not part—'tis death alone,
The laft fad hour, fhall tear thee from Sopheian!

Enter a Messenger.

   Mess. My lord, the country weftward, for fome
      leagues,

Is

Is all in motion. Through Moradia's plain,
Men hurry flocks and herds; their wives and
        children
Scream in the rear, or goad their camels on,
Laden with ftuffs of price, or houfehold lumber,
Caught up in hafte; all fpeeding toward the city.
    SOPH. Whence the alarm?
    MESS. 'Tis faid, that MAHOMET—
    SOPH. Sayft thou, that MAHOMET?—
    MESS. Yea, my good lord, attended by the
        nations,
An army as the fands unnumber'd, comes,
To add your Mecca to his length of conqueft.
    SOPH. Where be our treacherous fcouts? How
        comes it thus,
That notice flacks of duty?—Fly—away—
Send me the captain of the watch—Good CALED,
Speed to the feveral nobles of the city,
And bid them to the fenate; fay, ourfelf
Will hafte to join them—Speed, my friend!
                                    [Exit CALED.
Who waits?—

            Enter CAPTAIN of the Watch.

Captain, thy truft is great; fo is our confidence,
Alike repofing on thy faith and valour.
Set up a double watch on Uzza's tower;
See our gates clofed; and, on the inftant, cull
A chofen band for the patrole—Good captain,
Walk thou the round in perfon; if thou feeft
A face that catches at fufpicion, feize,
And bring him to our prefence.   [Exit CAPTAIN.

2   Enter

Enter another Messenger.

Now—what's the tidings?
  MESS. MAHOMET, my lord,
Greets you by his ambaſſador.
  SOPH. Conduct him—
Thou mayſt retire, my child; whate'er arrives,
Thou ſhalt partake it truely.   [Exit PALMYRA.

SCENE III.

SOPHEIAN alone.

So, now 'tis come—thy will, Omnipotence!
For thou doſt rule the hour, wherein SOPHEIAN,
Or his great foe, muſt fall!—If human juſtice
Might now decide—but O, 'tis weak, 'tis ſhallow—
Thy judgments ſink an infinite beneath,
And mock the mortal fathom!—
He comes, the ambaſſador—ha! on my credence,
And ſhews a preſence, that, from ruder ears,
Might well beſpeak his hearing!

SCENE IV.

To SOPHEIAN, ZAPHNA.

ZAPH. Thus Heaven's interpreter, to great
    SOPHEIAN,
Sends peace, forerunning peace.
  SOPH. I ſee his policy—
Where ſuch angelic envoys lead his miſſion,

He

He would infinuate that a god muft follow.
What would this new divinity ?

Zaph. My lord,
Spare mockery !—To any, fave Sopheian,
We fhould reply in thunder—but, to you,
Soft as the fouthern breeze !—To you, great
    Mahomet
Sends invitation, unity of fouls,
And greeting, given as to a fecond fon
Of high appointing Heaven !—He bids you fhare
Dominion, and the glorious toils that wait
The reformation of the world, the fellowfhip
Of faith, and heavenly miffion—

Soph. Faith, what faith ?—
Miffion from whom ?—

Zaph. From that Omnipotence,
Whofe power invefts him to the darken'd world.
As when fome comet, with portentous blaze,
Springs from the weft, and flames around the
    globe;
So moves the fword of our illuftrious Prophet,
Sufpended o'er the nations !

Soph. Is terror then the only attribute
That cloaths your Prophet ?—Speak, what won-
    ders wait him ?
Will the dead hear his voice, will nature bend
Obfequious to his bidding ? By what feal
Doth Heaven atteft his embaffy ?

Zaph. By conqueft !

Soph. So earthquakes yawn, to fwallow na-
    tions up;
Volcanos

Volcanos rage, and wasting plagues advance,
Commission'd to destruction!

 Zaph. Mahomet
Will best resolve those doubts—but, for the present,
He bids your gates unfold to his approach,
And that Sopheian meet his terms of love
With answering amity.

 Soph. Bear back his greeting;
And tell the robber, that Sopheian's answer
Lies in his sword.

 Zaph. You have a captive.

 Soph. True.

 Zaph. A fair one.

 Soph. So I think her.

 Zaph. What's her ransom?

 Soph. I weigh not worth with gold—to me she seems
Above all price; and Mahomet must find
New worlds to conquer, 'ere he can redeem her.

 Zaph. That reverend form—patience!—thou canst not mean—
Say, by what right thou darest to detain her?

 Soph. Even by that right, young man, by which your Prophet
Claims universal monarchy—by conquest!—

 Zaph. Know you her birth?—know you her merits?

 Soph. Yes——
She is your Sultan's daughter, and my slave—

    [Zaphna puts his hand to his sword.

What wouldst thou, boy? Shall I not use my slave?
Hath not your pious Mahomet his Haram,

       Where,

Where, while on earth, he antedates his heaven,
In all the lufts of his luxuriant riots?
    Zaph. You would not—durft not!—But I'm
        cool again—
Did not the law of nations—
    Soph. O, 'tis well—
I like thy fpirit, child ; and, though I hold her
Prized as my realm, I do approve thee yet
A mate to her beft worth.
    Zaph. You mock your fervant.
    Soph. No, by my life !
    Zaph. O fir, how low, how humbled,
The frail, rafh, heady thing, this toy of youth,
When fhown, and fhrunk in your fuperior prefence!
But, by that awful virtue, I conjure you,
Which guards your form, and opens in your afpect,
Do not defpife my tears—Is fhe not ?—O——
    Soph. Yes, by my honour, I do think her pure,
Even as the rofe of fpring, whofe folded bloom
Ne'er open'd to the breeze.
    Zaph. When time will ferve,
My life fhall thank you for it—O Sopheian !
Let me, now, ftep a minifter of peace,
Between your virtue and our conquering Prophet ;
Before whofe power, the kingdoms of the earth
Bend like the bladed harveft !—At his touch,
Your walls muft crumble, and your palaces
Sink to the pavement—Grant him but a con-
        ference.
    Soph. Never.
    Zaph. Then thus he fpeaks his laft decree—
If not the peaceful terms of pious friendfhip,

Vol. III.   C   Nor

Nor yet the dread of our impending arm,
Can bend the flinty temper of SOPHEIAN;
If not the wealth of rifled provinces,
Can bribe him to refign PALMYRA—then,
    SOPH. Then—what muft follow?
    ZAPH. Bid him, then, beware
The fate of his own children!
    SOPH. Amazement!
What children, fayft thou?
    ZAPH. Truft me, fir,
He vows, by all the fanctities of Heaven,
They both are living.
    SOPH. Living?—faid you, living?
My children!—both my children!—where?—
        O miracle!—
Indulgent powers!—What country?—have you
        feen them?
My fon and daughter too?—Alas—perhaps
Expofed to wretchednefs, oppreft with bondage!—
Inform me, youth—my children, my dear infants!—
    ZAPH. Ye powers, how kindred are the foft
        delights,
That flow from nature's feelings!—Sacred fir,
'Tis fure your children are moft fafe—the reft
Will be declared at meeting.
    SOPH. Hafte, kind youth—
Yes, we may meet—the fafety of my little ones
Hath whiten'd half his crimes—But mark me well,
For yet I truft not to your Prophet's faith,
Or his high boafted fable—bid his army
Repofe beyond the plain; he may, in perfon,
Enter with due attendance, and my honour

With

With equal hoftages fhall be impawn'd,
For his return in fafety.
   Zaph. Well, I truft,
Your terms fhall meet acceptance.
   Soph. Further yet—
To fhew, brave youth, the paffion thou'ft betray'd
For our fair captive, moves no jealous bearing;
Palmyra fhall prepare for thy return,
And in my palace wait a private hearing.
   Zaph. All thanks are poor—O, may your eyes,
       with joy,
From thofe, your loft and found, your twice born
       infants,
Behold a line of princes! May you live
Till honour can admit of no increafe,
And years difmifs you to the grave in peace!
                [Exeunt.

END OF THE FIRST ACT.

A C T   II.

SCENE I. The PALACE.

PALMYRA and ZAPHNA meet.

ZAPH. PALMYRA!—
PAL.   ZAPHNA !—
   ZAPH. Do I hear that voice ?—
Do I then hold thee ? gaze upon thofe eyes,
That open their returning dawn upon me ?—
O my life's life !—'twas a long night of abfence,
And bufied in fuch dreams of dire diftraction,
As thus to fee thee could alone compenfate—
Thus, thus to wake in blifs !—
   PAL. My love, my ZAPHNA !
My fears for you were twice my own diftrefs ;
For here, within, a friend of your's was bufy,
Who guefs'd your pains, and number'd all your
        fufferings.
   ZAPH. Would you believe I could furvive in
        pangs,
Greater than what expiring wretches feel
In the laft ftruggle, when the foul is parting ?
And yet, I know not how, fome ftrengthening power
Whifper'd a hope, and bid your ZAPHNA live.

PAL.

PAL. Bleſt be that power, for ſure he meant
    this meeting!
And, O my ZAPHNA, were my choice conſulted,
Better to die a thouſand deaths together,
Than live to part again.

    ZAPH. Part?—no, PALMYRA!—
That hope makes all my happineſs on earth,
In death my comfort, and my heaven hereafter.
Well did the faith of thy foreſeeing father,
Fill up his bleſt eternity with love—
Then, as my fair PALMYRA ſtood before him,
He caught the viſion of celeſtial beauty,
And drew his future paradiſe from thee!

    PAL. Delightful flattery!—And yet, my ZAPHNA!
Who knows but Heaven, indulgent to my wiſhes,
May, in the region of exalted charms,
Improve the pittance of PALMYRA's beauty,
And make me worthy thy immortal paſſion?
But tell me, haſt thou ſeen SOPHEIAN?—Say,
Will he reſtore me to my wonted happineſs,
Once more to liberty, to love, and ZAPHNA?

    ZAPH. So ſtands my hope—the reverend ſire
    conſents
To render back thy beauties, in exchange
For his own children.

    PAL. Are they living, then?
O the good man!—Methinks I ſee their meeting—
The royal parent, in his tears majeſtick,
Suſpended o'er his children; and the joy,
The extaſy, my ZAPHNA, of thoſe orphans,
Reſtored to ſuch a father!

C 3

ZAPH.

ZAPH. Ah—our fouls—
How much the fame! thy very thoughts are mine
And my heart melts with my PALMYRA's foftnefs.
A kindred feeling too—myfelf an orphan,
Dropt, as the Prophet faith, amid the ftorm
Of fome fack'd town, the child of war and chance,
Not worth a further fearch; and yet afpiring
To thee, bright daughter of the Dawn of Truth—
Star of that Heaven, who conftitutes thy fire
The Angel of his word!

    PAL. Thou art, my ZAPHNA,
Sufficient to thyfelf; the mighty heir
Of thy own virtues, feated firm and high
O'er all that's built upon the failing props
Of birth and empire!—Art thou not the arm
Of my great fire, Heaven's fubftituted bolt,
Wherewith our Prophet ftrikes the proftrate world?

    ZAPH. There is a fear—there is a fear, PAL-
      MYRA!—
The thought hath open'd fuch a gulph before me,
That my mind, plunging down her own conception,
Pre-occupies perdition.—

    PAL. What's fo high,
Whereto my hero may not lift his hope?—
What has he, then, to fear?

    ZAPH. Returning late,
From Tabuc, Dauman, Eyla, by my arms
Subdued—all flufh'd, and rapid on my way,
The Prophet met me; caught me to his breaft;
And, ere I bow'd myfelf to due proftration,
" ZAPHNA," he cried, " my ZAPHNA, by that
      power

               " Who

‘ Who leads the leaders of our hoſt ! demand,
“ And take thy wiſh.”—As ſudden, I replied—
“ Palmyra is the daughter of our Prophet !”—
I ſpoke, and ſought the earth—Deep ſilence follow’d,
When to my lifted eye, his cheek, all pale,
Uſurp’d a tranſient ſmile to ſmooth his anſwer :
I ſee,” he cry’d, “ I ſee that hour at hand,
“ Wherein thou wilt unthread this raſh requeſt,
“ And flee whom now thou followeſt !”
 Pal.. Ah, undone !
If Zaphna can be doom’d to ſuch a treaſon.
 Zaph. Forbear, my love !—to me would’ſt thou
  . impute—
Urge not to frenzy—To thy other creatures
Give other bleſſings, Heaven ! thou know’ſt that
  Zaphna
Can taſte but one—In her, as in the grave,
Is every ſenſe abſorb’d—to my Palmyra,
To this ſole point, whate’er I build for hope,
Here or hereafter, comes—ſap me this prop,
Heaven, earth, and all, are hurried from exiſtence,
And Zaphna ſinks for ever !
 Pal. Then, what more ?
Since that our hearts are ratified above,
Ere aught below ſhould wreſt the ſacred knot,
I’d prove a parent to my own affections,
And give where Heaven appoints.
 Zaph. Wilt ſeal that compact ? . .
          Pal.

PAL. Yes.
ZAPH. Nearly ?   [Opens his arms.
PAL. Dearly feal it !   [They embrace:
ZAPH. O the rapture !—
I doubt my time—the Prophet's on his way—
He will'd me to attend him ere his entrance,
And thence return the hoftage of his faith
To Mecca's chief.
    PAL. What here ?
    ZAPH. To thee, my love !
    PAL. Let it be foon, my ZAPHNA.
    ZAPH. Soul of my foul, ev'n wing'd by my
        own wifhes !
Adieu——
    PAL. May the good angels quit all other charge,
To take thee to their keeping.   [Exeunt feverally:

SCENE II.

A Street in Mecca.

MAHOMET enters crowned, and carried in a trium-
    phal chariot by feveral flaves, his captains, &c.
    attending. The Mob divide, and, as he advances,
    range on each fide of the ftage, and fall proftrate.

    MAHO. People of Mecca, rife !—your day is
        come,
Ye favour'd of the Heavens—my chofen brothers—
                                            Laft

Laſt call'd, yet firſt regarded!—ſee ye not,
As at the prayer of our primæval ſire,
Of Adam, firſt of men, your Caaba,
Your temple, once of golden architrave,
Dropt by the wondring ſtars in ſheets of light,
Fram'd by angelic builders—ſee ye not
Like glory now deſcending!—Long in night,
More dark and blacken'd by the guilt of man,
Did Mecca lie entranced, even from the flood,
Wherein her ſacred temple was o'erthrown,
With nature ſuffering wreck—till Abraham,
Great father of our father Iſhmael,
Directed by a ſtar, the holy Sheckinah,
As twilight glimmering through a duſky world,
Here built again your ſacred fane, reſtored
Of groſs materials—true—but more debaſed,
By future profanation—pagods foul,
The abomination of the times!—Yet, Mecca!
Ariſe as from the tomb—thou favourite city,
Ariſe as from the tomb!—Thy hour is come,
When this, thy hallow'd temple, ſhall be cloath'd
With more than priſtine glory!—Toward the ſun,
As when the Perſians eaſtward bend their heads
To his upriſing beam, ſo, turn'd to thee,
And to thy Caaba, the nations round,
Eaſt, weſt, and north, and ſouth, a proſtrate world,
Shall bend the diſtant knee!—Behold—the light,
The light is come upon ye—born by me,
Heaven's preſent Angel!—
The Mob ſhout, and cry, A Mahomet! a Mahomet!
a Prophet! a preſent Prophet! and again fall proſtrate.

SCENE

SCENE IV.

Enter Sopheian.

Soph. O profanation!—Hell, thy minifter
Ufurping godhead, and proftration due
But to the higheft !—Can I bear it ?—Shall aught
That's mortal, fway to this ?—My children, par-
  don !—
You are but two—thefe thoufands, thefe feduced,
My people, and my children too—Away,
Conforming bafenefs ! duty, to thy talk—
Let Heaven provide events !
   Mahomet defcends from his throne and advances
    toward Sopheian.
  Maho. Hail to the prince of Mecca ! thrice
   all hail
To Heaven's appointed, to our future Prophet,
Affumed to facred miniftry, the feal
And brother of our word !
  Soph. Away, impoftor !
Confufion to thy greeting !—Is it thus
Thou didft propofe to treat ? by fap and lure,
Thou fubtle miner ? didft thou hope, vain man !
I'd barter truth for treafon ?—never, never !—
I will not fet my fubjects to the fale,
Sons of my truft, for whom my years have travail'd !
Out of my realm, thou fcepter'd vagrant—hence !
  Maho. Stop, ftop the bolt, ye ready minifters !
Nor ftrike miftaking blafphemy—O ftop,
I do arreft your arm !—Know you not, then,
That Heaven hath fteel'd the heart of this his
  chofen,

In

In him to fhew the wonders of his might,
By quick converfion ?—
   Soph. O wily ferpent !—but I'll crofs thy wind-
      ings,
Even in their proper maze—My gentle people !
Lift not to this bad man—I am like yourfelves,
Simple and plain, and of fuch level fenfe
As Heaven gives honefty.—This arch-deceiver
Doth fay he's from above ; fo you, or I,
Might fay with equal right—who faw him go,
Or come from thence ? If this is Heaven's am-
      baffador,
Afk him for his credentials—Who fo fimple,
To give the flighteft value of his purfe,
Lefs the rich worth of his eternal faith,
Upon a wordy tale, no character
No token vouching ?—Bid the juggler fhew,
At leaft, fome tricks, fome flightings of his art,
To duft our eye of reafon.
   Maho. The deep Serene moves not at idle breath;
Nor will Heaven deign, by frolic, to indulge
The wantonnefs of man.   His Prophets come,
Each vefted in the proper attribute
That doth atteft his miffion.   Noah fo
Came cloath'd in juftice, and in clemency
The fon of Amram ; Solomon in wifdom !
But, vefted in the wonders of his power,
The laft and mightieft, I !
   Soph. His power !—wherein expreft ?
   Maho. The world hath felt the lightning of my
      eye,
And thunder of my arm !
Soph.

Soph. Such was the claim of Ammon's boast-
    ed fon ;
Such Nero's, when he ript his mother's entrails,
And laughing fet his native Rome on fire ;
Prophets and plagues alike !—Bend, bend, my
    people !
Kneel to this peftilence, this fiend fent forth
To blaft fair nature.—Heaven ! thy worfhippers
Do thank thee for creation—who is, then,
This image of thy power revers'd ? his tafk
To uncreate ; depopulate and wafte
The beauty of thy works !
    Maho. Defamer, no !—
For to the faithful I promulge glad tidings,
Due trophies, glory won of high exploits ;
Gcod things on earth, and endlefs joys hereafter.
    Soph. Have we then chaced thee to thy pa-
    radife,
Thou jolly Prophet ?—ftill, the flowing bowl,
The feaft, the rolling eye, and wanton touch,
To ftir decaying appetite above !—
Yet art thou juft in this ; thy followers,
Firft taught to caft humanity afide,
Are then rewarded with the blifs of brutes—
Fit heaven to fit earth !—luft, earn'd by blood !
    Maho, Curfe on thy fophiftry !—Doft thou
    not know,
The ways of fenfe are all the avenues
That lead to knowledge ? all the modes, whereby
Or earth or heaven can be reveal'd ?
    Soph. 'Tis falfe.
The man is foul alone ; a living foul !

His

His fenfes, appetites, his body, all
Scarce a thin furface to his deep exiftence;
His flaves, detach'd for grofs intelligence
'Twixt him and this flight world, his petty neigh-
     bour.
His proper faculties are inward, all
Internal to himfelf; the eye of reafon,
The touch that thrills humanity, the tafte
The appetite for goodnefs, whereupon
This embryon angel feeds, as in his fhell,
Till fledg'd for Heaven——
Said I, the fenfes were the flaves of man?
Too oft his tyrants, enemies at all times,
To be oppofed, fubjected, and repreft;
Soul againft fenfe to wage perpetual war,
'Till Heaven fhall quit the lumber : 'tis the cha-
     racter
That fevers man from beaft, and—fuch a Prophet!
  MAHO. Damnation!—Fiends and fire!—Down,
     down, ye thunders,
Crufh the blafphemer quick!—Mark me, ye
     nations!
Let late pofterity attend—I come not
In the weak coil of words, but ftrength of power;
To quell with arms, not fence at argument.
The world is warpt, and bids our flag expand,
The bloody imprefs that fhall feal our law,
Even to the end of things!—Who carps, who
     cavils,
I give his tortured carcafs to impalement,
His damned fpirit to the deep!—Away—
To arms, brave Ali!—to our hoft—lead on—

The morrow's fun beholds the truce expired,
And Mecca in the duft!—Go—leave me—

[His attendants retire.

Soph. Go, my people!   [Peafants retire.

SCENE V.

Mahomet and Sopheian for fome time continue filent,
    Mahomet looking ftern, and Sopheian with a
    contemptuous fmile.

Soph. Prophet, thou art moved—

Maho. Sopheian!

Soph. Say.

Maho. I came to thee in peace—thou haft
        murder'd peace!
I did intend thee honours, that might ftrain
The eye to upward gazing—Thy loved children,
Even as my own, I've fofter'd—
    Soph. That, indeed, bends to thy fervice.
    Maho. Hell! doft talk of fervice?
Thou haft expofed and fet at nought my miffion!
There's but one way——
    Soph. Declare.
    Maho. Embrace it inftantly—
    Soph. If not——
    Maho. Thou art a wretched father!—
    Soph. Ha!——
    Maho. And that lone trunk defcends into the
        duft,
No twig furviving.
    Soph. Thou art not fuch a devil.

                                Maho.

Maho. Doft thou not know me?

Soph. O, too well!

Maho. Enough——

Soph. Thou wouldft not yet—thou art, thyfelf,
       a father!
Thy child too in my power—beware of that !—

Maho. Fool, fool, to tempt me fo—I dare thy
       utmoft;
For thou art good, and can'ft not fwerve a hair
From the kind milk of nature.

Soph. Art inexorable ?
Take back thy child; with her my gems, my
       ftores—
Strip all, fave that which will not profit thee,
A little truth to cloath me.

Maho. 'Tis in vain—

Soph. Let me but fee them—'tis not much to
       grant—
But once to fold them in a father's bofom,
A firft and laft embrace !

Maho. Yes—when thy fon is writhing on the
       pale,
Wound up to agony; and thy chafte girl
To my licentious foldiers caft abroad,
As proftituted air—then—

Soph. O miferable !—
Idol of terrors, mighty fiend, yet hold—
       [As Sopheian fpeaks, he catches at Mahomet, and
          bends towards him in a fupplicating pofture.

Maho. What! have I found thee
At my feet, mine enemy ?—

D 2

Ha,

Ha, ha, ha, ha!—Ten thoufand curfes catch
    thee !   [Exit.
   Soph. The powers of hell are pitilefs; and
    Heaven,
Where pity is, we make our laft refource,
When elfe no arm can aid—O children, children !
Your fate is urgent; and the bolt once launch'd,
What prayer can intercept ?—Yes, to Omnipotence,
That inftant may be fpun into an age,
For grace to intervene.   O, then, be quick—
Let thy fwift power fill up my weak dependence !
Upon him, down ! o'ertake him in the midft
Even of his proud career ! his broad blown glories,
O blaft them, blaft the tyrant! ftaunch the fluice
Of the wide bleeding world, this day, this hour !
And let the faith of erring mortals know,
'Tis Heaven that winds thro' every path below.
                       [Exit.

END OF THE SECOND ACT.

                                        A C T

A C T   III.

S C E N E   I.

ZAPHNA and PALMYRA on one fide, and SOPHEIAN
flowly on the other.

ZAPH. JOY to our generous hoft—peace and
her train,
I truft, are near!—Ha, if I judge aright,
Joy hath no dwelling here—they are the characters
Of grief and deep difmay, that may be read
Throughout that reverend form !—Say, royal fir,
Have you not met ?
    SOPH. Yes, ZAPHNA.
    ZAPH. Treated ?
    SOPH. Yes.
    ZAPH. And how ?
    SOPH. What boots the tale ?—
    ZAPH. I doubt, my lord—
Pray pardon,—that your port hath haply feem'd
Too much aloft, unbending to our Prophet ;
For I did hear him, with an ample heart,
Speak of dear terms, and purpofed good toward
you.
    SOPH. I did defcend beneath a low man's level;
Befought, with tears befought him, for my children,
Even at his knee.

D 3

PAL.

Pal. O grace!—and what hath chanced?

Soph. Perhaps even now my son is on the pale;
And the chaste honours of my dearer daughter,
Thrown to the public camp.

Pal. And did you then,
Forget Palmyra—when the chains of one
Might ransom both your children?

Soph. I did add
Even all my treasures in exchange.

Pal. Ah, Heaven!—
I have then no father—Zaphna, thou art all,
The only friend that's left!

Zaph. Royal Sopheian—
I am your hostage; and, where I'm known, my honour
Unquestion'd as the light. I am more than hostage,
Bound from my soul to your best vantage ever—
I have served our Prophet from the earliest hour,
That arms e'er cloath'd an infant; a slight boast,
To say he's yet my debtor. I will seek him,
I will invest me with your suit—meanwhile
My faith remains your surety.

Soph. Generous youth!
Go—and the blessings of a forlorn father
Still wait on thee my son.

Zaph. Peace be your guest!
A quick return shall meet your amplest wishes.
                              [Exit Zaphna.

Pal. Alas! my lord, and hath my once fond father
Cast off his child? could a short absence thus
Efface great nature's imprefs?

Soph. Though I menaced—
Heaven knows how diftant from my heart!—to
    ufe thee
Below thy leaft defervings.—
  Pal. Could I think it?—
When memory goes back to its firft ftage,
It meets his kindnefs there, which thence came on-
    ward,
Encreafing as my days. My prate alone
Could caft his care, new form his face to fmiles;
I feem'd his little mint for daily pleafures,
Lived at his knee, and grew but in his eye.
Can I forget with what continued rapture,
He fince hath caught and held me to his bofom,
As from his being I were once again
To take new root?
  Soph. He knew, he knew, Palmyra!
Nature, tho' turn'd to favage, could not hurt thee:
Thence grew his confidence—And yet, fweet maid,
Would I might wean thee to my own affection!
For much I fear thy father—much I fear,
No child of mine fhall clofe my eyes in death,
Twice born, and now twice buried.
  Pal. O, my mafter!
Should a hair fall that hangs upon your peace,
On his own daughter, even upon myfelf,
I'll do you vengeance.
  Soph. Generous, gentle heart!—
Come, my beft child, and while our Zaphna's
    abfent,
Let's wear the hour, and mingle hope with tears;
D 4

Weep

Weep where we muſt, but ſmile whene'er we
     can,
Since woeful is the ſtate ordain'd for man. [Exeunt.

S C E N E   II.

M A H O M E T's Pavilion.

MAHOMET and CAAB.

MAHO. No, CAAB—If I forgive him !—
No more—his doom is ſeal'd ; for on his head
My greatneſs can alone take future growth,
Or needs muſt wither.   Didſt thou mark ?—
    CAAB. I did—
The imbitter'd envy of his taunts, the inſolence
Of his imagined triumph.
    MAHO. Curſe on his triumph! it ſhall ſink him,
          CAAB !—
My friend, I'll tell thee of this ſame SOPHEIAN :
From the firſt pluming of my young ambition,
He check'd its flight ; in war, in prophecy,
My deadlieſt lett ! In vain I ſought his friendſhip ;
He mock'd my dreams, and vilified my perſon.
'Twas needful, yet, to win him by my arts,
Or cruſh him by my arms. The laſt was doubtful—
And, therefore, to retain within my hands
A certain pledge of our projected amity,
I ſeiz'd the lucky vantage of an hour,
And ſtole his children—
    CAAB. Whom !

                              MAHO.

Maho. Be secret then,
Till time shall speak—even Zaphna and Pal-
            myra!—
    Caab. Say you, my lord, the children of
        Sopheian ?
    Maho. The same; and for that purpose brought
        them up
With all due preference; nay, loved them, Caab—
And from the dawn of young Palmyra's beauties,
Won by I know not what of infant sweetnefs,
I mark'd her for my bed; a favourite confort,
To give age appetite.   But now, my Caab,
I hate them both, the hoftile progeny
Of that old canker'd ftock! yet, for Palmyra,
There is a fort of malicious kindnefs,
That fuits our hatred well.   I muft enjoy her—
I elfe come fhort of my own paradife,
A Prophet to no end.
    Caab. My lord!
    Maho. Say, Caab.
    Caab. Think you, but if Sopheian knew the
        honours
You did intend——
    Maho. No more! I fee 'tis vain.
The fellow is in earneft; has ta'en up
Whims of I know not what, call'd truth and
            honefty—
A fool, and bigot!
    Caab. Yet, fuch weak propenfities
Have mainly ferv'd our Prophet.
    Maho. True, my oracle—
Though rancourous enemies when once attack'd,

                              They

They make faſt friends.   Why, what a deal of
        people
Have we religion'd into miſchief, CAAB—
To what the dictates of plain nature call
Theft, murder, rapine, ſacrilege!—yet theſe
Have faſhion'd all our heroes, ſet at gaze
The demigods of old.

    CAAB. Now, from my ſoul,
I do adore you; worſhip you with heart
Of true recognizance.   Your wiſdom ſums
Whate'er of power, or elevated attribute,
Is fabled in divinity.

    MAHO. Mark, CAAB!
Would'ſt thrive on earth, appear to look at Heaven,
As that were all thy bent; the ſeeming ſaint
Still makes the proſperous ſinner.
'Tis therefore, that, Prometheus-like, I've robb'd
Heaven's altar of enthuſiaſtic fire,
And have my faſts, my prayers, my zeal, and
        cant,
Spread hands, and whited eye-balls—morals too,
Good morals, CAAB! that have made good men.
My godſhip to a bett, but I, hereafter,
May have my martyrs too—What ſay'ſt thou,
        CAAB?
For, on my ſoul, I do begin to think;
I have but dream'd of ſleighting on the world,
And that I am ſent indeed.

    CAAB. Moſt high and mighty!
'Tis better as it is—for Heaven, belike,
Had given leſs latitude.

MAHO.

Maho. Say'ft thou, old chronicle?
Ha, ha, ha, ha!—But to our theme, my friend.
What with Sopheian?
  Caab. Bring your army on.
  Maho. That has its hazard.
  Caab. Poifon then—
  Maho. A dagger—
  Caab. A gentle cup—
  Maho. Blood, Caab, blood!
  Caab. My lord, you know I'm for the cabinet;
The fword's too bare a province.
  Maho. Yet, my Caab,
Thou couldft perfuade—
  Caab. Whom?
  Maho. Ali—no—what thinkft of Abdoramen?
  Caab. It will not do; he's not enough of faint;
Nor yet of finner for it—Say, 'twere Zaphna.
  Maho. Ha!—yes—I do conceive—O glorious
        mifchief!—
Come to my arms thou prophet of thy prophet!—
Zaphna hath fuch a gallantry of zeal,
Bid him but on, and in the name of Heaven,
He'd ftrike at Heaven's Supreme—This way, this
        way,
More from the light—until I pour into thee,
The horrors that are brooding in my foul,
To whelm our foes withal.
  Caab. Pardon, my lord—
I did not think—this will be parricide.
  Maho. Out fool—the nobler vengeance!—
        Further, Caab,
I have a lure to bow this youthful eagle,

                                A tempt-

A tempting lure—he loves Palmyra—fo,
The fifter's body for the father's blood!
It is a bargain feal'd—But ere he feize
His quarry, we muft gorge him—there's thy
            tafk—
'Tis but the fweet'ning of the facred chalice,
The cup of our commiffion, and all's fafe—
Then Caab we fhall mount as free as air,
To love and empire.
    Caab. I do think, my mafter,
If Zaphna does the feat, it were not fafe
He live to rue; they both muft fall together.
    Maho. Right—This once done, thou art thy
            mafter's mafter.
Ha! by my miffion—to our wifh—he comes—
Keep thee afide, my Caab.   [Caab retires.

SCENE III.

Mahomet retires to his chair; and, as Zaphna
    enters, affects to be wrapt in a vifion.

    Maho. Thy will!—in patience I refign me
            to it—
What, Zaphna! is it Zaphna thou haft chofen,
To be the voice, as now he is the arm
To propagate thy word?—I envy not—
I pity—Zaphna—O my fon, my fon,
The toils that win the trophies!—thou art young,
Unequal—pardon, Heaven—thy might, it is
Sufficient to him—What a combat firft
Muft wring his heart!—torn from itfelf—the will,
                            Self-

Self-will rent from him—by the will above
Supply'd—I fee—he draws the fword of Heaven—
He ftrikes—The foe is fallen—'tis finifh'd!

   While Mahomet fpeaks, Zaphna ftands amazed
    and agitated with various emotions ; then fpeaks,
    and falls proftrate.—

 Zaph. Thine and thy prophet's will,
Behold your fervant!

   [After a filent paufe, Mahomet pretends to awake,
    and feeing Zaphna, feems furprized.—

 Maho. How—Zaphna!
What doft thou here, young man ?
Thou art a hoftage—

  Zaph. 'Tis therefore I am come, my gracious
   mafter,
A fuitor for my hoft—

  Maho. Rife, Zaphna!—No—
'Tis ftrange—'tis myftical—'tis wond'rous all!—
Thy doing!—no, my child—for thou art come
Wide of thyfelf; thou know'ft not when, nor
    why—
Invifibly conducted.

  Zaph. Lo, great Prophet!
Your fervant's foul is wrapt in energy—
Strain'd to her wing, and panting for the flight,
Where you and Heaven appoint.

  Maho. What wouldft thou ? ha !—

  Zaph. The fcythe-drawn fword, to dart amid
   the legions,
Mow'd as the fummer's weed—to plunge the
   flame—
To ride the whirlwind—cramp'd within the pole,
To freeze, to fhiver, in the eternal bite

            Of

Of thawlefs winter—
Or boldly ftriding on the boift'rous furge,
My watry Pegafus wing'd by the winds,
To fcale the pale-ey'd regent of the night,
Revealing wonders !

    Maho. Apt—but foreign quite !—
Imagination hurries thee, my fon,
A thoufand leagues afide—'Tis not the plume
Of new-fledg'd youth, the riot of the blood,
Nor fiery fparks that mount upon the blaze
Of hot ambition ; fond conceptions all,
The quickening of mortality !—No more—
Heaven is not in them—'Tis a will debafed,
Sunk from itfelf; old nature turn'd and ftrain'd,
From wonted bendings; judgment quelled, and
            reafon
Led as a muffled babe—
    Zaph. O take me then,
Crufh me into oblivion, that no thought
May rife to further ferment !—

    Maho. 'Tis amazing—
Prodigious, what's ordain'd for thee, my child !
The greater heights, the lowlier thou muft fink,
Prepared for future foaring ; be a thing
Of fcorn to what is call'd thy nobler nature,
In thy own eye a bafe one.

    Zaph. O, pronounce !—
I am already all that Heaven would have,
Or nothing.—

    Maho. That Heaven thou ferveft, hath a foe.
    Zaph. A foe ?
    Maho. A dog !

                            Zaph

ZAPH. Perhaps, devoted—
MAHO. Stab him.
ZAPH. Whom?
MAHO. SOPHEIAN!
ZAPH. Ha!
MAHO. A scoffer—
ZAPH. Alas!
MAHO. A blasphemer of our law,
Cursing the earth he treads!—Thou musest,
          ZAPHNA.
     ZAPH. Not I—no—muse, my lord?—I would,
          I would
Be all obedience.
     MAHO. Take this poniard to thee;
'Tis consecrated steel—and thou the priest
Appointed to the sacrifice!
     ZAPH. His children?—
I trust not compass'd in the fire's offences.
     MAHO. No, they are ta'en to grace—Away,
          dispatch,
Or thou art lost for ever!
Follow him, CAAB—should he fail, enforce him.
                    [Exit MAHOMET speaking to CAAB.
     ZAPH. Ha!—Thoughts be still—A traitor—
          murderer—
A dark, a secret villain!—there's the merit!—
Down, down, rebellion!—Nature, who art thou
Whose sense would kick at Heaven? thou must
          thyself
Be slain, the previous victim; else this steel
Recoils, no purpose on the point. Help, Heaven!—
Quick, ZAPHNA!—or the combat fought within,
                              kills

Kills the whole man; and power will be as weak
As will, to this moſt dreadful taſk—O miſery?

[Exit ZAPHNA.

S C E N E   IV.

SOPHEIAN's Palace.

SOPHEIAN and CALED meet.

SOPH. Friend, are our gates ſecured, our guards
   diſpoſed—
All meaſures ta'en againſt ſurprize or treachery,
Where ſuch an inmate neſtles?

 CAL. All is done,
What diligence could act, or prudence dictate.—
The danger is not ours.

  SOPH. How's that, my friend?

  CAL. The common croud, who ever loved your
   perſon,
Wean'd of their ſuperſtitious awe of MAHOMET
By your laſt conference, have caught a rumour
Touching your long loſt children, and the danger
That threatens at their life—All fired, they run
To corners, and in ſudden whiſpers plot
The fall of the Impoſtor and his followers.

  SOPH. Ah CALED! wherefore do I know this
   buſineſs?
Which known, I muſt prevent.

  CAL. 'Tis therefore told,
To be prevented—

SOPH.

Soph. Does Chriſtianity
Enjoin ſuch heights, ſtupendous to our natures ?
　Cal. It does—whate'er of worth, truth, can-
　　　dour, honour,
Can be ſelected and ſublimed from things,
Through the whole man it raiſes and expands—
No out-let for evaſion, no compounding!
Your faith is paſs'd; and, to your ſtretch of power,
You are now the guardian of your foe.
　Soph. Yet, yet,
I could have wiſh'd—
　Cal. To what effect, Sopheian ?
The Almighty Faith of which thou art now pro-
　　　feſſor,
In the ſuſpended arm of feeble man
Arreſts all power; and to itſelf aſſumes
The ſcope of all events, even to a hair,
Which on the unbonneted or hoary head
Gives comfort againſt cold.
　Soph. And is it ſo ?
　Cal. All known, all noted, balanced, and ad-
　　　juſted,
As in a chymiſt's ſcale!—Man may intend—
That is his freedom, that his power—no more!—
Nor, from creation, hath the buſtling world
E'er ſway'd Eternal Wiſdom from his line,
An atom's deviation.
　Soph. If the end,
Muſt be, as it muſt be; what boots it, then,
To ſwerve from excellence ?
　Cal. Only to earn
The guilt, but not the iſſue of our purpoſe.

For will or nill, the fame effect fubfcribes
The over-ruling dictate. Fear not, then,
What the fpectator man may ftrive to warp
Amid the works of Heaven—Go thou ftraight on ;
And do, as honour bids.

SOPH. 'Tis right, 'tis great,
'Tis glorious!—and my wifh, fo prompt of late,
Shrinks back afhamed, nor dares abide the beam
Of fuch illumination. Hafte, my CALED,
Our word hath paft : our children let us leave
To Heaven—let's hafte, my friend, let's fly to fave,
To refcue their deftroyer.

CAL. I go, my lord.
SOPH. Soft, CALED—firft a word—

SCENE V.

As SOPHEIAN and CALED confer, ZAPHNA enters
at a diftance.

ZAPH. He's there—the accurs'd of Heaven and
of his Prophet !—
The trampler of our law, the victim due !—
Come, ye affociates of the clofe affaffin,
Diffimulation, fmooth-faced cruelty,
And lurking treafon !—aid my pious purpofe—
That I may fmile and talk, and fmile and ftab,
For Heaven, and for the word !—

[Exit CALED.

SOPH. ZAPHNA, welcome !
O doubly welcome now ; for I began
To fear for thee, my fon !

ZAPH.

Zaph. For me, my lord?

Soph. Yes—the unruly mob are ripe for mif-
      chief;
And, in their fury, bent to maffacre
Your Prophet and his train.

    Zaph. A tale worth liftening.   [Afide.

    Soph. But, thanks to Heaven! thou art return'd
      in fafety.
My children—do they live?

    Zaph. They do.

    Soph. Alas!
I fee thy plea hath been but half a winner:
But my Palmyra kindly hath engaged
To urge the dear petition to her father,
With all her winning rhetoric—Thou, my Zaphna,
Stir not to tempt the danger of the hour;
Already have I fent, and now I go
To quell this tumult.

    Zaph. Wherefore—why, my lord,
Wherefore to quell? does not your foul defire
Perdition to our Prophet?

    Soph. Front to front,
Or in the field, where open honour leads,
Yes, to the death I'd cope him—but not fap
By mineing treachery.

    Zaph. O Heaven!—But think—
Check fortune now, and what may follow?—ha!
Do you not hate, do you not fear him?

    Soph. No—
My towering faith informs, that guilt alone
Is real evil—What can man do, more

E 2

Than

Than Heaven gives scope? in that my truft is pillar'd.
I fear him not, therefore I cannot hate him—
The armed hand may ftroak the cockatrice,
Admire her fpeckled creft, and pearled fcale,
When fearlefs of her fting.

   Zaph. That ftrikes a light—
But O, from me how diftant!—juft of force
To dazzle, not to warm me.   [Afide.

   Soph. I muft hence.
'Till my return, this roof is thy afylum—
Would it were ever fo!   [Going.

   Zaph. Indeed, my lord!—
And do you wifh my fafety?—'tis too much—

   Soph. Ah, Zaphna, how unkind that queftion!
      —Yes,
Thou generous youth, would I might ever hold
     thee,
By all the twining bonds of dear affection!
Thofe children that thy Prophet would impofe,
Perhaps—I know not whom—a foreign offspring—
O Heavens, that I might win thee but from this—
I will not do thy ear offence, my fon,
To name him by his merits—why that figh?—
That thou, I fay, and thy Palmyra, here,
Might reign with me in Mecca; fhare between ye
My heart, my wealth, my fcepter!—What, in
     tears!

   Zaph. Oh, pardon——
   Soph. Nay, I muft prevent thy knee;
It is not in thy noble nature, Zaphna,
To want a pardon—but that I do love thee,

                        Let

Let this, and this, be witnefs!—Fare thee well—
                                        [Embraces.
May grace and honour guard thee!   [Exit.
  ZAPH. Guard me?—
That was his gentle prayer—O no, my father!
Fiends catch me firft, and may the Heavens guard
     thee
From traitors fuch as ZAPHNA!—Said I, Heaven?
Heaven! what is Heaven?—a prompter to ingra-
    titude?
To breach of faith, clofe couching treacheries,
And murders?—ZAPHNA then will none of
    Heaven—
He'll to the infernals firft, the place oppofed
To fuch a Heaven, and dwell condemn'd to virtue.

S C E N E   VI.

Enter CAAB cautioufly.

  CAAB. ZAPHNA!—my lord, my lord ZAPHNA!
  ZAPH. CAAB!—What doft thou here?
  CAAB. O, my good lord—the Prophet—
  ZAPH. Damn the Prophet—
Thee, and his other inftruments of practice,
The word he utters, and the heaven he worfhips!
  CAAB. O the good angel!—ZAPHNA!—Mercy
    take us!
Where have you caught this frenzy!
  ZAPH. Out, thou flave!
Thou under ferpent, poifoning as thou goeft

By curs'd infinuation ; leaving ftill
Thy venom in the track.
    CAAB. What this will coft !
When you fhall know—what grief, what penitence
    ZAPH. I care not—I renounce thy fect—thy
        mafter,
And thee thou image of his drofs ; his vile,
His worft impreffion.
    CAAB. What hath chanced ? I hope—
I hope you have not—I am fent difpatch,
To intercept the ftroke—and bring you to him.
    ZAPH. To intercept it, fay you?
    CAAB. Yea, my lord—
SOPHEIAN hath fent terms of due fubmiffion,
Of fuit and humble prayer to be received
To grace and to the law.
    ZAPH. Sayft thou, of fuit ?—
And terms—what terms, good CAAB ?
    CAAB. Nay, I know not—
    ZAPH. Pardon a young man's rafhnefs—Say,
        my friend—
    CAAB. In footh, 'tis but furmife.
    ZAPH. Of what? unfold—
    CAAB. It were not well.
    ZAPH. Kind CAAB—
    CAAB. Have you e'er
Remark'd a fort of kindnefs in SOPHEIAN,
Touching our fultan's daughter ?
    ZAPH. Often—yes—
He doth confefs as much.
    CAAB. I only know,
The man hath eyes, defires, and appetites ;

                        Whether

Whether the lady hath temptations too,
That I know not.
  ZAPH. Thou haft a further caufe.
  CAAB. No more in truth, than what my dif-
      tant ear
Caught of brief accents, when with MAHOMET
He held a private conference.
  ZAPH. In private?
  CAAB. Yes.
  ZAPH. And what didſt gather?
  CAAB. There, my lord,
Your pardon—
My foul's beſt worth could fcarce abide the charge
Of fuch a revelation.
  ZAPH. He did ſhew,
A face and port of fuch an open tendence,
I could not ſtray—I think—
If he doth hold me fair, and play me deep;
I will have fuch atonement of his treachery,
Such mercilefs account—
  CAAB. O, let not me,
Be author of ill thoughts—I may have err'd.
  ZAPH. Where ſhall I turn?—If I look up to
      Heaven,
I am confounded from his attribute,
Nor know the power I pray to—if on earth,
Defign, and craft, and covert policy,
Lie ambuſh'd in the focial face of friendſhip,
And trip at confidence.
  CAAB. Take patience to you.
  ZAPH. Why was I born?—O, what is man?—a
      thing,

E 4

Form'd

Form'd for the fport of fome facetious deity !
A veffel fill'd with adverfe elements,
Wherein his chymift would experiment
The wantonnefs of warfare.—In his infancy,
The bud how tender !—fhould he fcape the froft,
How fhort the bloffom !—bring him to the fruit,
He ripens into rottennefs !—Away
With fuch an infignificance—an edifice,
Built for the blaft, a voyage but for the wreck—
A voyage ? no—that hath its chart, its compafs,
A ftar whereby to fteer, and haply may
Attain fome haven—man is but a fkiff,
Tofs'd out to chance; his boafted pilot, reafon,
A fluggard fet to argue, not to act
Againft the tempeft of contending paffions.
Now here, now there, he's thrown; nor knows a
       fteerage—
No ground to anchor, and no fkill to guide;
The driving butt of every wind and tide !

                            [Exeunt,

END OF THE THIRD ACT,

ACT

ACT IV.

SCENE I.

M A H O M E T 's Pavillion.

To MAHOMET enter PALMYRA.

MAHO. **P**ALMYRA here !—Come to my
arms, my daughter.
PAL. If I muſt loſe your love—your bleſſing,
ſir,
Is yet a boon, which ſure I have not forfeited
By any lapſe of duty.   [Kneels.
MAHO. Loved and blefs'd,
Thou art thyſelf the bleſſing of the Prophet;
More loved, than ever father loved a child.
                              [Embraces.
PAL. You did refuſe to ranſom me—preferr'd
A foreign iſſue to your own PALMYRA ;
Although to poiſe the lightneſs of my worth,
The tender father added, in exchange,
The purchaſe of a realm.
MAHO. He is a villain—
SOPHEIAN is a dog!

PAL.

PAL. I know not that—
He has proved a gentle parent to your daughter;
The beſt of parents!

MAHO. How?

PAL. O, pardon, ſir!
If I have err'd, my guilt will ſtand reproved
In your exceſs of goodneſs.   I am come
An earneſt ſuitor to you.

MAHO. Say, fair pleader.

PAL. That of your bounty you would ſtraight
               remit
Thoſe children to their ſire, with all due circum-
             ſtance,
That may approve their birth.

MAHO. An hour ſhall ſend
My lateſt anſwer.

PAL. Let it be a kind one—

MAHO. Truſt me, he ſhan't repine.

PAL. Thus let me thank you.   [Bends her knee.
And ſhall I bear him back this kind aſſurance?

MAHO. Not ſo, my child—you ſtay with us.

PAL. Alas!—
My lord forgets his daughter is a captive.

MAHO. I here ſtrike off all chains, ſave of my
             love—
And that's a dear retention.

PAL. But, my lord,
Can you ſtrike off the chains of honour too,
That bind me to return?

MAHO. I can, PALMYRA;
Nor may the chance of battle give SOPHEIAN

                         A right

A right, fuperior to what nature gave
To me thy parent.
    PAL. Such SOPHEIAN's plea
For his own children.
    MAHO. He's an infidel,
A wretch anathemized! Compact and faith
With fuch a one, is impious.
    PAL. Ah, my father!
If Heaven's beft worfhippers make light of faith,
Is it with finners we fhould hope to find
The facred obligation?
    MAHO. Ha!—no more—
Haft thou caft off refpect and fair obedience—
All duty?
    PAL. Whom, my lord, fhall I obey—
My firft, or latter Prophet? You once told me,
That truth, faith, virtue, honour, were immutable,
Eternal in their natures: if you now
Would change that fyftem, when may I expect
Another variation, and fo onward,
'Till I am loft to all?
    MAHO. Confound the lecture ——   [Afide.
I grieve, my child, that weighty avocations
Intrude upon our converfe—Do thy pleafure—
I did but trifle——   [Exit MAHOMET.

SCENE II.

To PALMYRA; enter ZAPHNA.

ZAPH. Here! Art thou here, PALMYRA?—O
my charmer—

Thy

Thy prefence comes on my benighted foul,
Like a glad morning, to difpel the horrors,
Wherewith I ftood befet!—But fay, my love—
Haft thou confidered, in Sopheian's conduct,
Aught of uncommon tendernefs—beyond
What thy fuperior worth might claim from
      friendfhip,
Tho' that is much?

    Pal. Yes, Zaphna—yet, no more
Than my own heart did warrant me to anfwer;
Tho' that was likewife much.

    Zaph. Of fecret glance,
Complexion hurried, incoherent fpeech;
Sudden emotions half fupprefs'd, revealing
What they do feek to hide?

    Pal. No—never——Yes,
Something of this—yet little that I mark'd—
Sure nothing that could fpeak to thy fufpicions—
Why wouldft thou put me to ill thoughts, my
      Zaphna?

    Zaph. Didft thou hear aught touching a fecret
      embaffy,
Sent by Sopheian to the Prophet?

    Pal. When?

    Zaph. Within this hour.

    Pal. Indeed!—no, nothing of it.

    Zaph. Nor aught of terms intended?

    Pal. Not a fyllable—
What terms?

    Zaph. Suppofe his faith, his crown, his people,
      offer'd
For one rich jewel that out-prizes all.

                  Pal.

PAL. What jewel, ZAPHNA?

ZAPH. Even thyfelf, my love!

PAL. It cannot be.

ZAPH. But if it fhould—how then?—
Shall I not—

PAL. What?

ZAPH. Transfix the traitor's heart?

PAL. Alas!

ZAPH. Stab, tear the robber of my peace?

PAL. Ah, ZAPHNA!
My thoughts are driven amid a thoufand terrors.

ZAPH. Peace to thy breaft, my fweet!—'tis but
conjecture.
I have a hafty fummons from thy father,
And muft attend—

PAL. O think, till thy return,
No joy can enter where PALMYRA fojourns.

ZAPH. Thy ZAPHNA's life fhall wholly be em-
ployed,
To trade for comforts, and unlade the freight
Still where his foul hath anchor.

PAL. Fare thee well—
My ever loved, my friend, my father now—
Farewell, my only ZAPHNA! [Exit PALMYRA.

S C E N E III.

To ZAPHNA HERCIDES.

HERCID. Soft, ZAPHNA!—I muft crofs thy
hafte—

ZAPH. What's toward?

HERCID.

HERCID. That I would aſk of thee—I do adjure thee,
By all my watchful cares, which, from thy infancy,
Have been matured into a father's fondneſs,
I do adjure thee, tell me—

ZAPH. What, HERCIDES?

HERCID. Why hath an hour thus robb'd thee of
thyſelf?
Honour, late blown, and open in thy aſpect,
Shrinks like a famiſh'd wretch; while, from the
light,
Thine eye turns inward, cleaving to the gloom,
That broods upon thy ſoul.

ZAPH. Oh——

HERCID. Speak, my hero—
My ſon, my precious ZAPHNA!

ZAPH. Thou'lt be ſecret—

HERCID. Cloſe as the tomb, the marble ſeal of
ſilence.—

ZAPH. The Prophet thus—SOPHEIAN hath
blaſphemed
Heaven and the law——

HERCID. Proceed.

ZAPH. And Heaven hath doom'd
His fall, dreadful, and ſudden—

HERCID. Ha! by what means?

ZAPH. Even of this hand, HERCIDES.

HERCID. Merey, mercy!
O the eternal powers!—did MAHOMET
Enjoin—what, MAHOMET—thine arm for this?—
Moſt horrid!

ZAPH. Yes—thou ſeem'ſt amazed!

HERCID.

HERCID. Beware——
He comes—be filent—O beware, my ZAPHNA!
[Exit HERCIDES.

S C E N E IV.

To ZAPHNA enter MAHOMET.

MAHO. ZAPHNA, attend—and hear the leaf of
  Heaven
Denounced on thy rebellious head, outcaft
From grace, and from the law!
 ZAPH. What means my lord?
 MAHO. My fpirit went along—I did behold thee
Pale, trembling, weak, unworthy of the arm
Elected from above.
 ZAPH. O, had you feen
My pangs and ftruggles too—to pierce this heart,
Had been repofe to what I felt! And then,
He fpoke and look'd fuch things, fuch melting
   goodnefs!
It feem'd as Heaven did not enjoin, but were
Itfelf to feel the ftab.
 MAHO. 'Tis therefore, ZAPHNA,
The thunder-ftone juft launching to o'erwhelm
   thee,
Hath flumber'd in the hand. For O, already
Thou art enough undone—This night was doom'd
To love and to PALMYRA.
 ZAPH. To PALMYRA?
 MAHO. This night to love—the morrow was
   ordain'd
To glory and to empire.
ZAPH.

Zaph. O, my lord,   [Kneels.
Is there no place for pardon?
     Maho. Zaphna, Zaphna!—
To think but what a flood-gate Heaven prepared,
To pour his bleffings on thee!
     Zaph. O, my mafter!
But for one trial—for one hour's repeal—
I go, I run, I fly to execute
The thunder of thy word.
     Maho. Rife, rife—my prayer
Hath pull'd thy pardon down—The time was
          not—
Thy arm was check'd—The reprobate muft fall,
Spite of his late addrefs and feign'd fubmiffion,
Even at the altar of his gods—thofe idóls,
In whofe polluted and accurfed name,
He did blafpheme our Heaven!
     Zaph. It fhàll be done.
     Maho. Enough—that ftreet directs thee to the
          Caaba.
In the next hour he prays—
     Zaph. He dies!

          Enter Caab.

     Maho. Well, Caab,
Haft thou prepared our banquet?
     Caab. All is ready.
     Maho. Bid Omar, Abubeker, Abdoramen,
And old Hercides, to the feaft—Be fpeedy—
                         [Exit Caab.
Zaphna, be firm!

                                   Zaph.

ZAPH. O, doubt it not, my lord.

MAHO. Remember, that the Power who giveth
    life,
With equal right may inſtitute the means
Of death to all men.

ZAPH. It is juſt!

MAHO. And yet,
Thou doſt not ſeem to reliſh——

ZAPH. True, great Prophet!
I had rather ſlay a hòſt of men in battle,
Than one within his ward—But what were merit,
If duty did not ſway o'er inclination?

MAHO. Did not great Brutus bend in ſalu-
    tation,
When, for his dearer country, he did ſtab
The deareſt of his friends?—To ſerve her nation,
Heber's renowned wife betray'd· the faith
She gave to flying Siſera; and, through
The temples of her ſleeping gueſt, enforced
The inhoſpitable nail—And ſhall they act,
Beyond what Heaven's appointed champion may,
Arm'd by divine injunction?

ZAPH. Do not fear it.——

S C E N E V.

To them enter OMAR, ABUBEKER, ABDORAMEN,
HERCIDES, CAAB.

The Scene opens and diſcovers a table with a bowl and
    chalice.

MAHO. Health to our friends, aſſociates of
    the faith,

Chief captains of the hoſt of Heaven, elect
To ſpread his laws on earth! Sit, ſit, my brothers.

　　HERCID. Ha! that chalice there—I do not like
　　　　its ſanctity—
I knew a wretch once honour'd with that cup,
Whoſe following banquet was in Heaven—I fear,
I fear me, ZAPHNA, thou art not intended
To be a frequent gueſt.
　　　　　　　[Aſide, while the reſt take their places: they all ſit.
　　MAHO. Now to conſult, how nations, yet un-
　　　　conquer'd,
May ſooneſt be ſubjected—there's our bent;
Firſt to ſubdue, and then reform; the purpoſe
That conſecrates our ſword!—to this high miſſion
Let's drink a ſocial pledge—ZAPHNA, my ſon,
Take thou the cup of honour—nor conceive
That thoſe of riper years, but greener zeal,
Envy thy proud appointment!—Here, my friends,
To ZAPHNA the young leader of our arms,
Health, glory, and ſucceſs—Ha! Traitors—what!
Which of you?—Where's the wretch?—
　　　　　　　[Takes the bowl, and ZAPHNA the cup: as they both
　　　　　　　lift them to their lips, MAHOMET ſtarts up ſuddenly,
　　　　　　　and lets the bowl ſpill, while HERCIDES daſhes the
　　　　　　　cup out of ZAPHNA's hands. All the company
　　　　　　　riſe in amazement.

　　OMAR. What means our Sultan?

　　MAHO. As I held up the goblet to my lips,
Some ſlave among you took his poniard forth,
And ſtruck it to my heart.

　　CAAB. The Heavens defend—
There is no poniard here.

MAHO.

Maho. A sudden phantasie!—
Some short indisposition !—Break we up—
We shall soon meet—My friends, farewell to all—
Zaphna, you know your province !—This way,
    Caab.   [Exeunt.

SCENE VI.

Hercides advances, and the scene shuts.

Hercid. O fool, O villain that I am—curs'd
    caitiff—
A witless villain!—might I not have found him?
Heaven can't be with him—no, 'tis gross to sense!
That I could be so deep a mole—so hood-
    winkt—
Muffled to be bemired in guilt—O this
Entangling fiend, this ambient arch impostor!
My master, my dear master first betray'd,
His treasures plunder'd, and his smiling babes
Rent from his bosom!—this—Yet what is this,
To what ensues ?—Mercy !—I overheard them—
The young and noble son wrought by yon tempter
To massacre a father—his reward,
The incestuous knowledge of a sister—Heaven!
Wer't thou but open to the eve of penitence !—
How'ere, it is enough—the present burden.
I'll to Sopheian—I'll confess, unfold
The freight of my offences—further guilt
Can only serve to sink a lower hell,
And deepen my damnation !—   [Exit.

         SCENE

SCENE VII.

The Caaba.

Enter Mahomet and Caab.

Maho. Caab, my cloak—henceforth it is thine
        own—
An honourable badge of our affection !
Thy observation's juft ; there's no fure footing
On the loofe warrant of this giddy boy.
    Caab. No true dependence.
    Maho. Did he gorge our poffet ?
    Caab. I faw it in his lips.
    Maho. 'Tis well—there's one provided—and
        for t'other,
Rather than fail, myfelf will be the furety
Of his eternal reft—Do thou and Omar
Keep near, and wait the iffue.
    Caab. Yet, be cautious—
    Maho. Fear not—Away.   · [Exit Caab.
Sopheian once removed,
The force of the remaining world can't lift
Another bar like him to my ambition—
What's this I feel—this new intruder here?
Who cries, Forbear !—and would erect himfelf
Againft our great fupremacy of reafon ?
I'll none of thee, thou meddling counfellor !
Away—This is the hour—
Behind yon altar—there I may retire,
And watch the prompt occafion.
                    [Goes behind the altar.

SCENE.

SCENE VIII.

Enter Sopheian.

Soph. Adieu ye idols of my daily worſhip,
Falſe objeƈts of true incenſe, cordial prayer—
Alas, how ill direƈted!—Never more
Shall your waſte altar from Sopheian's hand
Receive the warm oblation.

Enter Hercides on the oppoſite ſide.

What art thou?
 Hercid. A villain—whom the Heavens, to
   ſave Sopheian,
Have turn'd to quick contrition—know you not
Hercides?
 Soph. How!—Hercides?
 Hercid. Soft, my maſter—
This way, for mercy's ſake!—I muſt be ſhort—
Perdition is about us—Haſte, O haſte! [Exeunt.

SCENE IX.

Enter Zaphna, looking about.

Zaph. He muſt be here—I held him in mine
   eye—
Yes,—in his ſanƈtum yonder—Ah, poor viƈtim!
What can thy prayers or faithleſs gods avail,
When ſuch a foe hath enter'd?—How is this?—
Although religion, love, and empire, urge me,

F 3   Though

Though heaven and earth call out and bid me
          ſtrike—
I have no ſtomach to't—I have been told,
That o'er the inſtant of ſome horrid act,
Voices not human have been heard to ſcream
Their nightly omens—ſpectred viſages
Glared on the eye—and ſudden lakes of blood
Have riſen athwart the proceſs !—
What a deep gloom dwells here to help devotion,
To awe the ſpirits down, and give the blood
Its reverential thrill !—My ſoul is caught—
Or is it cowardice that would unthread
Theſe ſinews from their bent ?—It muſt be done.
O, never holy prieſt, when on the altar
He laid the lamb, that turn'd a piteous eye,
Look'd gently up, and bleated for compaſſion,
E'er ſtruck with like reluctance—Yet it muſt—
No more of torturing doubts, of dread ſuſpenſion—
What muſt be done—once done—and all is finiſh'd!
          [Goes in behind the altar, and after ſome time returns.
What ſhould I think ?—
He did prevent my merit of its meaning ;
And made, what Heaven appointed for a murder,
Mere ſelf-defence—He aim'd his poniard well—
But from his hand I wrench'd the levell'd ſteel,
Struck the blow home, and caſt him on the pave-
          ment.

                              SCENE

SCENE X.

Enter HERCIDES.

HERCID. ZAPHNA, beware!—I muſt be ſud-
      den—

If thou ſhouldſt meet SOPHEIAN, touch him not—
He is thy father!

   ZAPH. Ha!—

   HERCID. Thy father, ZAPHNA—
Thine and PALMYRA's father! The impoſtor
Did know it, when he urged thee to the parricide—
Ye are the twain, of whom, when in your infancy,
He robb'd your gracious ſire, the prince of Mecca;
Himſelf the prince of devils! Hie thee hence—
Adieu—we muſt not be obſerv'd together.

                              [Exit HERCIDES.

   ZAPH. How the earth ſhakes!—what ſudden
      night comes on!

Where am I?—on the brink!—the flames beneath
Shew where to plunge—Catch me, ye circling
      fiends!

Wrap me with fiery ſcorpions! torture, tear
The hell-taught parricide!—
Is he among you? find him, ſearch him out—
No Prophet here!—Come hell—come thou
      long—

And we will ſweep him into ſuch perdition,
That our's ſhall be Heaven, from whence to look
On his deep hell beneath!   [Exit ZAPHNA.

SCENE XI.

Enter on one fide CAAB, on the other OMAR.

CAAB. Saw you the Prophet, OMAR ?

OMAR. No—not a creature pafs'd, where I kept
        watch.

CAAB. I faw SOPHEIAN, and young ZAPHNA
        enter,
But not a foul return.

OMAR. Hear you that groan ?

CAAB. I think the Prophet's voice.

SCENE XII.

To them enter MAHOMET, feebly leaning on the altar,
        with a dagger in his breaft ; they run to him, and fup-
        port him on each fide.

OMAR. Alas, our fultan !

CAAB. Ah, my royal mafter !

MAHO. Gently—O gently, friends !—
I totter on the fteepy ridge of life,
And the leaft fhove precipitates my being
Down, down, the deep immenfe—To fay, to fay,
When, where, and what's before me—'tis a lan-
        guage
New, wond'rous, horrible !—to human ears
Impoffible to utter—
Time's but a hinge, whereon mortality,
A narrow portal, turns—behind, before,
Lies the wide main of being !—O, I launch—

Support me—but a moment more—one moment—
'Tis all my univerſe!—For mercy, Oh—
Down reaching through the infinite abyſs,
To catch, to catch me, e'er I fall—Oh—   [Dies.
    OMAR. So—then our prophecying farce is over—
    CAAB. OMAR, not ſo—our Prophet cannot die—
Say he's retired—in viſion—or in trance—
Any invention that may ſerve to prop
Our new erected empire—Let us ſhade
His great remains; with utmoſt privacy
Convey him hence; and ſwear to hold this accident
A ſecret from the world.
                                        [Exeunt.

END OF THE FOURTH ACT.

ACT

A C T   V.

S C E N E I.

SOPHEIAN and CALED meet.

SOPH. JOY, CALED, joy! they're known, they're
         known, my CALED—
O fuch a pair!

  CAL. Whom?

  SOPH. Brave MOAWIAS,
And my fair AYETIA——
My ZAPHNA and PALMYRA!

  CAL. O grace! what of them?

  SOPH. Even my little ones.

  CAL. Say you?

  SOPH. The fame—the news hath made me ftrong
As in my prime of May—O hafte to find them—
The dear young traitors have efcaped their bounds,
And roam at large—I to the Caaba,
Toward MAHOMET's pavilion thou—
O hafte, hafte my kind friend!—

                   [Exeunt feverally.

                         SCENE

S C E N E II.

Enter PALMYRA.

PAL. What may this bode ?—I am undone—
    betray'd !—
Thrice did I meet him; thrice, with courteous
    action,
Woo'd him to conference; and thrice he started,
As tho' his eye had caught, within its glance,
A sudden basilisk—so struck with horror,
He from my presence shrunk, and vanish'd—
    Haply,
Some mood of his new jealousy—There,
Lo where he comes again !—sunk deep in thought,
Some grievous thought—within himself shut up,
And wrapt from every object—Stay I would not,
To give him more offence—first break my heart,
Wanting his healthful presence !　　　[Retires.

S C E N E III.

As PALMYRA retires slowly, and looks back,
    ZAPHNA enters.

ZAPH. Upon the rack, stretch'd to the utmost
    point,
That time allots mortality !—No respite—
A long, whole life of anguish !—'tis too much—
Thought will not bear it; and the fact commands
Dismission from above—Prophet accurs'd !—
But well the conscious fiend avoids this arm,

                    Train'd

Train'd by himself to murder—Wretched Zaphna,
From what a height, to what a depth of guilt,
Hath the swift current of one headlong hour
Hurried thee past repeal—from parricide,
To incest!—'twas the price—my sister's bed,
Bought with my father's blood!—which unenjoy'd,
I lose my purchase, and damnation comes
Shorn of its profits—Soft—forget her!—that—
To plunge at once the deep Lethean gulph,
A thousand fathom from the sense of things—
A mercy, next to bliss!—Ha, there again!—
Heaven would not, to the very teeth of guilt,
Impel temptation thus;
But that the fates, as though already past,
Have laid the deed to come—Palmyra!

      [While Palmyra advances slowly, and with diffidence,
        Zaphna speaks.

   Pal. My Zaphna!

   Zaph. O, Palmyra!—

   Pal. What would my love?

   Zaph. Didst thou hear aught?

   Pal. Of what?

   Zaph. Of something strange—

   Pal. No.

   Zaph. Of yawning earthquakes, and of deserts
      waste;
Of tempest-beaten gulphs, whose opening womb
Hath swallow'd all, nor left one mark behind
For fortune's future stroke.

   Pal. These are sad words—
Pity for whom they point at!

Zaph.

ZAPH. Wheresoe'er,
Heaven shield thy peace! for from this spot,
    PALMYRA,
We part, to meet no more—
    PAL. Save me, ye powers!—
Ah, ZAPHNA, wild are all thy words—thy looks,
Unform'd as clouds—and, as the rushing winds,
Unknowing whence they rise, and why they sweep
To desolation!
    ZAPH. No, PALMYRA!—fix'd
As earth's foundations, are the words I utter,
And sure as misery and death to mortals!
    PAL. Yet sure as misery attends on man,
We must not part, my ZAPHNA!—where thou
        goest,
Thither will I; the ground that bears thy couch,
Shall be a watchful pillow for my head;
Thy joys shall be my joys, thy griefs my torture:
In death conjoin'd with what of thee is mortal,
There will I make my grave; and with thy spirit,
Whate'er the lot, demand my Heaven hereafter.
    ZAPH. Why, of what kin art thou to me?
    PAL. Is love,
That sooths the warring elements, and tunes
The world to order, of no kindred then?
And am I not beloved?
    ZAPH. Too well, too well!—
    PAL. Ah, tell me not. Man knows not how
        to love—
And but the blush of maidenhood forbids
The fond unfolding, I could tell thee, ZAPHNA—

                         That

That where thy fex adventures but a ftep,
We go a league in love, and I the fartheft.
   ZAPH. What wouldft thou do?—ha! wouldft
       thou dare——
PAL. Yes——
ZAPH. Fearlefsly?
PAL. Without a limitation.
ZAPH. Fit thofe limbs for travel?
PAL. Yes—with thee.
ZAPH. What—to the brink?
PAL. And onward——
ZAPH. O ye powers?
Think—to forego dominion, pomp, all quality
And foftnefs of thy fex!
   PAL. Slight obftacles——
   ZAPH. O'er-journey'd then, or toil'd with fuch
      rude tafks
As penury enjoins—to lay thee down
On the cold healthlefs ground; the welkin wide
And dark, thy drizzly curtain——
   PAL. Hard, indeed——
If thou the fharer, ZAPHNA!
   ZAPH. Hunger-clinch'd,
Or fcant of fuch rude viands as do ftrive
With appetite——
   PAL. Yet, cherifh'd at thy fide,
This were a feftival.
   ZAPH. Refolved! determin'd!—
Thy hand then—come, at once—why doft thou
      linger?
E're this we fhould be wing'd upon the way,

To leave reflection and remorse far off,
The laggards of our journey.

 PAL. But ZAPHNA——

 ZAPH. O trifler——fare thee well——

 PAL. I will——Come on——

Who lingers now ? Away——but thou art so rash,
So full of starts, that sally up to frenzy——
'Tis this that frights me.

 ZAPH. Take me to thee then,
And mould me as thou wilt.

 PAL. Yes——witness Heaven !
In lieu of all, I take thee——hence, and ever,
            [Embrace.
My lord, my husband, father, brother !

 ZAPH. Ha !
Off, hold thee off——Perdition on the name !

 PAL. The matter——what——why ZAPHNA——on
   my knee,
Wherein have I offended ?

 ZAPH. Who inform'd thee ?

 PAL. Of what, my life ?

 ZAPH. Thy life !——O angel innocence——
Thy death, thy deep damnation !——Nay, hold off,
Nor touch pollution——Villain that I am,
Thy honour's grave, the gulph that would devour
The worth of thine eternal soul——Thy brother ?——
I am——indeed——thy brother !——

 PAL. Shield me, Heaven !

 ZAPH. Saidst thou not, father too ?——Alas,
   PALMYRA !
Thou hast no father———   [Weeps.

 PAL. What's befallen ?

              ZAPH

ZAPH. Juft butcher'd——
Even by thefe hangman's hands.
    PAL. My father ?——
    ZAPH. Murder'd——
    PAL. It is too much—O ZAPHNA, cruel
        ZAPHNA!——
    ZAPH. The good, the kind old man—the fa-
      cred fource,
That lent us both a being—ftopt for ever!——
The generous, great SOPHEIAN!
    PAL. Ah, my ZAPHNA,
Thy health is fhaken much, o'erfway'd by croffes——
I too have caught the malady—my brain
Begins to turn.
    ZAPH. Omnipotent! whofe pardon over guilt
Reaches a length immenfe, be near me now——
O fave me from that prefence!—Down, PALMYRA,
Low as the earth, before the facred fhade   [Kneel.
Of thy great fire—'Tis juft—I feel his vengeance,
Forerunning his approach—it bears upon me——
It whelms, it crufhes me!——

S C E N E IV.

Enter SOPHEIAN in hafte,

He runs and embraces them.

    SOPH. They're here—They're found——
O let me fold them, let me wrap them inward;
Return them to the womb of yearning love,
The heart's warm feat of life! there feed my
      young ones,

And

And cloath them with my vitals—My PALMYRA—
My ZAPHNA—my PALMYRA—my long loft—
O children twice conceived—the happier birth,
To greet my years—new infants of my age—
I have it not in words—'tis here—'tis here—
The welcome of my babes!—Kneel ye, my children?
Now all the bleffings of the dews that fall
In our Arabia, all the fweets that rife,
Be in you, and about you, till your virtues
Grow as in paradife, matured to Heaven,
Without a bloffom dropt—Thefe arms are aged,
In fondnefs overftrain'd—Nay, rife, pray rife,
And blefs me alfo—

   ZAPH. That which is not to be, and that which is,
Struck from the rank of things!—
It muft—yet cannot——
Thefe are the very megrims of exiftence;
The dizzy rounds of thought, that foundering
       drown
In their own whirlpools.
   SOPH. How, my fon!—Why ZAPHNA—
   ZAPH. Nay—by your pardon, fir—I will dif-
       pute it
Againft all tricks of fophiftry—To fay
That things without, are not within us—lo,
Thofe racks, thofe wheels—there's no fuch thing
      —'tis here!—
'Tis the mind's bed whereon the body lies,
Stretch'd out in anguifh!
   SOPH. I am loft to this.
   ZAPH. But have you heard the like?
   SOPH. Of what, my child?

VOL. III.   G   ZAPH.

Zaph. Perhaps a fable—Clytemneſtra too
Was but a mother, and the ſtory ſays
A bad one—in his father's quarrel too
He ſtruck—O wretched ſon!—and he ran mad
      for't—
I have not read of any ſon ſo loſt,
As to aſſault a father—if you have,
I'll liſt—and weep the while.
    Soph. Alas! Palmyra.
    Pal. My lord.
    Soph. Doſt thou know aught of this?
    Pal. In truth,
I am myſelf beſide the ſenſe of things.
You ſay, you are my father—Pardon, ſir;
Your goodneſs makes you ſuch to every orphan—
But, if I claim you by a nearer title,
Then who is Mahomet?
    Soph. A murderous faulcon!
Who ſeizing on the neſt of my delights,
Bore off the mother with her little ones,
And left me reft indeed——How fares my
      Zaphna?—
His eye is much diſtemper'd.
    Zaph. Within the map of our mortality,
Is it not to be found—the land of ſleep?—
Or if a ſtranger, and in foreign climes,
I have dream'd thus—would it were morning!—O—
My head—light, light—thy arm, ſweet ſiſter.
    Soph. His health—kind Heaven, be it thy
      care!—My daughter,
Lead him to ſome repoſe—

SCENE

SCENE V.

ZAPHNA goes out led by PALMYRA. HERCIDES
enters haftily to SOPHEIAN.

HERCID. Beware, my lord, the furety of your
          perfon !
The moon doth wax in labour; all abroad
Is buftle, all confufion ; throughout Mecca,
Each houfe is left the watch of its own fires,
And the wide air is peopled.—
    SOPH. What is forward ?
    HERCID. Some cry, The Prophet, where's the
          Prophet ? Each
Inquires th' alarm, none anfwers—this way now,
And that again, the tide of concourfe flows,
Unknowing why.   To MAHOMET's pavilion
I flew ; affright and bufie confternation
Was vifaged in his train.   I prefs'd to enter ;
When Abdoramen barr'd me with his hand,
And to my ear—" The Prophet is intranced—
" To Heaven, perhaps, upon a fecond embaffy"—
He murmur'd and retired—Is ZAPHNA fafe ?
    SOPH. Here, in my palace.
    HERCID. From what perils fcaped—
Amazing providence !
    SOPH. But much difplaced,
By conftitution, or ill reft; and fomewhat
Tending unto delirium—he did talk
Of actions dire, dark treafons, and of parents
By favage children flain—

G 2

HERCID.

HERCID. Ha! pauſe awhile—
It did occur—I have it—On my ſoul
The impoſtor is no more !—I do remind me—
Slain by miſtake—as mercy ſhall o'ertake me,
Fallen in the toils he pitch'd !—
    SOPH. Who, MAHOMET?
    HERCID. Even ſo—I do remind me—Every
        noon,
Was't not your uſe to worſhip at the Caaba?
    SOPH. It was—
    HERCID. There was your hour of ſlaughter
        fix'd—but then
This Prophet for the fiends, being ill-aſſured,
Of his young votary, not vers'd in blood;
In perſon hath adventured, and ſo fell
Even by his own appointment.
    SOPH. I do think,
It bears a face.
    HERCID. Upon my life, a ſure one !
When in the temple I did warn your ſon
To ſpare a father, I do mind the horror,
The wild aſtoniſhment his eye did utter.—
As though the deed had overrun prevention,
And caution came a laggard.

SCENE VI.

Enter CALED.

    CAL. Health to the prince of Mecca ! may his
        reign,
Peaceful and late, know every night like this,
                Without

Without a rival!—Mahomet, 'tis thought,
Is fallen—for certain, fled. His votaries,
As people all appall'd, converfe in murmurs;
And·fudden rumour thins his hoft.

 Soph. O friend—
Come to my breaft, and fhare its exultation.
[Embrace.
'Tis elfe too mighty; this concurring flood—
Peace, and my children too!—

 Cal. What—found? reftored?
The fame, and both?

 Soph. How kind this focial tranfport!—
Yes, Caled, both, the long loft little ones,
The individual pair—Hercides here
Confirms the wondrous blefling.

 Cal. Ha—Hercides!——
Soft—let me view him well—I would not rafhly—
The blood of innocence, 'tis dear above—
The fame, by all my hopes.—Villain accurs'd!
[Seizes him, and draws a poniard.
Be fhort—if that thou own'ft a prayer—if Heaven
May lift to fudden penitence—this inftant—
'Tis all the wealth thou haft, wherewith to quit
Thy manifold incumbrance.

 Soph. Friend!—Hercides!—
What may this mean?

 Cal. Away, Sopheian—
He dies on thy approach!

G 3   SCENE

SCENE VII.

Enter ZAPHNA and PALMYRA.

ZAPH. My gracious lord, if malady may plead
                              [To SOPHEIAN.
For errors not of will——   [HERCIDES kneels,
    HERCID. Ah, ZAPHNA—will you,
Will you behold the fosterer of your youth
Butcher'd by sudden hands?—your fond pre-
        ferver—
The breast whereon your infancy was laid,
Rent in your presence?
    ZAPH. Who avows a deed
So horrid?
        [Lays his hand to his sword. SOPHEIAN prevents him.
    CAL. Off, rash boy!—thou mayst avenge,
Not save him—who advances, by my life
But quickens his perdition!—Patience, friends,
You know him not—this caitiff—Come, to
        shrift—
It boots thee not to hesitate—dispatch
Thy villainies at large!
    HERCID. Oh, Heaven already
Hath heard the deep detail—
    CAL. Know'st thou this prince—
    HERCID. My first, and worthiest master.
    CAL. Had a brother?
    HERCID. Ay, fir, the noble JOSEPH—you do
        press me,
Even to the quickening of my crimes.

                              CAL.

CAL. O wretch,
How didſt thou find them natured to each other?—
Of ſouls adverſe—or twined in amity,
As brothers ſhould?

HERCID. No loom of ſhuttled threads
E'er wove ſo cloſe a web.

CAL. How grew their difference?-

HERCID. Shame would ſupprefs the mèmory—
          'Twas then,
When the profane impoſtor firſt commenced
His dream of Heaven, into my ſecret ſoul
He warp'd his gliding legends—I did think,
That evil was the bleſſed act òf ſaints,
When hallowed in the purpoſe.

CAL. Hear you that, ZAPHNA?

ZAPH. I do hear it feelingly.

HERCID. This my dread lord, and his all noble
          mate,
This bond of brotherhood, this brace of pillars,
On whom Arabia built her neſt of odours,
Was I inſtructed to divide.

SOPH. O Heavens!

HERCID. To him I forged a tale of pregnant
          luſt
And treaſons, working in the faithful breaſt
Of his moſt loving brother—while, to JOSEPH,
I framed ſuſpicions dark, and deeds of blood,
Thro' envy ſtirr'd of his ſuperior virtue.
Thus the thrice valiant JOSEPH was o'erſway'd
To flee the place of his reſpect and ſafety;
And by the abſence of his potent arm,

G 4

Left

Left the ufurper free in his career
To luft and to ambition.

    Cal. Fare thee well—
The tale is told—Heaven take thee to his mercy!

    Soph. Pernicious flave—O treafon to my peace!
'Tis loft for ever—Fool, moft credulous fool,
Fit ftuff for knaves to work upon—O brother,
Then thou art wrong'd, dear brother of my foul,
Wrong'd paft the reach of penitence!—Ha, caitiff,
This youth and maiden too?

    Hercid. My gracious lord,
I do confefs, to form them in the faith,
Young profelytes for Heaven, I did affift
To tear them from thy arms—yet, Heaven alike
Will witnefs for me, that my love to both,
Did pafs a parent's fondnefs—from their infancy,
Oft in my arms, and never from my heart,
I watch'd their ways, and warded all their dangers;
Yea, to this day, when on the verge of death,
From Zaphna's lip I dafh'd the poifon'd cup,
Even in the tyrant's prefence.

    Cal. Good, my lord!
Such deeds as thefe, to nature's not impaffable,
Have a ftrong pleading.

    Pal. Might I find acceptance.

    Zaph. Let my knee fpeak.

    Soph. O Zaphna—O my children!—
You know not whom—it is a fum immenfe,
That counts our loffes; uncle, brother, father,
All the dear ties!—thy precious father, Zaphna,
Shorn by this flave.

    Zaph. O grace, O earth, O Heaven!
Am I not then your fon?

Soph. Thou art indeed,
Son of my foul, loved heir of my adoption ;
But he thy nobler, more exalted fire,
By nature as by worth.
    Zaph. Your fervant ever—
Hear'ft thou, Palmyra ?
    Soph. 'Tis a tale, my children,
Full of fond tears, and we will pay them amply.
    Pal. to Cal. If, fir, you deem me worthy of
            a claim
In that dear kinfman ; pardon my inquiry—
You feem no ftranger to him.
    Cal. True, kind maid !—
And yet to fpeak the wonders of his pilgrimage,
His wrecks, his fcapes, viciffitudes extreme,
And feats in foreign climes atchieved, the burden
Would charge a wakeful liftener—Foot by foot,
Together have we trod the maze of fortune ;
And arm in arm, with froft upon our helms,
Abode the tentlefs field—The reft is mournful—
Let his laft charge fuffice—" Since Heaven," he
            faid,
" Forbids thefe eyes the profpect of a brother,
" More long'd than light—be thine that bleffing,
            Caled !
" Convince him of his fervant's faith—his in-
            nocence—
" But no reproof, my friend !—And in thy fojourn,
" If thou fhouldft meet with fome unhappy
            orphan,
" Heir to his fire's misfortunes—then, my Caled—
" Think of my child, and take him to thy bounty !"
                            Zaph.

Zaph. It is not to be born——

Soph. Enough, enough!——
This ftrikes at life.

Caled. Alas, his vifage turns!——
I have gone too far——My lord, my royal mafter,
Pardon the fond deceit !——he lives——your fervant,
Your Joseph lives——ill meriting fuch goodnefs.

Soph. Sayft thou, great oracle?

Caled. He ftands before you.
    [Throws off his difguife; Sopheian, Zaphna, and
    - Palmyra ftand fome time amazed: then So-
    pheian rufhes to his arms, while Zaphna and
    Palmyra kneel befide them.

Pal. Ah——

Zaph. Heavens!——

Soph. The mighty powers of grace——I have
    him !——
Off——
Let my eye make him fure, that every fenfe
May feize its proper blifs——'Tis he, 'tis he——
Hear it, ye tribes of Ifhmael!——Lo, Arabia !
Lo, thy returning Phænix——O, my Joseph,
No more of parting——never crofs my ear,
Croak fuch a raven more——but thus, ftill thus,
                        [Embrace.
Even in the fleep of death, together wedded,
Till the laft peal fhall wake the world.

Caled. Thefe fobs——
Thefe tears arreft my utterance——let them anfwer.

Soph. Joseph——behold thy children!——

Caled. O fweet maid !——   [Embraces Palmyra.
May Heaven enfold thee with a love like mine,

              And

And clasp thee to his grace—ZAPHNA my
    child ! .   [Embrace.
  ZAPH. O, sir——
  CALED. Why weeps my boy?
  ZAPH. Unwonted feelings these, that wring the
    heart
With such a straight embrace.
Sons, brothers, sires, to me new comers all !
Yet nature knows, and opens for their entrance;
But answers to them with a voice so loud, .
It tears the mansion inward !—Late, your ZAPHNA
Wanted a friend—and now, he has a father !—
  SOPH. JOSEPH, thy compact—take PALMYRA
    to thee;
And when thou wouldst prefer the maid in mar-
    riage,
I claim her for my ZAPHNA.
  ZAPH. Sir—to speak—
  SOPH. I see, thou canst not; thy too grateful
    heart
Is overcharged—O JOSEPH, O my brother,
Thus, like two confluent streams, in these our
    children,
And theirs descending, we shall flow together,
Smiling through time, and reach into eternity.
  CAL. Heaven, thou art mighty and confess'd
    in this !
With what an arm, through what a mortal maze,
Hast thou led forth thy servants?—Rise, HERCIDES!
Errors that meet reluctance in the will,
Give place for reformation—Still be near,
And let thy ZAPHNA find a father in thee.
                      PAL.

PAL. But what, alas, your cenſure of PALMYRA,
Whoſe life hath been one error?-
    ZAPH. This, my love—
That from our preſent ſenſe of previous ſlidings,
We gather cautious ſteps, and upright treading—
ZAPHNA hath taken a leſſon from his faults,
Beyond all rules of ſtern philoſophy—
Untutor'd as I am, and new to learn,
Where, or to whom, revealing Heaven hath ſent
His outward lumination, ſure I am
His inward is to all men. Is it reaſon?
No—'tis the Boſom'd God, the Living Senſe,
That feels, not argues upon guilt or goodneſs.
'Tis our Internal Chymiſt, ſkill'd to try
The bullion'd droſs, or gold, of every faith,
By the quick touch of his approved aſſay.
If that All-actuating Power, who form'd,
And fills mankind, hath ſtoop'd to their inſtruction;
'Tis to refine the principle he gives,
And not to quell the native ſenſe of goodneſs.
In vain we would The Eternal Unit part—
One in the Heavens, and in the feeling heart!
His laws to his impreſſions muſt be kin :
Where GOD's without, he ſpeaks the GOD within.

T H E

Earl of WESTMORLAND:

A

T R A G E D Y.

PERSONS.

OSBERT, King of Northumberland.

BRUERN, Earl of Weſtmorland.

OSRIC, Earl of Mancheſter, and Friend of BRUERN.

EDWIN, Son of BRUERN and ROWENA.

IVAR, King of Denmark.

HUBBA, his Brother.

ROWENA, Wife of BRUERN.

LORDS of the COUNCIL, OFFICERS, SOLDIERS, MESSENGERS, NUNS, ATTENDANTS.

SCENE, the Suburbs of YORK.

Earl of WESTMORLAND.

A C T I.

SCENE I. The Suburbs of York.

Enter Osric and Edwin.

Edwin. WHERE would you lead, fir—
whither do we travel?

Osric. Hold, we are near the appointment of
our journey.
Where do we travel, fay'ft thou?—O, my foh!
To fave a treafure, more than mines can boaft;
To feize, to fnatch her from impending war,
And give a mother to the arms of Edwin.

Edwin. A mother, fir!—My mother, fay you?

Osric. Yes.

Edwin. O yet beware, how you excite defires
In a fond heart; a fenfe of new delights,
To pine with eager and with empty longings!
A mother!—Are you not my father, then?

Osric. No, Edwin, no—far other than thy fire,
I claim thee as the child of my adoption,
Heir of my heart, and of my foul begotten.

Edwin.

Edwin. O, fir, the creature of your goodnefs
    ever !
But then my parents—will you not inform me ?
  Osric. Search not too deep; behind their ho-
    nour'd names,
Lurk deadly dangers.—O, thou noble youth !
There is a fecret—and, for thy dear fafety,
I wifh it ever fo—for my fad heart
Mifgives me in the iffue.—This fame Osbert,
The king, who long hath fill'd Northumbria's
    throne,
Did wrong thy valiant fire: thy fire, provoked
Beyond the bearings of a faint-like fufferance,
Wrench'd the avenging thunder from Heaven's
    hand,
Levied fierce war, and rent his country's peace.
I was his friend, the inmoft of his foul;
And ere his daring purpofe was avow'd,
In fecret he configned thyfelf and mother,
Her to my care, and thee to my adoption—
For well he knew, tho' loyalty withheld
My hand from his rebellion, yet my heart
Rank'd on his fide, and bled amid the battle.
  Edwin. A caufe, you fay, there was—and O,
    I hope,
A worthy caufe,
  Osric. A caufe there was, my Edwin !
But not the varying circumftance of things,
Not nature can afford a worthy caufe,
For warring on our country—Think of that—
And if—as haply thou fhalt hear a tale
Too foon for thy repofe—then, Edwin, then,

Supprefs

Snpprefs the vengeance rifing in thy bofom;
And, to the judgments of vindictive Heaven,
Permit the crimes of man.
    Edwin. O, tell me all!—
    Osric. I fear I have reveal'd too much already.
    Edwin. What can you fear from me?—Fear
        not your Edwin!
Am I not as the creature of your goodnefs,
Form'd by your hand, and charm'd to your di-
        rection?
    Osric. The beft of mortals have their hour of
        frailty—
Fear, Edwin, fear yourfelf!—I do remember,
When yet thou had'ft not breathed five hours of
        life,
A fervant bore thee in thy fwathed attire
To the great hall, wherein thy father fate
With many noble friends—An aged pilgrim
Stood at the gate: all piercing was his eye,
But calm his afpect; and his ftaff appear'd
A prop for piety, and years well fpent,
And wifdom, to repofe on—He approach'd;
And having eyed thee with a look, that feem'd
To penetrate and found the depths of time,
He laid thy fingers on his palm—he paufed,
And then to thefe prophetic words gave utterance:

      Little, feeble, mighty hand!
    Thou fhalt fave a finking land;
    On the falt and circling flood,
    Build thy country's wall with wood;
    Build the wall of wide renown—
    And give one head to Britain's crown!

Yet, 'ere this or that be done,
The Raven muft obfcure the fun,
Filling nations with affright,
Covering Britain broad as night!
Thou fhalt pierce him as he flies—
On his fall fhall Britain rife!

Yet, O yet, 'ere this be done,
Thou, the fubject, and the fon,
Shalt lift thy fell and fatal dart,
To pierce thy king and father's heart!

EDWIN. Ha! what a fudden terror fhakes my
    limbs,
And freezes to my heart!—Father, and king!—
Murder my father!—lightnings ftrike me firft.
Prevent this parricide—lop off thefe hands;
Tear my heart forth; nor leave a power to act,
Or think fuch horrors!

    OSRIC. Peace to thy heart—thy father is no
        more!

    EDWIN. He fell not then by my mifdeed—
        thank Heaven!

    OSRIC. No. But thy mother now demands our
        care.
This way, my fon.   [Exeunt

SCENE

S C E N E II,

THE INSIDE OF THE ABBEY.

ROWENA, and NUNS ranged on each fide, with
Tapers.

ANTHEM.

Here, in every facred aifle,
Solemn walk, and filent cell,
Truth and Peace ferenely fmile,
Hope and warm Devotion dwell.

Safely landed, here we mourn
Foundering mortals, left behind ;
Wretches, on the deep forlorn,
Toft and wreck'd with every wind.

What has Grandeur to fupply,
What has Pleafure to impart ?—
Mere illufion to the eye,
Real anguifh to the heart !

Here, from time and tranfience won,
Beauty has her charms refign'd ;
Heaven already is begun,
Opening in an humble mind.

Fount of Truth, Seraphic bowl,
Pour the nectar from above !
O, defcend into the foul,
Thirfting after life and love !

H 2

Death

Death is conquer'd, time is paft,
Heaven is prefent to our view—
Welcome, welcome, joys that laft!
Short feducing world, adieu!

[*The Nuns retire.*

Rowena *advances flowly, and fpeaks.*

All hail Devotion, hail thou wing'd for Heaven,
Divine ambaffadrefs! Here let me dwell
With Solitude, thy fifter, and the train
That wait on thy uprifing—Patience, Peace,
And Refignation calm, and Charity
Whofe love enfolds a world.

A Nun *enters.*

Nun. Madam, an antient man,
His look importing hafte and earneft fuit,
Entreats admittance.

Row. Whence?

Nun. From Osric, as he fays, late Earl of
        Manchester.

Row. Say'ft thou, from Manchester? Quick,
        give him entrance.   [*Exit* Nun.

S C E N E III.

Osric *enters.*

Row. What would'ft thou, ftranger?

Osric. O, all-beauteous faint!

Time

Time cuts each lingering preface from my
     tongue—
Ruin has fpread her baleful wings around,
And I from far have haften'd to preferve thee.
   Row. Do I not hear a voice, that ufed to make
The widow's mufic—tuneful as the fall
Of waters on a burnt and thirfty land ?
If thou art Osric, fay—at once inform me;
Or if his angel, I will kneel to thee.
   Osric. Hold thee, Rowena!—Yes, I am that
     Osric,
Nor yet immortal.
   Row. Wherefore, then, thefe weeds,
Thrown o'er thy virtues, like a mifer's cheft
Rufting on treafure ? Some mifhap has found thee;
Why elfe an abfence of twelve tedious years ?
Where haft thou been, what diftance has withheld
     thee ?
And why now here, why thus, and at this hour,
When Apprehenfion, fearful centinel,
Stands all alarm'd upon the gloom of night,
And ftartles at events ?
   Osric. The tale is long—time ferves not now
     for utterance—
Even, while we fpeak, deftruction rufhes onward !
Danes, Dacians, Goths, collecting all their powers,
From Wefer to the cold Septentrion ftar,
The fons of winter, pour fuch legions forth,
As, number'd, never yet have met in arms,
To fpeed perdition ! Swift, O hafte thee hence!—
Friendfhip attends to guide thy facred fteps
To fome afylum; and, to guard thee forth,

H 3

Waits

Waits a young champion, valiant as his fire,
And gentle as thy felf.

 Row. What champion ?—Ah !
I will not hope it—no, I will not, Osric !
Yet thy looks fpeak—and lives my Edwin, then—
My child ?—O, call him, give him to my tears,
To my heart's yearnings !—Yet, do not call him ;
No, rather keep him from my arms for ever !
Perhaps he knows, knows all the piteous tale
Of his unhappy parents—how the ravifher,
This king of fatyrs, ftole upon the hour
Of faith, and holy hofpitality—
My hufband abfent, every power away,
That fhould have guarded innocence and virtue
From brutal force, from horrid violation—
And ftain'd the chafteft, whiteft page of life,
With foul difhonour !

 Osric. No, he knows it not.

 Row. Why, where has he efcaped the fhafts of
   flander ?
Is there a tongue that fpeaks Rowena's name,
But aptly tacks pollution to the found,
And taints the paffing breeze?—Who knows nought
   elfe,
Is learn'd in my misfortune; and the fhame,
That fits between the low abafed brows
Of his fad mother, fhall attaint my child,
And blaft his filial virtue.

 Osric. Think not fo.
For thou art all one excellence, too pure
For groffer imputation !—
Thefe many years, the bufy, meddling world,

          Has

Has talked itself to filence; and thy fon,
Hath ever lived, till this important hour,
A ftranger to thy name.——
Soon as thy mighty hufband fell in battle,
Upon that bloody day, wherein he made
His laft dread effort to revenge thy wrongs,
Driven from my country, from my native honours,
I fled, thy little fon within my arms;
And in the court of royal Ethelred,
Till now have fojourn'd—EDWIN, gentle youth!
Approach, my EDWIN!—draw with reverence here,
And bend thee as to Heaven!

S C E N E IV.

EDWIN advances with flow reverence.

Row. What lovelinefs!——
Fond, fond refemblance! gefture, form, and grace,
Like my loft lord!—ideas, once fo loved,
Nor yet forgotten!—Parent nature, how,
How doft thou ftir me! how awaken all
The tender, dear diftractions! O, my child!
                                        [Embraces.
    EDWIN. Your pardon, madam—I am much
        unfkill'd,
And new to all the duties of a fon;
But in your face, as in the front of Heaven,
There is a language that befpeaks my foul,
And dictates more than outward forms can reach!
Here, at my heart, you pull the vital cords;
            H 4   Within

Within I know and feel from whence I am,
Part of your being—But—O mother!—
    Row. What says my child?
    Edwin. Had Heaven so will'd, how doubly
        bleſt were Edwin!
My father—what of him?
    Row. Thy father?—ah, that I can only ſay,
Thou had'ſt a father!—His paternal lips
Have held fond talk with thy unthinking days,
For he did love thee with a mother's feeling;
And that ſtrong arm on which the nations hung,
With thee hath toy'd away the ſmiling hours,
And grew around thy ſlumbers—Me, even me,
He loved—too fatally he loved thy mother!—
The nobler paſſions of humanity,
Bore his bold veſſel with too ſtrong a wind—
We were his ruin—O, my child, my child!
Thy father loved too well—and we have loſt him.
    Osric. Bright ſaint, let other hours indulge the
      ſcenes
Of fond remembrance—now, the times are urgent!
Haſte, haſte, Rowena, 'ere the ſpeedier foe
This night, perhaps, ſhall ruſh around theſe walls,
And intercept our journey.
    Row. Ah, my lord,
Fly thou—and with thee be my Edwin's ſafety!
But take no thought for one ſo loſt as I am.—
I cannot, muſt not fly.
    Osric. Say you, Rowena?—
We have miſtook your meaning.
    Row. No, good Osric—

My

My reft is fix'd even here; and Heaven, I truft,
Is the next manfion that receives Rowena.

Osric. It muft not be—Already, I behold
The powers of hell unbound ;
They rufh to earth, and with them bring along
Hair ftarting horror, fear, and hate, and rage,
And wild ey'd famine, and wide-reaching wafte,
And luft and rape—by whom thy wrongs, Ro-
      wena,
Are multiplied on thoufands.

Row. Not fo, I hope—around this hallow'd
      pile,
Oft hath the rage of battle felt rebuke';
While each licentious foldier ftood abafh'd,
Or bow'd at diftance—From the penfive fhrines,
The twilight arches, and the fhadowy domes,
Religion throws a far-forbidding awe
On all beholders.

Edwin. Alas! my mother, have I found you
      then,
To part with you fo foon ? like chearing light,
But for a moment fent to blind-born eyes—
Juft come, to fhew the bleffednefs of fight,
And bid them clofe for ever !

Osric. Soft!—fome lights approach,—
This way they move—Thy chamber, hafte, Ro-
      wena !
An hour fhall fend us to thy laft refolves.
               [Exit Rowena. Back Scene clofes.
'Tis Osbert—that is he—This way, my fon ;
I would obferve him.   [They retire.

SCENE

S C E N E V.

Enter OSBERT attended.

OSBERT. Hafte, Wolford !—gather up our
     . fcatter'd foldiers,
Call the militia in—alarm the country—
Line the wall round—and bar the maffy gates—
Confufion ! to be thus furprifed !
No word, no warning of the coming danger !—
Our fcouts, are they gone forth ?
  OFFICER. They are, my liege.
  OSBERT. Throw open all our magazines of
      arms ;
We want new levies—and proclaim rewards
To old and young, to every trade and rank,
Whofe arm fhall lift a fword in our defence.
Where's Anulph, Adelfrid ?
  OFFICER. They are fled, my lord.
  OSBERT. O recreant flaves ! they've eat our
      honey up,
And now forfake the hive—Quick, what's the
      news ?

Enter an OFFICER.

OFFICER. Retire, my liege, retire—'ere morn-
      ing dawns,
The foe is on us.
  OSBERT. Let them come, my friends.
Short is the conning of a foldier's leffon—
If not to live, why then, to fall with honour.

Retire,

Reti.e, and leave me to my thoughts a while—.
> [Exeunt Attendants.

'Tis finifh'd—Thou haft found me, Heaven !—
Where now,
O, where's Northumbria's guardian, where is
WESTMORLAND,
Whofe arm launch'd forth the thunder of the war
And crufh'd invafion ?—where my guilt hath
fent him,
By my foul rape of his moft chafte ROWENA,
Difhonoured to his grave !—Where too is MAN-
CHESTER,
My throne's beft prop, the wifdom of my council ?
Him too I have caft off; and given, in place,
Riches to knaves, to cowardice commiffion,
Office to ignorance, and truft to traitors.

SCENE VI.

OSRIC and EDWIN come forward.

OSBERT. Who aft thou ?

OSRIC. A Briton.

OSBERT. Subjeft to whom ?

OSRIC. My country, and the law.

OSBERT. Hath not thy king a name ?

OSRIC. Yes, I remember now—his name was
OSBERT,
Till loft to fame, and of himfelf forgotten.

OSBERT. Ha ! know'ft thou not, that chaftife-
ment attends
The voice of infolence ?
> OSRIC,

I

Osric. The voice of truth!

Osbert. O, it is
A voice, to which I have been long a ftranger!—
Pride, ftand aloof! ye vifionary forms
Of titled majefty, away! while thus,
Thus to my arms I take one honeft man,
More worth to kings than empire! [Embraces Osric.

Osric. Saints of Heaven!
Is this Northumbria's monarch, this our Osbert,
Whofe heart fo long was fhut from all accefs
Of alienated worth?—Rowena!—Westmorland!

Osbert. I underftand thee—
O, feverely true! Heaven pardon and redrefs!

Osric. Then pardon thou—my liege, my ftill
  loved lord! [Kneels.
Pardon a rafh and moft licentious tongue,
That thus, with unexampled boldnefs, durft
Defame thy virtues, and traduce my mafter.

Osbert. Ha! Manchester!

Osric. The fame—Why turns my prince
From his old man?

Osbert. Ungrateful to mine eye,
Is the cold vifage of the friend I have injured.

Osric. No more!—I fwear,
Thus to have found thee, to thyfelf reftored,
Is every lofs retrieved—'tis more than empire!
It is thy better birth-day, hail'd and hymn'd
By angel forms, and heavenly winged faints,
That guard a Britifh throne!

Osbert. My father!—Come,
Come to my heart, and plant thy virtues there.
    [Embrace.

      And

And O! thou fage of years, thou fon of wifdom,
If there is aught in art or arms to friend us,
One caft of helpful council—ftretch thy hand,
And fave a finking realm!

  Osric. One yet remains,
One laft expedient, one of mightieft proof—
But ftrange to power, and ftill to kings ungrateful.

   Osbert. O name it!

   Osric. Wherefore do I fee thee thus,
With luke-warm foldiers, thinly fown around thee?
Where are thy fons, thou father of a people!
That now fhould combat for their own inheritance?
O! to the fouls of unpoffeffing flaves
No lofs can come, and every lord is equal.

   Osbert. What's to be done?

   Osric. Yet, ere the morning dawn,
Summon thy fubjects, yield them their dear rights,
The rights of men free-born—the fons of Heaven,
Who hold, in common with the proudeft kings,
The gifts of nature, 'and the claims of reafon!
Would'ft thou have foldiers faithful, daring,
         dauntlefs;
Give them a ftake to fight for—Is it gold,
Office, or honour, or the brighter prize
Of animating glory?—No—'tis more!
'Tis LIBERTY, my prince, affured by law,
And circled from encroachment!—Never fell
Army, or empire, 'ere the fatal day,
In which they fell from Freedom!

   Osbert. O, enough—all, all fhall be amended,
As thou, my friend and father, fhalt appoint.
But fay——

‡

What

What youth is that whofe form attracts our eye,
And bids it note him ?

  Osric. Mine, my gracious fovereign.
  Osbert. Is he thy fon ?
  Osric. I have no other child.
  Osbert. Son, worthy of the fire !—Approach
    brave youth !
And fay how beft a monarch may prevail,
Who means to woo and win thee to his friendfhip?

  Edwin. My gracious lord, the little worth I
    boaft,
Will fave the feeking.

  Osbert. O! we truft not thee,
To fpeak thine own defervings ;.well we know,
Honour ne'er rifes in its own report.
But if we yet furvive to-morrow's fun ;
If, by thy wife and warlike father's councils ;
If, by thy arm, thou offspring of the brave !
It lie in valour, or in art to fave ;
Thence, every joy and every equal care,
From both I gather, and with both I fhare—
With him my fcepter, and my heart with thee ;
Thou my loved brother, and my father he !

         [Exeunt.

END OF THE FIRST ACT.

           ACT

A C T II.

S C E N E I.

OSBERT and OSRIC.

OSBERT. STILL living—and fo near me?—
O, the rapture!—
The dear diftrefs'd!—Will you then plead my
pardon?
Will you not tell her—nay, enforce it, OSRIC;
Pour all the abundance of my foul before her—
Tell her, her fafety lies within thefe walls;
My crown is hers, my life her beft protection.
  OSRIC. Mean you to wed her, then?
  OSBERT. Would'ft thou not, my friend,
Afpire at Heaven, if diftance did not bar thee?
Wed her!—yes, OSRIC—for a fingle day,
An hour of blifs in her fociety,
I'd barter every year of life to come—
But, O my crime—that outrage on her honour!—
Her peace, her beauty, and her fpotlefs innocence,
Rent and polluted by my brutal paffion!—
What fhall I plead?—Pardon fhe never can—
Tell her, in that, we are already wedded;
For OSBERT hates himfelf.
  OSRIC. I will, my lord.

OSBERT,

OSBERT. Nay, but this night—this very night,
    my OSRIC!—
Fate may difpofe the morrow to another.
Tell her this inftant hour ftands fingly up
'Twixt life and death, time and eternity,
Connubial honour and the blot of ages!
Away—my peace attends on thy return!—
Some angel fit upon thy charmed tongue,
And teach thy breath perfuafion.   [Exit OSBERT.

    OSRIC. ROWENA married, and a queen!—'tis
    well—
The foe expell'd, my prince return'd to virtue,
Her honour refcued, and his fault forgotten!—
But, EDWIN!—there's the gulph—this dread pre-
    diction!
For OSBERT wedded, then becomes at once
His king, and father; fo may fate be anfwer'd!—
'Tis but in man, throughout the maze of life,
To mark the clue of his peculiar duty—
'Tis Heaven's to wind and guide the thread at
    pleafure.   [Exit.

S C E N E II.

Enter WESTMORLAND and ETHELWALD.

ETHEL. I fwear it is too much—Again per-
    mit me
To gaze, to feaft my fight—again fall proftrate—
            [Kneels.
To kifs the fteps of my reviving lord—
My lord, my long loft lord—to touch, to clafp him,
           That

That every fenfe may fwear—'tis he, indeed;
And not fome phantom of illufive joy,
That would abufe his fervant!
    WEST. To my arms——
To your returning mafter, rife, my friend,
My long tried ETHELWALD!
    ETHEL. Dead! wept! entomb'd!—
Your folemn trophy rais'd!—all the fad rites,
Of dirge, and mournful obfequy!—yet thus,
To fee, to feel, that things impoffible
Appeal to demonftration!
    WEST. Lift, my friend,
And lofe thy wonder.—
Fame fays, that, on the eve of holy-crofs,
Cover'd with wounds, along the blood-ftain'd
       bank
Of fouthern Tyne, thy haplefs mafter fell.
He fell, indeed!—confufion followed ftraight,
And rout, and darknefs, that difpers'd alike
Victor, and vanquifh'd. Yet, not fo retired
One faithful foldier—he, o'er heaps of dead,
Sat mournful, till the moon fhould lift her lamp,
To light him to his lord, whom foon he found—
From my pale head he loos'd the mangled cafque;
And, bending o'er me, thro' the filent night
Pour'd forth his loud affliction. To his plaint,
And the cool frefh, I rais'd my ponderous lids,
Then funk again—Tranfported, all in hafte
He ftript my arms, and on a headlefs trunk
Beftow'd the rich endowment; bound my wounds,
And, with a finewy, and a dear embrace,

Upborn, convey'd me from the field of death,
To a near hamlet.

ETHEL. Pay him, bounteous Heaven!—
Let me not tafte of death, till I become
A fervant to that fervant!

WEST. Senfe, and health,
With time, return'd; till when, I held my fecret.
Then did I give my fortune to the winds,
That threw me on the Dane—him long I ferv'd,
Led forth his battles, and enlarged his bounds;
And, in return, he comes, my foldier now,
To free my country, and to right my quarrel.

ETHEL. Alas! my mafter, is it in thy leading,
That fuch a hoft of foes comes banded onward,
To lay fair Albion wafte?

WEST. No, ETHELWALD—
My foldiers ftep as though on holy ground,
Smooth as a mift that moves upon the morning,
Dropping kind dew on every head, fave one—
For there our vengeance levels—he, your king!—
Your precious OSBERT!—lives he?

ETHEL. He does.

WEST. Thank Heaven for that—O, fnatch him
        not, ye fiends!
Set him but firft within my reach of fight,
And if he fcape this arm—live, OSBERT, live!—
Bow, world, before thy lord—for he's immortal!—

SCENE

S C E N E   III.

Enter Hubba.

Hub. I have traced and found thee, Westmor-
land!—O friend,
Does this beseem the general of our armies—
Thus to forsake his camp, alone, unguarded ;
And cast his valued person on the edge
Of danger, and of darkness ?
  West. O, my Hubba,
There is, there is a cause!—
  Hub. Wherefore that sigh,
When fame, when friendship, and when Denmark
        wait,
But till the morrow's sun shall light the world,
To give Northumbria's scepter to your hand,
And crown your arms with conquest ?
  West. O friend, friend !
My steps have long been strangers to ambition—
I seek not fame, nor royalty.
  Hub. How, Westmorland !
What else is worthy of a warrior's notice ?
  West Vengeance.
  Hub. Vengeance ?
  West. Vengeance, my royal friend!—O, ge-
        nerous Hubba,
Oft was I on the point to tell thee all,
To pour my anguish in thy friendly bosom—
But shame withheld the tale.

Hub. Long have I mark'd
The labours of thy foul, the big emotion;
But fear'd to afk, although I wifh'd to eafe thee.
    West. The hour is come that muft reveal my
        wrongs,
Loud as their cry for juftice—Lift, my friend,
It is a grievous tale—I once was held,
Fair, brave, and young, the hope of my loved
        country,
Her firft in arms, and honour'd as her king.
Upon a time, I faw a noble maid,
Daughter and heirefs to the earl of Devon;
I faw, I loved, and woo'd, and won her to me—
But, O, to fay how bleft—new-budding youth
Would run to age, in numbering o'er her beauties,
And never feel decay!—
Where'er fhe moved, the gladfome eaft went
        with her,
And rofe in morning·comfort on my fight.
At length, this angel, placed on earth, brought
        forth
A fon, a little cherub to the world,
Cloath'd in the brightnefs of his mother's beauty.
So, all was full, rhe focial, the humane,
And every cordial amity!—Two years
Pafs'd blifsful on, and fmiled.—But then!—
    Hub. What then?
    West. Ay, then arrived that hour, that fatal
        hour,
Which hell caught out, and mark'd for my un-
        doing—
When, in a vifit, as from friend to friend,

King

King Osbert fought my caftle, I was abfent—
But my too charming bride !—dark envy faw,
And figh'd—his crown feem'd poor—high paffions
    rofe,
That fwept faith, friendfhip, Heaven, and earth
    before 'em.
To fue, was vain—he knew it vain—what elfe ?
Force, guilty, ruffian force—and I was ruin'd !—

    Hub. O, honour, virtue !—what, Northumbria's
        Osbert ?

    West. Even he—the fcepter'd ravifher, the
        robber—
The luftful, lawlefs ruler !—Go, my friend,
We have a bufinefs here of private claim,
But dear import—return thou to the camp,
Prepare our deftined embaffy to York,
And challenge forth whoe'er, in fingle fight,
Shall ftand his country's hope—he fhall be met,
And thefe the high conditions—if we conquer,
Then, Osbert cedes, and fair Northumbria's crown
Is left at our difpofe ; but, if we fall,
We fwear to abdicate his throne for ever,
And leave the land in peace.

    Hub. It fhall be done.

    West. Osbert, I think, will not confide his
        crown
To any fecond arm : for he is bold ;
Though guilty, warlike as the fons of earth,
Ere nature knew decline—my vengeance then,
With fudden tranfport fhall fpring forth, confefs'd,
And gripe its quarry.

I 3

Hub. 'Tis moſt likely—O,
May all the powers that war on perfidy
Succeed your hope !—Adieu.   [Exit Hubba.

West. My Ethelwald,
Are we not near the place that holds my treaſure—
The bleſt abode, where my Rowena dwells,
And confecrates the ſhrine ?—

Ethel. We are, my lord——
Yon pile, yon happy pile, contains the faint,
And lifts our earth to Heaven.

West. Your arm, my Ethelwald,
For l am ſudden faint with doubt and joy,
And trembling expectation—
Now walls, kind walls, be faithful to your truſt;
Give but theſe eyes to fee her once again,
And I will cafe your ſpires with beaten gold !—
Lend me thy cloak—Attend a-while without—
Yon gate invites my entrance—   [Exeunt.

S C E N E   IV.

An Apartment in the Abbey.

Rowena and Osric feated.

They rife and come forward.

Osric. Yet, give me leave—
Row. No more—I pray, no more !—
Honour !—ſhame to it, for it ſticks on guilt,
And leaves reproach to virtue ! I will none on't—
My lord, my lord, I am married to my grave,
And will no other huſband.

Osric.

Osric. Wondrous creature,
All fainted excellence!—I did but wish
My country wedded to her peace in thee;
To fee thy bright example, as a glafs,
Rais'd to the public eye, where every foul
Muft fhame to look, or drefs itfelf to virtue.

  Row. Alas! good Osric, I have no fkill to
        queen it;
And if the little virtue Heaven has lent,
Will ferve to pilot on one humble bark
To its laft port, it is a tafk fufficient—
So much for royalty!—And, for the reft,
I had rather mix me with the loathfome dead,
And yield my living body to corruption,
Than turn my foul into the bed of fenfe
Still more detefted.

  Osric. Yet, Rowena, yet,
There is a claim, your country has a claim—

  Row. A claim!

  Osric. Yes, lady,
Of retribution—that you feal her peace;
A kind reverfe of bleft profperity,
In recompence of all the mighty ills,
You brought upon her.

  Row. I, Osric, I?

  Osric. Not the famed Helen, whofe deftructive
        charms
Laid Afia wafte, and made all Greece a widow,
Caufed equal defolation—Still, methinks,
I fee thy hufband in his vengeance rife
Loud as the thunder, furious as the whirlwind;

I 4   O'er-

O'erturning armies, and our tower-fenced towns,
In undistinguished ruin !
    Row. No, MANCHESTER—He warr'd on guilt
        alone,
The friends of violence, the foes of virtue !
    Osric. Against his country, and her lawful
        king—
    Row. His country's lawless tyrant !
    Osric. He is penitent—
As pilgrims sworn to wander thro' the world,
Their bare feet weeping blood on every flint,
For one false step.
    Row. O name him, name him not !
    Osric. How!—cannot piety, like thine, so
        rais'd
O'er all we deem of angels—fast, and prayer,
And vigils, that already hold in Heaven
Their nightly converse—cannot these afford
One drop of mercy to repentent frailty,
That kneels and prostrate falls beneath thy feet
For blest forgiveness ?
    Row. O, OSRIC !—
My friend, my father !—well, I will confess it—
To thee I will confess—days, nights, and years,
I have strove, and combated, and pray'd for help,
And waked, and watch'd, and wept, and wish'd to
        pardon,
To quell the swelling hate, the big resentment—
In vain—still faithful to the dread remembrance,
The giant wrong returns too mighty for me—
His name, his dire idea !—'tis my curse,
The spectre of my thoughts, my detestation,

8

My

My daily, nightly horror!—
Heaven, pardon thou!—But where?—O! where's
       the power,
Shall wash my stain away?
   Osric. Thy stain, thou mirror of divine per-
      fection!—
Thy stain?
   Row. Indelible,
It sticks—'tis rooted in my name, my memory,
Deep as existence—O, the ruthless ravager,
Who kills for ages!—Seest thou, Manchester,
These organs, once so pleasing to the eye,
Now to the soul they hold abhorr'd, and loath-
      some?
This body of pollution, 'tis my burden,
A load irreconcileable—till death
Shall mix and crumble it with kindred dust,
That no discerning finger may point out
Where lie the ruins of the lost Rowena.
   Osric. Faireft, my suit, I doubt, was over
      earneft,
But did not mean offence—Repose attend thee!
Heaven's happiest visions open in each thought,
And furnish out thy slumbers!   [Exit.

S C E N E   V.

Westmorland enters, and bends on one Knee.

   Row. O! once, indeed,
I had a husband—his all placid face
Was as a little Heaven, new planeted

                With

With twin bright stars; and beauty from each
    limb,
As through a summer casement, look'd abroad,
And found no rival.——
Ha! what art thou——   [Seeing WESTMORLAND.
That thus obtrudest thy irreverend step
Upon the sacred vigils of the night ?——
Com'st thou in friendship ?   [WEST. kneels.
    WEST. From that sacred breast,
Heaven's choicest seat, far, far be dread and
    danger !
In friendship ? yes—with awe—with adoration.
    Row. Whence?
    WEST. Peace be to your gentle heart !——
I bring a token, and from one, who once
Was honour'd with the highest, dearest claim,
That ever did enrich a mortal—one,
Who once did boast ROWENA for his blessing—
Her long lost, her life-wedded WESTMORLAND.
    Row. If, O if—
Celestial messenger ! thou dost descend,
To tell my hour's at hand—I hail thy summons !
My soul is on the wing to meet my lord,
Where all cares end, and love alone's immortal.
    WEST. He lives—thy happy husband !——
He lives, he comes !——Already has he past
A length of distant lands—already reach'd
The beach that beetles o'er that envious sea,
Which roll'd between you !——
    Row. Living !——landed !——
Did'st thou say, landed ?
    WEST. Yes, within this hour——

I

This,

This, this exalted hour, this hour of blessedness!
Prepare to hear, to see, to hold—
    [WESTMORLAND rises—the cloak drops,
 Row. Ah, Heaven!
O'erwhelm me not with hopes of happiness,
That mock a mortal's reach!—Am I awake?
In life, or death, that form should be remem-
    ber'd—
It breaks upon me—O the gracious figure!—
'Tis he, my lord, my husband!—
Shield me, give me room!—
His presence fills the place—but leaves our air—
Too thin for breath—I cannot—oh— [Faints.
 WEST. Here end me, nature!—I have lived
   my length,   [Catches her.
Have climb'd the zenith of my Heaven—and hence
'Tis declination all—Wake, O wake, my love,
Star of sweet influence! Ye silver lids,
That chamber up the morning, open straight,
Open your gates, that I may see my day.
 Row. This crown is hot—it sears me to the
   brain!
Yon is a brighter, for 'tis gem'd with stars!—
Away—unhand me, ruffian—thou a king!
Have I not sworn it? I will not be wedded.
     [Breaks from him.
 WEST. Alas, she raves—
 Row. Indeed—eyes mock me not!
If it is he, I'll have him!— [Runs into his arms.
 WEST. ROWENA, dearest!——
Why wilt thou pluck up sorrow by the roots,
      With

With such deep heaves? Why drown me with thy
　　tears?—
This paffion quite o'erbears my growth of joys,
Which elfe had reach'd the ftars—Ah, thofe dove
　　eyes,
How they do fpeak!—
Wilt thou not know me?

　Row. Art thou not my lord,
My wedded lord, fair Albion's arm of war?
And am not I thy true and humble wife,
Sworn fervant of thy will? I think, even fo.
But whether fo it be, in life or death—
Awake, or over-watch'd—in footh, I know not.

　West. O, thou fair creature,
Whom nature form'd fo exquifitely apt
To fill the deep defirings of my foul,
Made up of love, and peace-born bleffednefs!
Do I then hold thee?—painful, painful rapture!

　Row. Lord of my life, haft thou alone the
　　power
To pafs the bourn of pale mortality,
Whence none return befide? or has the grave,
Cold and infenfible till now, relented,
Warm'd by my fighs, and quickening to my
　　wifhes—
And given thee back, thus lovely, to the light,
Thus, thus, to my embraces?　　　　　[Embrace,

　West. My heart's bleffing!—
The feafon ferves not now—we fhall have time,
We fhall have time for all the wond'rous tale—
To talk, to liften, mingling fweet regards,

　　　　　　　　　　　　　　　　　And

And looks, and fmiles, and queftions, from that
      tongue,
Tuned, as the harp of David, to expel
All anguifh from the foul !

  Row. Delightful intercourfe,
Foretafte of Heaven !—But then—

  West. Why that look averted ?
Then !—What of then, thou deareft ?

  Row. Then, my Westmorland,
How fhall I dare to lift a face of fhame
To that majeftic brow ?—And yet, I truft,
'Tis not the tranfience of external beauty,
A form alone that won thee to my wifhes—
No, thou didft wed a more effential wife,
The heart, the immortal foul of thy Rowena,
Still thine, and unpolluted.

  West. Ha !—yes, thou fhalt have vengeance !—
      Say'ft thou, deareft ?
O, no, thou art all, from violence, from Osbert,
From mortal touch, all pure and unpolluted,
As fnow new fifted through a northern fky,
And kift by the cold breeze—thy chafter breath
Would ferve to light the veftal fire anew,
And confecrate its flame.

  Row. Our Edwin lives—

  West. For that I bow to Heaven—
There undivided, clafp'd within our offspring,
The fondeft wifh my foul ere form'd is anfwer'd.

Enter

Enter ETHELWALD.

ETHEL. My lord, beware!—Juſt iſſuing from
    the town,
By diſtant torch-light I diſcern ſome troops,
That this way bend their motions.

    WEST. Then, ROWENA,
We part for ſome few hours—To-morrow's ſun
Shall light me to my love; and I will lift her
To ſuch a height, ſo near divinity,
The bending world ſhall look with wonder up-
    ward,
And worſhip while they gaze!

    Row. O, my life's lord——
Grandeur and I have vow'd a wide divorce—
I can't ſupport the ſtedfaſt ſearching brow,
The world's broad look—I ſink to death be-
    neath it!
Ah, might I wooe thee to the kindly vale,
The ſweet deſcents of life!—there Peace keeps
    home,
Nor ever viſits at a lordly manſion;
But with the loves and joys, and downy hours,
Bounds o'er the green, and laughs within the
    cottage.

    WEST. Then, be it ſo—
Soon as one urgent debt is paid to honour,
Adieu the cares, and coils, that worldlings dreſs
In rainbow robes, and falſify with titles!
Far from the ſcenes of frenzy, let us fly

To

To some fair Eden of primeval innocence,
Where my Rowena's presence shall bereave
The fox of fraud, the tyger of his fiercenefs;
Shall tune all paffions of the foul to peace,
The waves, the winds, and war-worn elements,
To their firft order——Thou, like finlefs Eve,
New from the hand of Heaven, returning blifs
To that fond bofom whence fhe drew her being;
My vital confort, my far dearer part,
Warm at my fide, and panting at my heart!

[Exeunt.

END OF THE SECOND ACT.

ACT

A C T   III.

S C E N E I.

The Council Chamber.

Osbert, Osric, Edwin, and Lords, rising from
Table.

Osbert. THE dawn has almoſt ſtolen upon
our councils.
Here break we up ; and let a ſhort repoſe
Fit us for weightier toils.
[Exeunt all but Osbert and Osric.
No ray of hope, thou ſayeſt—
No glimpſe, however diſtant, that may ſerve
To light me to my wiſhes ?
Osric. None, my lord.
Cold as a marble emblem of the dead,
By ſome chill vault incircled from the world,
Rowena's every ſenſe is ſhut, alike,
To love as to ambition—Yet the turns,
The ſtrange events that lodge within the womb
Of wide futurity, alike forbid
Deſpondence, as preſumption.
Osbert. There I caſt
One little grain, where hope may yet take root

In

In poffibility—For, O my friend,
My father! who haft given me, by thy councils,
My better birth—a birth, wherein alone
Exiftence can have worth, my birth in virtue!—
Already does my foul attempt for freedom ;
And, from the fetters and the gloom of guilt,
Gets all aloft, and foars within my bofom.
I feel new being, joyous, calm, humane,
The kindly offices of man to man,
How fweet the intercourfe!—of kings to all,
Thrice bleft prerogative!

   Osric. True, my loved liege—
When monarchs ftoop to act, and feel like men,
They rife a flight o'er angels.

   Osbert. Yes, my Osric,
The foe who meets the ardour of to-morrow,
I think was born when lucklefs planets ruled.
I pant for day—I pant, to fhew my people,
What deeds their king fhall dare in their defence,
The firft in danger, as the firft in office.
But I detain thy age from needful reft ;
Thy couch expects thee—this one warm embrace
Shall yield thee till the morning.

   Osric. Firft of kings,
Thrice valiant Osbert,—may thy future reign
Rife, like the coming fun, upon the world,
Chearful to man, difpenfing light and life!
And after a long courfe of wide beneficence,
Retire, when late, to Heaven, and fet in glory!
                         [Exit Osric.

Enter an OFFICER.

OFFICER. My liege, as weftward we held on
   our rounds
Near the York Minfter, we efpied a man,
Of port majeftic, and of fhining arms,
Dazzling the night. He would have pafs'd our
   guard;
And Anulf, Ethelbald, and valiant Ofwald,
Fell by his arm—At length, by numbers quell'd,
He waits your pleafure—
 OSBERT. Give him entrance. Ha!—

S C E N E II.

Enter WESTMORLAND in Chains.

A majefty indeed!—though fome lorn cloud
Appears to have informed his manly brow
With well acquainted forrow!——Say, brave
   ftranger,
Who, and whence art' thou? Silent!—then,
   perhaps,
Some dear and facred grief fits heavy on thee,
That fhould not be prophaned by vulgar ears.
Leave us together.   [Exeunt Guards.
Now, declare thyfelf—
And if thou beareft up but to thy feeming,
Noble and virtuous, though thou fhould'ft be
   found
My foe profefs'd, know OSBERT for thy friend.
 WEST. Thy foe profefs'd!—

OSBERT.

Osbert. Of Denmark, art thou?

West. Yes.

Osbert. What—of the powers now banded
    againſt Britain?

West. A leader.

Osbert. Speak thy purpoſe.

West. Thus ſays the Dane; and what my
    tongue declares,

His ſcepter ratifies—Not luſt of fame,

Or empire, bears us to Albion's ſhore;

But juſtice on a ſingle head—Grant that,

And Denmark is your friend.

Osbert. Have ye, for this, o'erſpread our ſeas
    with fleets,

Our land with arms?

West. We have.

Osbert. Name the offender.

West. Nay more—

We aſk, but what by law of arms we warrant—

The guilty and the injured, man to man!—

The reſt let fate decide.

Osbert. 'Tis granted, chearfully.

West. And ſurely—is it?

Osbert. Yes, if there's truth or honour in the
    land;

In Heaven, or earth, aught binding.

West. You will not ſhrink—

Osbert. No—though ourſelf ſhould anſwer thy
    bold ſummons.

Thou haſt our faith—I ſwear it, by my head.

West. 'Tis there our vengeance levels!

Osbert. Inſolent!—

K 2

And

And who is he, that dares impeach a monarch ?
And more prefumptuous ftill, that fingly dares,
In equal field, to meet the arm of Osbert ?
    West. He ftands before you——
    Osbert. Ha!—thy name ?
    West. 'Tis Westmorland !—

A long paufe.

Now do you know me ?
    Osbert. Westmorland !——
Had yawning hell
Caft all his fiends upon me—neither depth,
Nor height—the univerfe could not afford
A fpe&tre, like thyfelf, to fhake the nerve,
And blanch the cheek of Osbert !
    West. O thou fell tyger, hungry as the grave,
Gorged with the lives of innocence and honour !——
What can'ft thou anfwer, thou imperial fpoiler,
To me, thy fubje&t ?—now thy flave—in chains——
Alone—unarm'd—yet, by thy proper guilt,
Exalted as thy judge—an awful judge,
To fink thee to perdition !
    Osbert. I had made——
I hoped, I trufted, I had made—my peace
On earth, in Heaven !—but, like a baneful blaft,
A fudden peft, thou art come to wither up
All the wide harveft of my ripen'd hopes——
Thou plague, thou hell of Osbert !
    West. Yes——
Beyond this life—while there's a place for being——
War, hateful, deadly, and determined war,
Muft be the lot of Westmorland and Osbert !

Heaven

Heaven can't contain us; nor the fuffering earth,
And keep her elements at peace—
The feat of memory is curs'd that holds thee—
O I would chafe thee to the verge of thought,
There pufh thee off, and blot thee from creation—
Though I leapt after!
   OSBERT. Rebel, I thank thee—thou doft well
        expunge
My fingle fault by thy fuperior wickednefs!
To thoufands—to thy country falfe, thou traitor—
Who never wrong'd thee!—
   WEST. Ha!—yes—it may—it may be fo—
Devil!—'tis thou haft damn'd me then—Yet,
        wherefore?
The very wren would rouze at fuch a wrong;
Would guard his little neft from violation,
And plume himfelf againft the princely eagle!
In fuch a caufe, all ways, all means, are lawful—
Truth does avouch it—vengeance! it is my food,
My thirft—High Heaven, who gave a world to
        man,
Gave it in common—trafh not worth contention!—
But chaftly paled the bridal bed around,
With fanctities and honours, whofe offence
Is deeper than damnation!
   OSBERT. O, thou haft,
Thou haft, indeed, been injured—paft repeal,
Or the world's recompence!—What's to be done?
   WEST. The duty of a king—
One act of juftice—let it mark thy reign—
Let not a nation fink for thy tranfgreffion!—
For once give anfwer to the call of honour;

K 3

And

And as thou haſt been ever bold in ill,
Be bold for once in honeſty!

   OSBERT. O! no—
Yes—any other arm but thine—or thine,
Though doubled, ſo thou drop thy dread ally
That combats for thee HERE!—O no, I cannot—
I will not fight thee!—

   WEST. Then, periſh Britain,
Or caſt the tyrant out!—War, paſs thy bounds!
Range vengeance, wide as air! cruſh, cruſh the
     world,
So thou but wrap him in the general ruin!—
Art thou, art thou a man—a king—a warrior—
A champion, choſen to breaſt thee to the breach?—
And doſt thou quail, and ſkulk behind thy people?
Doſt thruſt the ſucking babe, and fear-frozen
     mother,
Betwixt thyſelf and danger?

   OSBERT. Oh!——

   WEST. Thy oath is paſt, thou muſt abide the
     venture.
Take arms of vantage, caſe thee round in ſteel
Of proof impenetrable—give me, but,
Naked, defenceleſs, but to have one ſtroke,
One grapple for the bleeding cauſe of honour,
And I acquit thee—from the firſt of time,
Through all eternity, I ſeal thy pardon!

   OSBERT. Well—when?—it ſhall be done!—
     Thou haſt me ſhort,
A little ſhort of recollection now—
Time ſoon ſhall ſerve—I ſwear it—arm to arm,
Great, injured man!—thou ſhalt be ſatisfied.

WEST.

WEST. Wilt thou?—And I will thank thee in
    the grave.
OSBERT. I will——
WEST. Well—hold thee to thy pledge—thy
    faith—thy manhood—
I may expect thee, then—
OSBERT. Yes—elfe, may Heaven
Stand in thy place for vengeance!

An OFFICER enters.

OFFICER. My liege, the foe approaches, and
    is now
In fight of York——
OSBERT. Moft noble ftranger!—for an hour
    or two,
You muft confort with patience—Guards, con-
    duct him;
And fee that he be treated with attention,
Becoming princely dignity and honour.
           [Exeunt WESTMORLAND and Guards.

S C E N E   III.

Enter OSRIC and EDWIN, with Citizens.

OSRIC. My lord, they come apace, the ftorm
    bends this way!
Mine be the walls, mine and the citizens—
But hafte with EDWIN, hafte to horfe, my liege!
Array your foldiers in the fquare, and hold them

K 4

Ready

Ready to fally on the firft advantage.
Hafte, valiant OSBERT !   [Exeunt feverally.

S C E N E IV.

The FIELDS before YORK.

A DANISH March and Mufic.

IVAR, HUBBA, and Soldiers, enter with the Great
Raven-Standard of Denmark.

HUB. How fair to fight, how chearing to the
        fenfe,
Thefe fields throw fragrance to the vernal breeze,
And greet our foldiers with a fweet falute !
  IVAR. It is a tempting invitation, HUBBA—
This favourite ifle, this daughter of the gods,
Retires with confcious beauty from the world;
Like fea-born Venus, rifes from the waves,
And chaftly courts the foldier's arm to clafp her.
  HUB. IVAR, thus far, the voice of honour
        calls ;
And friendfhip anfwers to the glorious fummons,
To pluck oppreffion from the feat of power,
And fubftitute the injured : 'tis an office,
Worthy the delegates of Heaven.
  IVAR. True, brother.
Nor do I grudge Northumbria to her WESTMOR-
        LAND,
Our brave, unhappy friend—But then, my HUBBA,
In Britain's heavenly fphere, there are more ftars

7

Than

Than 'gem the crown that WESTMORLAND muſt
     wear;
Nor can we want a cauſe, while great ambition,
That made a god of Grecian Philip's ſon,
Inſpires with equal ardour.

  HUB. O, beware!—
If theſe your counſels, let your breaſt conceal them;
Nor truſt them to the ear of WESTMORLAND.
I know how dear he holds his country's health;
Nor would I wiſh his valour for our foe.
Think how his arm might ſway the ſcale of Britain!
A name is light, yet his outweighs a legion.
There's not a Dane throughout your numerous
     hoſts,
But looks to him, as to the god of battles;
And wears ſome favour, letter'd with his name,
To charm misfortune from them.

     SOLDIER enters in haſte.

  IVAR. How now? thy looks ſpeak haſte—
What tidings, ſoldier?
  SOLD. O, my ſovereign lord!
'Tis rumour'd, that our leader, in the night,
Adventuring near the city, was beſet,
And, all unſeconded, is either ſlain,
Or captive now in York.
  IVAR. The ſword of Denmark
Shall richly pay his ranſom—
Now looſe the war, impetuous as a flood,
And thou hot ſun be quench'd, and ſet in blood.
  (Sound Trumpets)   [Exeunt.

                   SCENE

S C E N E V.

The Inside of the ABBEY.

ROWENA and Nuns.

Row. Pafs but a little time, and all fhall be,
To every purpofe of this prefent world,
As though they had never been!—Build on,
      projection !
Pile, avarice! ambition, fcale the clouds!—
It is but as a dream of varying fancy ;
A breath—and all is vanifhed !
Hear me, my children!—Lift, ye hallow'd virgins,
O lift, and take my laft inftructions with ye!—
Ha!—did ye mark that groan ?

   1ft Nun. No one is near——

   Row. Methought it came attended by a voice,
That echoed—" Take her laft inftructions with ye."
   1ft Nun. Hark—hark !
               [Charge, drums and trumpets at a diftance.
   Row. Defend us, Heaven !—the noife of battle!—
                      [They look out.
The form of coming war, how dreadful is it !—
Wide on the right, no opening fpot can fhew
What ground they tread.—Alas, alas, for York !
She cannot ftand the fhock—her ancient towers
Already feem to fhake at their approach,
And bow to her foundations. [Sound, beat, and clafh.
   1ft Nun. Look !—O look !—
   Row. Ha!—Yes—the town too iffues to the
      battle—

                              On

On either part, the kings ride foremoft—Now,
Now they have mark'd each other for deftruction—
He's down—the Dane is down!—
Now Osbert is unhorfed—
O bravely refcued!—
And fuch a fair deliverer!
Ha!—'tis my Edwin!—Turn, thou infant warrior,
Nor tempt the random blow——
Ah, rafh, rafh boy!—
See how he throws himfelf amid the battle,
And makes a mock of danger—
O, fave him, fave him, Heaven!—They gird
   him in—
A child againft an army!—
He's down, he's down, and I will look no more—
What dreadful founds are thefe?—

        [An approaching tumult.
See, Edith, fee. [A Nun goes out, and inftantly returns.
 2d Nun. They come—they are at our doors,
A band of ruffians!—Save us, madam, fave us!
 Row. Quick, to the gate, fly fome one!—make
   it fure,
But for a few fhort moments—For myfelf,
Blow tempeft!—nature, wreck!—it matters not—
'Tis finifh'd—I am fecure—But, O for thefe,
Thine own devoted—O, or never, now
Infpire, thou Living Strength! a wondrous deed,
A courage not their own—Say, my fifters,
What would ye do, from luft and violation,
What dare, from fuch a loft eftate to efcape?
 1ft Nun. Put us to proof.
 2d Nun. We dare the laft extremes.
 3d Nun. Tortures, or death, or worfe.
           Row.

Row. One dear embrace—
For now we part no more!—and thus, and thus—
[*Embrace.*
We bind us to each other, in a knot,
More firm than that which winds the world to-
      gether,
For ours is tied in virtue.
O, if they yet furvive—my child, my hufband!
In whom my foul lives, feelingly transferr'd
Through all their faculties—protect them, Heaven!
Quit, quit all care of me, and take the dear ones
To your peculiar guardianfhip!
Hark!—for now   [*The noife approaches nearer.*
Our trial is at hand—Are ye prepared?
[*Draws a knife.*
  Nuns. We follow you to death!
[*The Nuns do the fame.*
  Row. And fuch a death,
As fhould preferve the very life of virtue,
[*A fhout at the door.*
Were fcarce a fin—They come!—Sifters, away!—
'Tis triumph all above, when Virtue wins the day.
[*Exeunt.*

END OF THE THIRD ACT.

A C T

ACT IV.

SCENE I.

OSBERT enters.

OSBERT. WHAT art thou, Time?
　　　　Thy many ages paſt, were once to come;
And now, are—nothing!—What thou art at preſent,
We cannot, if we would, retain—The morrow!
Ah, who would wait the coming of the morrow,
But that Hope bears him to ſome promiſed bliſs,
That yeſterday ne'er knew!—The morrow comes;
And, like its predeceſſors, merely ſerves
To count our cares—Where's he, who would recall
The happieſt term of time once paſt, or wiſh
To plant it in the days of life to come?
But what is life to come, where hope comes not?—
ROWENA, injured ſanctity! in thee
The world is bankrupt; and for aught that's now
Contained beneath yon ſtar-ſet canopy,
I reck not—For the reſt—the dread hereafter!—
A life of guilt were haply beſt atoned,

Se

So Heaven in mercy warrant, by a death
Of juſtice, and of honour !—Who attends ?

Enter OFFICER.

Take this ſeal, ſoldier—go, and bow thee down
Before our noble captive ; give him freedom,
Arms, and ſafe conduct to Saint Cyprian's Grove—
Say, we have buſineſs for a ſword like his,
And wait him there.   [Exeunt ſeverally.

S C E N E II.

OSRIC and EDWIN.

OSRIC. But to be loofed to ſuch ungovern'd
          ſorrow—
'Tis deſperation !—'tis the anarchy
Of minds o'erthrown, where paſſions ride aloft,
And the fair fields of ripening virtue lie
Defaced beneath the tempeſt !
     EDWIN. Pardon, ſir !—
I would—I will obey you—are you not
My only parent, now ?—O, happy father !
You lived not to behold this day—the loſs
Of your child's mother—of your loved ROWENA—
Of all that earth could boaſt of Heaven—of all
That life could give of joy, or death take from us !—
But the cold grave, with its unfeeling ſhrowd,
Now ſhuts you from the ſenſe.—
     OSRIC. Yet, EDWIN, yet,
She may be ſafe : they would not, could not per-
          petrate
                              A deed,

A deed, of such reproach to manhood—no!
Your eyes shall yet behold her.

    EDWIN. Never, never!—
O sir, till I beheld her angel-face,
I knew not what it was to have a mother.
I had laid up, within my fond conception,
A thousand promised scenes of joys to come,
Delights of filial sweetness; days, and years,
Spent in the glad officiousness of duty,
Made happy by her smiles—O, mother fair!
Why died I not in thy defence?
For O, this weak unexecuting arm
Was impotent to save thee!

    OSRIC. 'Twas Heaven's will—
What lay in man to do, thou didst, my EDWIN!
The king hath summon'd us to council, here—
If thou dost prize my safety, dry thy tears,
And keep their source a secret.   Retire awhile,
To calm this storm of overbearing passions.

[Exeunt.

S C E N E   III.

A GROVE.

OSBERT enters, and walks some time disturb'd.

    OSBERT. My hand, my heart, be firm!—It is a
        period
Of infinite import—a mighty summons!—
The voice of equity, the sense of honour,
Rouze up the man, the soldier, and the king,

To

To fill the hour with deeds of anſwering greatneſs.
Heaven take the iſſue to thine own direction !

S C E N E   IV.

WESTMORLAND enters with the Officer.

OSBERT. My noble friend, moſt welcome!——
    You withdraw.   [Exit Officer.
WEST. And is it come, the thirſted hour ?—O
    tranſport !
Art thou mine, vengeance ?—what ! the ſacrifice
Within the graſp of honour ?—Haſte, call forth
Thy guards——
Thy champions choſen to anſwer to the fire
That rages in my heart, thou yet art mine !——
Tho' the ſwift bolt ſhould ſhoot between us,
    OSBERT !
Thou art mine for ever !——
   OSBERT. Be it !—Thou ſeeſt I have ta'en no
    vantage, WESTMORLAND,
Of aid, arms, time, or place—fair, equal, all,
And ſecret—Silent, art thou ?—then, come on ;
                      [Draws.
And let us prove the proweſs of an arm
So far renown'd—if mine betray me not,
Thou ſhalt be well encount'red—What impedes ?—
For injured honour—for revenge—come on !——
   WEST. Amazement holds me—Is it poſſible !——
No vantage, doſt thou ſay—and this right hand
Arm'd by thyſelf againſt thy proper boſom ?
'Tis contradiction to eternal order——

                            Could

Could aught fo guilty be fo brave?

OSBERT. Thou feeft—

WEST. So like a foldier, like a king,
True to his oath and honor!—OSBERT, art thou?
It cannot be!—What, OSBERT!—he who laid
My world of joy—of honor wafte; and in
One cruel hour of his licentioufnefs,
Who did devour my infinite of years;
And caft the peace of mine eternal foul
To defolation!

OSBERT. Oh!—no more—come on,
And rouze thee, like the lion, with the lafh
Of wrongs, thus treafur'd to the hour of wrath,'
And retribution.

WEST Yet thou haft my thanks.
I ever held thee bold; for this once, OSBERT,
I hold thee noble.   , ·

OSBERT. Art prepar'd?

WEST. Yes, yes,
The world impels; fame, honor, rolling down
Thro' late pofterity, demand it of me.

OSBERT. They do.—Come on.

WEST. Thus then,—to clofe the wound
Thro' which difhonor iffues to the world!—
Reft you, my liege.   ,   [They fight.

OSBERT. No, fate is bufy, WESTMORLAND
And we will know the iffue

[OSBERT is wounded—WESTMORLAND fteps back
concerned, and OSBERT leans upon his fword.

OSBERT. WESTMORLAND !—
Thy debt is paid ! and what remains for me,
The next dread minute muft unfold !   [falls.
   WEST. Alas !
Unhappy man !—my wrath that, giant-like,
Beftrode the world, and call'd the nations up,
With thee is fallen, and has expir'd before thee !
O that the breach of honor had been clos'd
Without this bloody cement !—that my fword
Had reach'd thy guilt, but fpar'd thy noblenefs !
   OSBRT. O WESTMORLAND come near—thine af-
       pect tells me
I have thy pity,—If I have thy pardon,
Seal now a blefs'd oblivion of all injuries !
   WEST. Heaven fhower on both a pardon full and
       free,
As that I grant to OSBERT !
   OSBERT. Once moft lov'd,
And ever held in honour—noble WESTMORLAND !
O, had not paffions hurried me to deeds,
Detefted by the doer—what a race
Of kindred glory had we run together !
   WEST. Alas ! the fteps that prefs the paths
       of error,
  Are not all thine,

OSBERT

OSBERT. My brother!—haft thou too had thy
    faults ?—
Then lend thine arm to frailty—Let me lean
On that forgiving bofom—O, thofe tears,
Thofe tears, my WESTMORLAND, they fall up-
    on me,
Like Heaven's indulgent dew—each drop, of
    power
To wafh a ftain away !—This fignet—take it—
Thy paffport hence—I had to tell thee much—
Of love—of noblenefs—o'ercome—yet ftrug-
    gling—
A moment—life's no more—It anfwers not—
Sad tidings, too———
They had unman'd thee !—thy ROWENA is—Oh—
                      [Dies.
  WEST. Gone!—art thou gone for ever?—OSBERT,
    OSBERT !—
To kill thee once, I would have given a world;
And now would give, thou nobleft, firft of men !
A thoufand worlds to have thee back again. [Exit.

S C E N E V.

A Pavilion in the DANISH Camp.

IVAR, HUBBA, and Danifh Officers.

HUB. O ftain to manhood!—'tis a blot, my
    brother,
That covers Denmark !—yes, it is a deed
That ties the worth and frefhnefs of our fame
To deteftation !—What, to wrong a fex,

                    Sacred

Sacred to arms, and guarded by their weaknefs—
The murder of defencelefs women !—Gods,
Of virgins too, devoted to your altars !
It is a war with Heaven and earth !

    IVAR. Advife,
How may we caft the unworthy imputation
From our own honours.

    HUB. Will you, to your fervant,
Permit this dear concern ?

    IVAR. Moft willingly.

    HUB. Arnold, be thine the care to feize on all
The perpetrators of this deed—to York
Convey them——Kenulph, be it thine,
From the fad afhes of yon pile to cull
The facred reliques—fee them clofed in gold,
Fit emblem of the purity that pafs'd
Thro' fuch a fire !—   [Shouts.

    IVAR. What new alarm ?—See, foldier, whence
           thofe fhouts,
That echo through our camp ?

           Enter OFFICER.

    OFFICER. My royal lord !
'Tis faid our general approaches, free,
And fafe, from York.

    IVAR. How, fay'ft thou—is it poffible?
By mighty Thor, he comes !—'tis he—

                        SCENE

SCENE VI.

To them WESTMORLAND enters.

IVAR. My friend!

HUB. Great father of the war,   [Embrace.
Moft welcome !
Free, arm'd, unhurt ?

WEST. It is a ftory,
Full of ftrange accident.

IVAR. Come you from York ?

WEST. I do—where OSBERT fell beneath my
      hand,
In equal combat flain.

IVAR. Proclaim it to the Heavens !
Sound, found it, every inftrument of triumph !
Hail him ye hofts—our general is a king,
Northumbria's monarch ! Thus let me falute
      him,
With earlieft gratulation.—

HUB. O, my friend—
Soul of all honour !—may thy empire fpread
Wide as thy worth and glories !

WEST. Thanks to both,
And grateful retribution—Ha !—
Eyes fee amifs—or hence be dark for ever !—
Thofe ruins !—Speak, who burnt the hallow'd
      pile ?

HUB. Truft me, my noble friend, we both are
      guiltlefs—

L 3

Both

Both were in battle fallen, when this dire act
Of outrage and dishonour was committed.

 West. O, if Arabia's spicy nest be desolate,
Where is my bird, the Phænix of its odours?—
Who can inform me?—

Ethelwald enters.

Ethelwald!
Where is thy precious charge, thy mistress?—
  Silent!—
Alas, there's desolation in thine eye!—
Speak, I conjure thee—yet, while I have power
To ask, or sense to hear thee.

 Ethel. O, prepare—
Prepare to pardon, then, this tongue accurs'd
'Bove all that e'er were doom'd to speak of woe!—
Rowena—your Rowena is—

 West. What?—

 Ethel. Dead!   [Westmorland falls.

 Ivar. He stirs not.—General!

 Hub. Most noble Westmorland!—
Nor hears.—The tempest-brooding calm is on
  him;
And it may break in violence, self urged
Against his precious life.

 Ivar. Remove his sword.

 Hub. Down, art thou down?—amid the world's
  wide forest
The stateliest pine o'erthrown!—O conquering
  grief!

Before

Before thee falls, who ftood the force of thoufands,
He moves.—Friend !

   ETHEL. Mafter!

   IVAR. Royal WESTMORLAND !

          [They raife, and feat him on a fopha.

   WEST. Alas—the lot of man is frailty !
I murmur not, that I was born to fuffer—
But this was fuch a ftroke !—my heart, to this,
Lay quite difarm'd and unprovided !—ETHEL-
      WALD !
Speak, fay what envious cruel fiends have brought
This fudden night upon us ?

   ETHEL. O, my loved lord !—the day was fcarce
      difclofed,
When, in contempt of all the powers of Denmark,
Bold OSBERT fallied forth.   Never was field
So fought—until, on either part, the chiefs
Sore toil'd, or fallen, were carried from the battle !
Then, round yon pile, were gather'd, as from hell,
The infatiate furies, Cruelty and Luft !—
What could ROWENA do ?—the thunder flept,
Nor Heaven defcended on the wing to fave her.—

   WEST. Proceed, proceed—my foul is in thy
      tidings;
And every liftening pulfe fufpends to hear thee !

   ETHEL. When fhe perceived no help was near,
      fhe call'd
Her virgin train around her.   Straight fhe drew
A knife, now facred to the caufe of virtue,
And bade them mark her—Yet, while they beheld
That face, whereon, like firft created nature,
Beauty divine was vifibly impreft,

At

At once 'twas chaos all!—her cheeks, her lips,
She gafh'd, fhe mangled!—and, to knowledge, now
ROWENA was no more!—
    WEST. Powers immortal!—
    ETHEL. Then rofe the daughters of her bright
        example
High o'er their fex, o'er all that e'er was famed
In ftory!—each was a ROWENA, now!
In rufh'd the ruffians—but, when they beheld
Beauty to horror turn'd, their boiling lufts
Froze inward—back they flunk—but foon return'd,
Laden with ftubble, and with kindling brands,
That caught the pile around—As incenfe breathed
In morning facrifice direct to Heaven,
ROWENA, and her train of maiden-faints,
Afcended wrapt in flames!—and I but fcarce
Efcaped to bring the tidings.
    WEST. Mighty being!
Parent of good! for my ROWENA, thanks!—
You thought I fhould be troubled—not the leaft—
I never knew an hour of peace like this!—
All, all, within, is ftill, amid the tempeft,
The wreck of human nature!
    IVAR. Your looks are much difturb'd—Retire,
        my friend.
    WEST. Is the king come?—are all our friends
        invited?
Sit, fit!————
Sound trumpets, bear the triumph of my joys
Upon the chariot of the air, to Heaven,
And tell them, 'tis the bridal day of WESTMORLAND!
Mark ye, the king looks fad—I cannot blame him—
                  What,

What, what is empire, to a bride like mine!—
See where she sits, the queen of health and beauty
Dealing out joys, as plenteous as the spring
Throws odours to the breeze!—Approach not,
   friends,
Lest you be lost, like me, beneath her charms—
Her sweets oppress! they grow too mighty for me!
Joys insupportable!——
  Ivar. Help, bear him forward.
How strong this passion shakes him!
   West. Osbert, thy hand—ruin hath recon-
    ciled us—
What a dark journey do we go together!—
Ha, who are these?—their hands are weighty
   on me!
O, treacherous Danes!—
I have lost my powers—they bind me to a rock—
See, see the Magic Raven, how he plumes!—
How he prepares his beak!—Ungrateful bird!—
I, who have fed him with the spoil of nations,
Am now become his prey—
Loose me—he searches to my inmost bosom—
He tears my heart—he gorges up my vitals!
         [Faints.
  Hub. Alas! and is our Denmark so accurs'd,
There to bring ruin where she meant to rescue?
  Ivar. Soft, he revives; his eye is more com-
   posed.—
How fares our friend?
   West. O, ye have kindly brought the dawn
   about me—
Reason's returning beam, to guide our passage;
          The

The fun, that lights this little world of man.—
Patience, good Heaven!—I will abide your pleafure.

   Hub. Unhappy, honoured, injured WESTMOR-
     LAND!
What fhall your afflicted fuppliants plead,
In mitigation of your juft difpleafure?
Here are our fwords—and, if thou canft not
     pardon,
At leaft revenge!—

   WEST. No—take them back—Alas!
I am, myfelf, the frail one of my kind,
The very child of error—There is, yet,
One fuit wherein I'd move ye.

   Hub. Say on, and think your will but told
     again
In our obedience.

   WEST. Thus it is—Since things,
By fome o'erruling hand, have turn'd averfe
To my foul's purpofe; and that I, once deem'd
My country's guardian, fhall in ftory now
Be held a traitor to her peace—I would
Hence forward fpare the expence of blood—To
     York
Difpatch your herald—
And challenge forth whoe'er, in fingle fight,
Shall ftand his country's hope. Ourfelf will meet
     him,
And thefe the high conditions—If we conquer,
The gift of fair Northumbria's fcepter, then,
Is left at our difpofe—but if, and who
Shall bar Almighty Pleafure?—if I fall,

You

You fwear to abdicate her throne for ever,
And leave the land in peace.

   IVAR. It fhall be done.
Say, is there aught befide ?

   WEST. Not now.   I feel
A drowfy weight fteal o'er my travel'd foul.

   IVAR. Adieu!

   HUB. May all
The peace that refts with virtue, aid your flumbers!
               [Exeunt all but WESTMORLAND.

   WEST. Falfe Danes! I know ye now—thofe
      ruins!—Soft,
That runs again to madnefs—O, thefe fields,
Thefe fields of blood, whence are they?—is it
     WESTMORLAND
That brought fuch carnage on his country?—How,
How does that feel!—
This hoft of fiends I have conjured up—but how
To quell them—there's the talk!—to lay the hur-
     ricane
That wrecks thy peace, fair Albion!
My country, fear no more from my hoftility—
Send but a toilet-champion to the field,
And to his ftainlefs fword this breaft fhall be
As paffable as air!
         [Repofes on the fopha, and the fcene clofes.

SCENE

SCENE VII.

FUNERAL PROCESSION, and DIRGE.

I.

Wretched mortals, doom'd to go
Through the vale of death and woe!
Let us travel sad and slow.

II.

Care and Sickness, Toil and Pain,
  Here their restless vigils keep:
Sighs are all the winds that blow,
Tears are all the streams that flow!
Virtue hopes reward in vain—
The gentlest lot she can obtain,
  Is but to sit and weep!

III.

Ye dreary mansions of enduring sleep,
Where pale mortality lies dark and deep!
Thou silent, though insatiate Grave,
Gorged with the beauteous and the brave;
Close, close thy maw—thy feast is o'er,
Time and death can give no more!

IV.

In ROWENA thou hast
Thy consummate repast!

All

All that earth could boaſt divine,
All we held of Heaven is thine !
Time and death no more can gain——
They have all perfection ſlain !
O Grave, thy feſtival is o'er ;
The beggar'd world can give no more!

Song of Consolation.

I.

Ye deſolate mortals who ſtray,
Dark, devious, and wilfully blind ;
  O turn, and diſtinguiſh the way
That leads to the bliſs of mankind !

The titles ye falſely aſſign,
With their ſymbols are ever at ſtrife ;
  And death by appointment divine,
Is our birth and our portal to life.

II.

The Framer of Nature from chaos and night,
Who drew yon fair ſyſtem of order and light,
On extremes hath the plan of his univerſe
      built,
On frailty perfection, and pardon on guilt ;
And through the ſhort tranſience of death and
      of pain,
Appoints human weakneſs to riſe and to reign.

C H O R U S.

CHORUS.

'Tis Virtue, 'tis Virtue, o'er grief and the
grave,
That rifes fecure, and fublime;
The prize that Eternity watches to fave
From the wrecks and the ruins of time!

END OF THE FOURTH ACT.

ACT

A C T V.

S C E N E I.

The LISTS, between the CAMP and the TOWN.

IVAR and HUBBA, with Danifh Officers and
Soldiers.

IVAR. **I** See they do accept our fummons.—Say,
Are hoftages exchanged ?
OFFICER. They are, my liege.
IVAR. And all due ceremonials elfe performed?
OFFICER. Duly performed.

S C E N E II.

Enter OSRIC with Britifh Lords and Officers.

OSRIC. Princes of Denmark, hail !—I will
not afk,
Wherefore your warlike vifitation—No—
The mighty never want a caufe for quarrel.
I hold me to this queftion—do ye vouch
The meffage of your herald ?

IVAR.

Ivar. Yes.

Osric. Repeat it.

Ivar. If Heaven fhall blefs our champion's arm
    with conqueft,
The gift of fair Northumbria's fcepter, then,
Is left at our difpofe—If Denmark fall,
We fwear to abdicate your throne for ever,
And leave your land in peace.

Osric. We do accept you—but with this ad-
    dition,
That they whofe champion falls this day in battle,
That inftant quit the field.

Ivar. Agreed.

Osric. Then let 'us march without the lifts,
    and there
Affirm the compact with our mutual fanction.
Heralds, prepare the field—call in the champions,
And hold them ready, at the trumpet's found,
To fix a nation's fate.   [Exeunt.

Enter Westmorland.

West. If death fhould be no more than fo—
    to loofe
The care-ftretch'd rack of thought—to fink at once
In fweet oblivion—'tis the hope—the Heaven,
That Guilt fighs after !—Clofe thefe eyes—
    but fhut
Their living telefcope—and all is darknefs !—
Let death but fhut the world from every fenfe,

8

The

The foul—what then of her?—when the hearing,
Sight, touch, and tafte, her wonted minifters
Of light, of knowledge, and of action, perifh;
What is it then that wins yon diftant worlds,
And takes the rounds of varying nature in?—
The eye?—O no—'tis dark amid the noon,
Till the bright foul, its animating gueft,
Look from the lids, and waken to perception.
It is the foul that fees, then—and this eye
Is but her glafs occafional, to view
This outward world, perhaps not obvious elfe:
But let her forth from this her prifon houfe,
She fprings upon new worlds, whofe light is life,
To which the fun is darknefs!—Then exiftence
Is fure—but whether, or for blifs or woe?—
Be it—Heaven's will is beft—and bounty wide,
Where there is leaft to merit.

S C E N E IV.

EDWIN enters on the other fide: he walks flowly by,
and looks ftedfaftly on WESTMORLAND.

WEST. Sweet youth!—Say, wherefore am I
      fingled out,
To ftand within thy gaze?
  EDWIN. Becaufe, till now,
I have fcarce beheld the prefence of a man;
And joy that fame muft wait upon my fall,
When dignified by you.
  WEST. Good Heavens!—art thou,
Art thou my fell antagonift?—Fair flower,

Avoid my cruel froft!—Retire, my child,
Nor break thy mother's heart!

EDWIN. Intend you this,
In fcorn, or in compaffion ?

WEST. Both—but moft
In anger, that the Britifh fons of war
Should fend their ftripling, their Adonis forth,
Where their beft power would fhrink.

EDWIN. Your caufe is weak,
Tho' ftrong your arm—fo are we better weigh'd,
Where juftice, to my weaker arm, has join'd
A caufe invincible—My injured country
Already fits triumphant on my fword ;
And lifts the laft, the loweft of her fons,
O'er thee, the firft in Denmark !

WEST. Child of glory !
Happy the boaftful climate of thy birth !
And thy glad parents—thrice, thrice bleft are
          thofe,
Of whom thou wert begotten !—Had'ft thou,
          Heaven,
Ordain'd a fon, one fon like this to WESTMORLAND,
His lateft hour had bleft thee, and been happy.

EDWIN. Have you no fon ?

WEST. I have.

EDWIN. How bleft were I,
To be that child, and kneel to thee, my father !

WEST. Reach me that valiant hand—Had fate
          not doom'd
That one of us, this hour, muft fall in battle ;
O, I had held thee at my heart, as near

As

As is the blood that warms it.—Of Northumbria
Art thou?

   Edwin. I am.

   West. I too am Britain-born.

   Enter an English and a Danish Herald.

   Eng. Her. The princes, valiant combatants,
      salute you;

And round the panting barrier thousands wait,
Whose fate feceives decision from your arms.

   Dan. Her. Sound trumpets, found the charge!
      [Exeunt Heralds—Trumpets found—Edwin draws.

   Edwin. O, honour'd chief!—tho' my dear
      country lifts

This sword impulsive on thee; yet, I feel,
'Twould be more grateful turn'd upon myself—
Less wounding far, than pointed at thy bosom!—
Come, come on!

   West. Soul truly noble!—This to prove thy
      force.   [Fight.

   Edwin Unworthy triumph—barbarous man!—
      that stroke

You took defenceless!—

   West. It is accomplish'd!—Yes, thou glori-
      ous youth,

We both have reach'd our wish—I came to die,
And thou to conquer!

   Edwin. Ah, what myftery?

   West. But that the icey hand of death is on me,
I could unfold—My friend will tell thee all,
The noble Manchester—

Edwin. Thy friend?—Great powers!

West. Draw near—Thou haſt a heart replete
    with greatneſs:
If thou doſt hope to wed ſome heavenly maid,
To be as bleſt as once was Westmorland,
Lay me, O lay me with the dear remains
Of my loved angel, my triumphant wife,
My deified Rowena!—

Edwin. Thine! what—thine!

West. Thou ſeem'ſt amazed.

Edwin. If dead men riſe to life,
Thou art——

West. Ha! what?

Edwin. Thy ſon—his name was——

West. Edwin.

Edwin. My father!—O my father, my dear
    father!—
Curs'd hour, curs'd hand!—O ſir—O firſt of men!
Give me that wound, if you would have me
    happy—
Loſt, ruin'd Edwin!—loſt, undone for ever!

West. Art thou my ſon, then?—my Rowena's
    child?—
Thy goodneſs, Heaven! it is too mighty for me—
Come to my arms—cloſe—preſs into my heart!—
                    [Embraces.
Hold off, and let me gaze again upon thee!
Thou art, thou art my ſon, my joy, my rapture,
My better ſelf—thy country's Westmorland!—
Why doſt thou weep?—by honour's holy bands,
I ſwear I would not change this day for ages—

This

This glorious day, wherein thy fire is made
Triumphant o'er himfelf!

   Edwin. My father!—Oh—
Thofe too kind words go pointed through my
        bofom—
They reach at life; and facred nature lies
O'erthrown, and bleeds her laft—

   West. Thy hand, young hero—child of ho-
     nour, help me!   [Sinks down.

S C E N E V.

Enter Osric.

   Osric. Health to our champion! to his arm
     for ever,
Succefs like this—and be his living name
The firft in Britain's ftory!—Silence!—tears!—
Whence, wherefore?

   Edwin. O—touch not this parricide!—
Your friend!—my father!—look, O look, where
     bleeds
The lord of loft Rowena!

   Osric. Westmorland!
What, Westmorland?—The powers!

   West. As I do think—my friend,
The noble Manchester!

   Osric. Help there, in hafte!—Fate, fate, thou
     art Almighty!—
Strength, honour, prowefs! what is now your
     boaft,

M 3

When

When proftrate thus your mighty one is fallen,
When here lies WESTMORLAND ?—Help, bear him
    gently,   [Soldiers bring in a chair.
So—there—How fare you ?

    WEST. As a lonely man, ·
Unfkill'd to fteer his courfe, juft launched from
    fhore,
And never to return.—O gentle MANCHESTER,
Through what a wondrous whirl of varying fortunes,
Thy friend has paft, this day—a lover bleft—
A captive—then a conqueror—then a king—
And now, what thou beholdeft here!—ETHELWALD,
My faithful ETHELWALD will tell thee all—
O, I have been to blame—too late, my brother,
I faw, and would repeal—but deeds were done—
And fate refufed to cancel—What remain'd,
But to atone in part ?—The Dane was falfe—
And thus, to bind his fate, I chofe to perifh,
A victim to the land my life had injured !—
My words grow painful—Noble, noble MAN-
    CHESTER,
Regard thy gracious fon—
No more—I faint !———

    OSRIC. Alas, my friend !

    EDWIN. My father !———

    WEST. My fpirit returns—the afpiring lamp of
    life
Brightens its lateft blaze—I fee, they come,
Again they come, the invaders of Northumbria !
Treaties—leagues—what are ye ?—O my country,
How art thou wafte !—Fair Albion, land of beauty !

Owls

Owls build within thy lonely palaces,
And weeds o'ergrow thy pavements!—Ha, he
            comes!—
My child, the ftar of Britain, EDWIN comes!—
I fee, like lightning, he divides the night—
He darts, he rufhes on them—Ho, for Freedom!—
Down with the traitorous pair—the Magic Standard,
Grafp it, 'tis thine!—Refpiring LIBERTY,
Juftice, and golden Commerce, how ye walk,
And brighten o'er the land!—Releafe me—oh!—
Pardon I feel is paft above—more—more—
Wondrous, unfpeakable!—I come—and leave
This leffon to the world—that Heaven is all,
And man is—nothing!————Oh!   [Dies.

CYMBELINE:

A

TRAGEDY.

PERSONS.

CYMBELINE, King of BRITAIN.

CLOTEN, Son of the QUEEN.

LEONATUS.

BELLARIUS, a Hermit.

ARCHIMNESTOR, an Alchymist.

FAUSTUS, Servant to LEONATUS.

CAIUS LUCIUS, General of the ROMANS.

CLODIO, Lieutenant-General.

QUEEN, Wife of CYMBELINE.

IMOGEN, Daughter of CYMBELINE.

PRIESTESS in the Temple of ANDATE.

LORDS, OFFICERS, SOLDIERS, ATTENDANTS, &c.

CYMBELINE.

ACT I.

SCENE I. The Palace.

The Queen and Archimnestor.

Queen. THIS way—apart—
Here, take this golden earneſt of
my favour.
I know that thou art ſkill'd, from cauſe to con-
ſequence,
Through nature's longeſt chain—Where are the
drugs?
Arch. They are of dread import—Think,
royal miſtreſs,
Death and the fates are theirs. They ſend of
errands
That cannot be recall'd; to worlds remote,
Of which we know not. Whom they are to ſend—
Queen. Befits not thee to aſk—ſuppoſe a rat,
Or ſomewhat nobler—Heaven, without com-
punction,

Kills

Kills thousands by the hour—The best must fall;
The manner matters not.—These juleps, come,
Instruct me in their virtues.

    ARCH. This falls on nature like a depth of snow,
Unfelt, though weighty—silent as a thief
By night, it steals the mental treasures forth,
And leaves the house asleep—This smiles; but
        holds,
In every drop, a death; in every death,
A thousand racks, impalements, all the pangs
That science yet hath learn'd, by fire or cord,
To wring from nature.

    QUEEN. It is enough—Retire.
                     [Exit ARCHIMNESTOR·
Empire is now our own, while thus, like fate,
We deal out death to all, who would oppose
The greatness of our purpose.

S C E N E   II.

CLOTEN enters.

    CLOT. O mother, she is gone—she's lost for
        ever!—
    QUEEN. What means my son?
    CLOT. My love, my IMOGEN,
Britain's bright heir, my promised wife, is lost,
Is married to another—to the wretch I most detest,
That foundling, that accursed LEONATUS!
O, she is gone, and with her too is gone
All prospect of the throne!

                                 QUEEN,
      3

Queen. Not fo, my child—
A froward foolifh girl, fhe's well away !
Whine for a wench ?—my boy fhall have a thou-
　　fand..
Be fecret and fecure ; for here I vow,
Ere yet our horned moon fhall fill her orb,
To feat thee, fcepter'd, on the throne of Britain.
They come—Be patient, and rely on me.

S C E N E　III.

Enter King, Imogen, Lords and Attendants.

Cymb. Give me room, gods !—What, here—
　　within my palace !—
Wived, wedded, coupled to a dog—our daughter!
Such a broad act !—'tis worfe than to offend
Within the very aim of Heaven's hot bolt,
When launch'd to crufh tranfgreffion.
　　Imog. O, my father !　　　　　　　　[Kneels.
　　Cymb. Our daughter, art thou ?—Britain's on-
　　ly hope,
Sole heir of our dominions ?—Gods—O gods !—
So match'd, fo pair'd !—the offspring of our
　　throne
Caft on a dunghill—married to a wretch,
Whofe hopes are lefs than air; whofe whole pof-
　　feffion
Shrinks from a grafp; who wants a name to tell
He fprung from human race !—
A foundling-villain ; one compofed of fcraps,
A poverty of manhood !

　　　　　　　　　　　　　　　　　　Imog.

Imog. O, fir—my royal mafter !—

Cymb. What, confefs it ?—

Out, thou vile ftain, thou foulnefs of thy race !—
Thus let me fcour the blot.   [Offers to kill her.

Queen. Forbid it, Heaven !—   [Interpofes.
Gentle, my lord ! the princefs, as you fee,
Is all fubmiffion ; mourns, and weeps, and prays,
And only waits to know your royal will,
Whereby to fquare the line of her obedience.

[Imogen rifes.

Imog. No, madam ! let him ftrike—he is my
king ;
He is my father too.   He would have yoked me
To that fame fon of yours !—My life is his,
But not my truth ; my death he may command,
But not my proftitution.

Cymb. Degenerate girl, who wouldft have fill'd
our throne
With beggary and bafenefs !—

Imog. No, my lord—
With goodnefs and with glory ; with a man,
Who, that he is a man, is the beft praife
And pride of human kind ! I would have given,
Grace to your crown, protection to your age,
Truth to your truft, and conqueft to your armies.

Cymb. Poifon and poniards, rather—Out up-
on thee !—
A fpecious, popular, and fecret traitor !
Fond, foolifh wench, he prizes not thy love,
But as thou art the ftep to his ambition.
Now, by the powers I hold from earth and Heaven,
As father and as king, I do divorce thee

From

From all affiance with that foundling flave,
That hated LEONATUS!—Come, thy hand—
Here, CLOTEN, take her to thee—
   IMOG. Hence, low wretch!—
Exchange an eagle for an owlet!—No.
     CYMB. Hear me, thou rebel!—I had once a
          fifter,
Fair to all eyes, and dear to every heart:
Like thee, fhe proved incontinent; nor fought
Our will in wedlock—To the laws I gave her:
At the dread fhrine of our avenging Goddefs,
I faw her blood let forth—I faw the flames
Afcend her pyre, and in one blaze involve
Her and her unborn babe.
    IMOG. O tale of woe!—
O barbarous brother.!
    CYMB. Hear me—What withholds,
But that I yield thee, alfo, to the claims
Of fteel and fire?
    IMOG. Thrice welcome, fire and fteel—
So that my fufferings might atone the fins
Of my dread fire.
    CYMB. Mark, lords; and you, my fubjects—
This traitrefs, this young parricide, who would
Untimely pufh her father from his throne,
And, with her paramour, ufurp dominion;
Henceforth, an alien to our blood and crown,
We caft her off—and, in her room, adopt
This fon of our fair QUEEN, the princely CLOTEN.
With love and fealty, alone, we claim
All future kindred—fuch, alone, fhall heir

                              Our

Our heart and empire! I will hear no pleadings—
Follow me all, and leave her to her fortunes.

[Exeunt.

S C E N E   IV.

To Imogen Leonatus.

They run and embrace.

Imog. My lord, my every love, my Leonatus—
Thou world of Imogen, who doſt comprize
Whatever nature, in her various round,
Can cull of good—thou fullneſs of my ſoul,
At once the ſource, and the ſatiety,
Of all my wiſhes !—
O, we muſt ſever—we muſt part, my love,
As in the laſt vain gaſpings after life,
When ſoul and body ſunder!

   Leon. O bower of bliſs, on whom eternal
      ſpring
Hath laviſh'd all its fragrance, ſayſt thou, part ?—
To part with thee, in life or death, were worſe
Than all the gather'd heap of mortal ills,
That life or death can threaten.

   Imog. All is over—
All is diſcover'd, ſweet, and we muſt part !
If Heaven has joy, within the ſeeds of time,
For truth, and faith, and infinite endearment,
Then we muſt meet again !—Away, away—
Even while I, thus, would cling to thee for ever,

My

My fears, that one look more may prove our laſt,
Turn me to frenzy !—While we talk, the ſtorm
Comes on apace; and, ere one fond adieu,
May break upon thy head !

    Leon. Let us haſte, then,
And, glutton-like, at one ſhort meal, devour
Our hoard of promis'd bliſs—Come to my arms !—
O thus, for ever thus, that I might hold thee—
Wrap thy exiſtence inward to my ſoul,
Even as the claſping rind contains and folds
The fragrance of the cedar !

SCENE V.

Enter KING, QUEEN, CLOTEN, Lords, Guards,
           Attendants.

    Cymb. Tear them aſunder—quick—your office,
        guards !
Diſarm, ſecure the traitor.
    Imog. At your peril—.
Guards, touch him not—Sir—lords—Britons—
        he is,
He is my huſband—my eſpous'd, my heart's
        beloved,
My Leonatus !——
    Cymb. Seize him, I ſay——
    Imog. Forbear, I charge ye !—What—
Your chief, the guardian of my father's throne,
Britain's firſt boaſt, the glory of your country !—
    Cymb. Guards, traitors, ſlaves—your lives ſhall
        anſwer this !

Vol. III.   N   Seize,

Seize, ftab, difpatch him—
                    [Guards turn their weapons on Leonatus.
    Imog. Mark your princefs, firft—
Behold this poniard!—by the Power ye worfhip,
By your tremendous Goddefs, great Andate—
On your firft motion to attempt his life,
His precious life,—this paffes through my bofom!
    Cymb. Villains! I fee ye are confederate all,
Againft your king. 'Tis well. Thus far I par-
        don—
I grant the traitor's life; but far removed
From Britain—By Andate too, I vow,
If his returning ftep fhall ever dare
To prefs our fhores, that moment is his laft—
He dies, I fwear—his blood fhall pay the trefpafs,
Although the blood of this unduteous girl
Should mingle with the ftream!—
    Leon. Yes, Cymbeline,
Deluded prince! your foldier will depart,
But take no traitor hence. Be well aware
Of thofe he leaves behind! and, O, ye gods!
Grant, that my honour'd father, and my king,
May not find fpeedy reafon for repentance;
Look round for help in fome diftrefsful hour,
And call, but call in vain, on Leonatus.
    Cymb. Away with him—to fea, to banifhment,
Diftant as winds can waft!—And you, our Queen,
Take this young rebel into clofe reftraint,
And fee her chamber'd!   [Women lay hold on her.
    Imog. Sir, my king, my father!
Will you not grant your child one laft adieu,
Perhaps—O Heavenly powers!—perhaps, for ever.

    I   Cymb.

Cymb. Keep them afunder—Bear them cff,
    I fay,
Far from each other!
    Leon. O, thou departing light of all my life!
Muft I then lofe thee, Imogen?—Night hangs
On every road from hence!—Beyond this fpot,
The world alike is wafte; a worthlefs blank,
A wild of defolation!—
    Cymb. Hence—away—
Away with them.—
    Imog. My lord!—   [Struggling with her women.
    Leon. My only life!—
    Imog. Adieu!
    Leon. Adieu!
O Imogen!—
    Imog. O Leonatus!— [They are taken off feverally.
                [Exeunt Cymbeline, Lords, and Attendants.
    Clot. Now, mother, there is room for hope.
    Queen. No, Cloten!
This was befide my aim—I had him fure,
Juft on the brink, from whence this foolifh king
Unwillingly hath fnatched him—Here is gold—
Hafte—find that one-eyed ruffian, with his fellows,
Train'd and inured to blood!—If he fcape thus,
'Tis ftill in fate to crofs us.
    Clot. What if I go along?
    Queen. Difguifed?
    Clot. And mafqued?—
    Queen. 'Tis well!—Difpatch, my fon—
                        [Exeunt feverally.

N 2   SCENE

SCENE VI.

A Country on the Shore of the River
THAMES.

Enter CAIUS LUCIUS, CLODIO, and other Roman
Officers.

LUCIUS. Neptune hath smooth'd our way; the
    gods of wind
And waters have conspired to make our passage
As speedy as propitious—Valiant CLODIO,
While yet our legions disembark, appoint
Such train as may befit thy embassy
To Britain's neighbouring court—This pacquet
    bears
The will of Cæsar, and thy full instructions.

CLOD. A Briton, here, informs me, that the
    house
Of CYMBELINE is all in wondrous ferment,
Raised by a son of fortune, who hath wived
The daughter of his KING—one LEONATUS.

LUCIUS. How! LEONATUS?

CLOD. Have you knowledge, then,
Of this adventurer?

LUCIUS. Yes, a dear remembrance—
So hath the world's sole ruler, great Augustus,
With many of the noblest sons of Rome.
So fair an outside, and such worth within,
Endows no second man.

CLOD.

CLOD. You ftretch him, fure,
Beyond his limits.

LUCIUS. No—At Actium, CLODIO—
But you, as I muft think, were not at Actium—
There, this unbearded boy, unbearded then,
With wonders took the eye of Cæfar captive.
The battle done, he call'd, and queftion'd him
Touching his birth and country; when the youth,
Blufhing, replied, that, as he knew no fire,
He was not worth a name—" Be henceforth, then,
" The fon of Cæfar," cried our emperor,
And named him LEONATUS.

CLOD. Let him pafs;
For, till this hour, to me he has been namelefs.

LUCIUS. The daughter of his king?—Now, on
                my foul,
If I did deem aright, he might have had
The daughter of our emperor, the firft
In beauty, as in birth.

CLOD. O, Momus, hear !—
Julia prefer a favage, to the choice
Of Rome's unrival'd demigods?

LUCIUS. Believe me,
I was not fingle in fuch thoughts.   But then,
Drawn by fome ftrong attachment back to Britain,
He quitted the warm fhine of Cæfar's favour,
And left the emulators of his virtue
To wonder and to mourn—We fince have learn'd,
The Scots, a wild and warlike race of men,
Sprung from an ifle that conftitutes the brink
Of our expanded world, beyond whofe verge
Nature herfelf has nothing to behold,

N 3

Save

Save air and ocean—thofe fierce men, I fay,
Broke in, on Britain.   All, from end to end,
Was flight and panic; till this LEONATUS
Alone made head, and drove thofe boifterous
        kerns
Back to their wattled hives.   And well, I deem,
Well he may match the daughter of the man,
Whofe crown he has redeem'd.

SOLDIER enters.

SOLD. A noble prifoner waits.
LUCIUS. Conduct him to us.

S C E N E   VII.

LEONATUS enters.

LUCIUS. Immortal powers! the very man we
        dream'd of.—
My friend, my beft beloved, my LEONATUS!
                                [Embrace.
By the gods, welcome—welcomeft of aught
The gods themfelves could fend!—Whence, from
        what chance,
What happy chance?
   LEON. O LUCIUS, fon of Rome,
Beft loved, and beft refpected—you behold
A wretched outcaft, thrown, as with a fling,
From all his heart holds dear.
   LUCIUS. Banifh'd?
   LEON. Even fo.

LUCIUS.

Lucius. O, Capitolian Jove, thou dost infatuate

Those thou wouldst ruin !—Cast their shield
away !—
What now shall guardian their abandon'd side,
Against the sword of Rome ?—My Leonatus,
The valiant Clodio.   [They salute.
Say, my soul's elect,
Where may your purpose bend ?

    Leon. In sooth, I know not—
To Gaul—or possibly, to Rome and Cæsar.

    Lucius. If you are not upon the spur from
            hence,
We would entreat your sojourn with our love,
Till we may burden you with some dispatches
To Cæsar and our friends.

    Leon. Alas, for me,
The world affords no wish, no way from hence, .
Save what may serve a friend.

    Lucius. Within the minute,
My thanks and I attend you.   [Exit Lucius.

    Clod. Noble stranger !
Your aspect bears a seal of such mishap,
As saddens all who see.   May any cause
Be worth this sum of woe ?

    Leon. If, to have lost
Whatever earth can yield of estimation,
Or fancy frame in Heaven, be worth a sigh—
Then mine are honest tribute.

    Clod. Sir, you are young ;
Just at the tide of spring, that overbears
The flats of common sense—Oft have I known

                    Untutor'd

Untutor'd paffion, defperate from the lofs
Of the moft flight and worthlefs thing on earth,
A woman——

   Leon. A woman!—Does your fentence, judg-
      . . ing fir,
Extend beyond the ftews?

   Clod. Throughout the world's
Wide orbit.   Nature form'd their flippant fex
Upon the model of the fea-born dame,
Whofe knowledge takes in all of gods and men,
From Mars to foft Adonis.

   Leon. Fie, fie!—this foul opinion
Strumpets thy mother in her urn.

   Clod. My mother
Stood on a line with her, the chafteft fhe,
Whofe fond inamorato, in his brain,
Now figures for a phænix.   I fap not
The credit of a fingle fair; but mourn,
That any gallant man, fhould tie his faith,
His peace, and valued honours, to a thing
That none alive can keep—Place me a cloud
'Twixt Dian and Endymion, my eftate,
My manhood for the pledge, that I transfer
The horns from her to him.

   Leon. O, I do know,
I do know one—but fuch another, till,
By the fame pattern, nature fhall renew
The beauty of her works—like to that one,
Another can't be known!—By great Andate,
The fight would throw a rein of dumb reftraint
On that licentious tongue—One chaftening look,
One aweful glance of her reproving eye,

Would

Would freeze the hotteſt libertine of Rome
To ſtill and downcaſt reverence !
 CLOD. Is ſhe native
Of any world yet known ?
 LEON. Your Italy,
A ſtranger to her virtues, as you ſay,
Records her name—'Tis IMOGEN !
 CLOD. The peerleſs heir of Britain !—O ye gods,
A plumb, a province, for the wiſh'd encounter !
 LEON. Away, ſlight, empty braggard !—what
   couldſt thou,
Where even Hyperion, or the Roman Jove,
Born, as to Læda once, on downy pinions ;
Or, in his ſtill more tempting form of gold,
Though dropt into her lap, in all his glory,
Should find her truth more ſtrong than his ſeduction?
 CLOD. She is a woman ſtill—I go, this hour,
To CYMBELINE from Cæſar—Had I means
Of fair addreſs, I, here, would freely gage
My villa, rated at the rich return
Of fifty annual talents, that I bring
Sure proof ſhe renders up her chaſteſt hoard
To my free arbitration.
 LEON. Inſolent !——
Thou dareſt not gage.
 CLOD. By Jupiter, I think
You will not dare the trial.
 LEON. To convince thee
Of thine own arrogance, and my contempt,
Thou ſhalt have letters to her—Mark me, yet ;
On thy return, the convict of thy folly,

'Tis

'Tis not thy villa only—no, thy blood
Shall pay the penalty of this prefumption!—
Prepare to anfwer with thy fword.

 Clod. Agreed.

 Leon. Till then I hold no converfe with a
  ruffian,
Though dignified by Rome.—I'll fend the letters.
       [Exeunt feverally.

END OF THE FIRST ACT.

ACT

ACT II.

SCENE I.

LUCIUS and LEONATUS.

Lucius. O No, my LEONATUS!
Indeed it was not well—had I been
present
This wager had not past.

Leon. Why, honour'd friend?
From brutal violence, or saucy insult,
She is well guarded in her father's court—
What is there then to fear?

Lucius. Ill blood, at least—
And possibly the venture of a life,
That is most dear to LUCIUS!—This same CLODIO,
For skill in weapons, and a bearlike boldness,
Is rank'd among the foremost.

Leon. Never, yet,
Was I confronted with a son of Rome,
So rudely manner'd.

Lucius. All, of Cæsar's court,
Are not of Cæsar's confidence, nor yet
Of his commissioning; howe'er, by means

Of

Of fecond links, and golden interventions,
A brute of fortune mayn't be far from favour.
The firft of Clodio's faults is, want of virtue ;
The fecond, that he hates it in another.
Agrippa link'd him with me in commiffion ;
Nature forbids all further tie between us.

    Leon. Let him be weigh'd, before you hold
        him worth
Another word—But fay, my noble friend,
Is war determined againft Britain, then,
In all the bloody procefs and extent
Of military licence ?

    Lucius. War, or tribute—
Such is the will of Cæfar ! Yet we bear
The Roman fword, but, with more furety,
To plant the Roman olive.

    Leon. Tribute, Lucius !
Do ye infift on tribute ?

    Lucius. Some light matter—
But as a term that may exprefs fubmiffion.

    Leon. O, 'tis in that, in that alone, my friend,
That tribute turns to lead !—A drachm of weight,
A ftraw, a feather, to a freeborn mind,
Becomes a mountain's burden, when impofed
The badge of vile dependence !

    Lucius. Noble creature !
Conceive me as the duteous minifter
Of Cæfar's will, not mine.   And yet my will
And power are now intent to place a friend
Even on the throne of that unthankful country,
From whofe rejecting arms he late was caft,
A hopelefs exile !

Leon.

Leon. How!—reftored to Britain?—
Revenge?—my Imogen?—imperial power?—
And Cæfar's favour?

Lucius. All, by holy friendfhip,
I fwear it, all are thine.

'Leon. Alas!' my Lucius,
I did but fum the bright temptation up,
Juft to behold the value, for a moment,
Of what I muft rejeƈt.—
Say Lucius, that fame Roman, who derived
His name of glory from Corioli,
Was he not banifh'd?

Lucius. Yes.

Leon. And turn'd his fword
Againft his country?—

Lucius. True; and, thereby, fhew'd
To thanklefs Rome, the richnefs of the pearl
Their pride had caft away.

Leon. And was enroll'd
Among her heroes?—

Lucius. Truft me, with the foremoft.

Leon. O wayward man, deluded, by the glare
And wildfire of ambition, from the path
That Goodnefs brightens with unfetting glory!—
The Line of Duty is a Rubicon,
Whofe bounds no power, in earth or Heaven, can take
Or give a right to pafs!—True Honour, Lucius,
From the beginning to the end of things,
Goes hand in hand with Virtue!

Lucius.

Lucius. O, the gods!
Let me behold him—Let my wonder mark
The greatnefs of your works!

SOLDIER enters.

Sold. The legions are all landed, and attend
Their general's voice, for march, or for en-
        campment.
Lucius. I come.   [Exit Soldier.
My Leonatus, while I touch, and talk,
                        [Takes his hand.
And breathe within the region of thy virtues,
I too, methinks, grow greater than Auguftus;
And feel, in thefe expandings of my foul,
That honour's more than empire.   [Exeunt.

S C E N E II.

The Palace of Cymbeline.

Queen and Cloten enter oppofite.

Queen. Well, Cloten—haft thou?—How is
        this—a face
Of damp and difappointment!—O, thou fhouldft
Have come, with triumph, prologue, in thy looks;
And blood-befprinkled garments, to forefhew
The important deed was done!
Clot. Perdition catch him!
And dangers, great as he has juft efcaped,

For

For ever clofe him round, that no curs'd chance,
No fudden arm may fnatch him from the brink,
Till he is funk, paft fight.
  QUEEN. What, fafe, unhurt?
The lion fcaped the toils?—nay, then, our clue
Of fate again is ravelled.
  CLOT. I had gotten
A pack of blood-hounds, ftaunch, as ever open'd
On the hot fcent of near appointed flaughter.
We took us to the Thames, plied fail and oar—
Forward we fhot, purfued—our eyes o'ertook him,
Held him in view, and gain'd upon our prey;
Till, juft as when the frighted hare appears
Within the ftraining greyhound's jaws—damn'd
        hap!—
A Roman galley croft, and took him in;
And all our tugging rowers fcarce avail'd
To warrant our own freedom.
  QUEEN. Soft, the KING.

S C E N E III.

Enter KING, IMOGEN, Lords, Guards, &c.

  CYMB. So near, and landed, fayft thou?—This
        is magic.
No word of preparation, or approach!
Our watchers have confpired, with winds and feas,
To bring this ftorm upon us.—What's their power?
  MESS. About five legions, fheath'd in arms of
        proof,
And clofe-appointed.

                              CYMB.

Cymb. Give us but note for double that
        amount,
And we will charge them to the beard.—Cingetorix,
Light up our beacons, give the alarm throughout.
And, Cadwal, call our train'd brigades together.
My Queen!—although thy Mars is not, as when,
A ftripling, he afpired to win a plume
From the firft Cæfar; they fhall find him, yet,
Equal in clofing arms to aught that's lefs
Than their almighty Julius. Gods! I thank ye
For this addition of a late renown,
Though at the ftake and peril of our crown.
                              [Exeunt all but Imogen.

    Imog. All is in uproar!—here and there they
        run,
They know not whither; or, in fixt affright,
Freeze to the fpot they prefs—Alack, for them!—
But, wherefore am not I in like alarm?—
O greater woe!—to me no gain can come;
And I am already funk fo low in lofs,
As mocks at lower—Time and life, what are ye—
While fill'd with thought, yet emptied of the
        thing
That made your value? Time, and life, and
        thought,
You are my wretchednefs.—O Leonatus!

SCENE

S C E N E IV.

A Servant enters followed by CLODIO.

SERV. Madam, a knight of Rome attends your
     pleasure,
With letters from my lord.   [Exit.

  CLOD. Nay, change not, lady—
The noble LEONATUS is in safety,
And honour'd me with these.   [Gives Letters.

  IMOG. Thanks, courteous fir!—
O, learn'd, indeed, were that astronomer,
Who knew the stars as I his characters;
He'd lay the future open—Wax, thy leave.
Bleft be the bees that made these, locks of counfel!
Good news, good gods!   [Reads.

  CLOD. All of her, that is out of door, moft
     rich!—
If fhe be furnifh'd with a mind as rare,
She is alone the Arabian Bird; and I,
In rafhly feeking after my own fhame,
Have loft myfelf—Audacity befriend me!

  IMOG. Moft welcome, worthy fir!—for my
     dear lord
Here fends thrice happy tidings, that he is near,
And well, and well protected in the love
Of the moft noble LUCIUS—Generous fir,
You have chear'd a hopelefs mourner—welcome,
     welcome!

VOL. III.   O   Have

Have you aught elfe, in kind commiffion, from
My Leonatus; or, if not from him,
From your kind felf?—as, how he look'd, or talk'd
Or fmiled, or moved; or, with what circumftance
He gave this bleft remembrance—Thefe are things,
In love's fond lore, of infinite import,
Though nothing to you wife ones.

    Clod. Royal lady,
I blufh to find myfelf not duly verfed
In this fweet erudition.   I have nought,
Worthy of like memorial, to deliver,
Save, that our friend, our happy Leonatus,
Bade me renew the plightings of his faith,
Upon this peerlefs wax.
               [Offers to kifs her hand—fhe withdraws it.

   Imog. How, fir!—I find you grow alike for-
          getful
Of me, and of your meffage—Here—who waits?

    Clod. Your pardon, fair!—wherein have I of-
        fended?

    Imog. Is it the cuftom, for your Roman dames
To be fo ill refpected?

    Clod. Gracious goddefs!
What you mifdeem for infolence, with us
Marks the fubmiffive fign of adoration;
And the fair hand of our imperial Julia,
Is daily worfhip'd by the lips of thoufands.

     Imog. Fafhion may change with fancy—Gentle
        fir,
I truft your knowledge will excufe our wants,
And yet conform to what it finds—Still, welcome!

                             All's

All's well, I hope—pray take my power for yours,
And to your full content.
　　Clod. Surpassing creature !
Were I commission'd to call forth the winds,
From east and west, to winnow her throughout,
The gods, the gods, I find, have made her chaffless.
　　　　　　　　　　　　　　　　　　　　[Aside.
Consummate queen ! scepter'd in every soul
'That bends before perfection !—there is, yet,
One favour—
　　Imog. Ask with confidence—believe it
Already granted.
　　Clod. I am come, express,
From Rome to Cymbeline, and bring a coffer
That bears the seal of Cæsar, yet inviolate.
Within, 'tis freighted with some rich contents
Of rare device, and precious estimation ;
Gifts from Augustus to your royal sire,
Your princely self, and his adopted son,
Your peerless Leonatus.—For this night,
I wish them safe ; and safest I should deem them
In your protection, lady.
　　Imog. Send them hither ;
And, for the sake of that most valued part,
Respective to my lord, I'll see them stow'd
In my own chamber.—I will answer, truly,
To your best trust—and so, good sir, good night !
　　Clod. My soul bows down to thank you. Peace,
　　　　　and slumbers
Sweet as your graces, wait you till the morning ?
　　　　　　　　　　　　　　　　　[Exeunt severally.

S C E N E V.

**Enter King, Queen, Cloten, Lords, Guards,
and Roman Herald.**

A Parchment, with a large Seal, in the Hand of Cymbeline.

CYMB. It is the feal of Cæfar—Tell me, herald,
Who comes with thefe credentials?
    HERALD. The valiant CLODIO, fecond in com-
        mand
To our moft noble LUCIUS.
    CYMB. He is welcome—
We are prepared to hear him—let him enter.

S C E N E VI.

Enter CLODIO with a Train of Romans.

CYMB. Firft, CLODIO, for thyfelf and thofe
        brave Romans,
Our Britain greets ye well—Our further anfwer
Waits to be meafured by your errand—Say,
With us, what would Auguftus?
    CLOD. Thus, faith Cæfar:
Nature, through Heaven and earth, hath form'd
        her works
In due fubordination.   One Supreme
Rules each appointed province.—Sol, who now
Drinks at the nether ocean, through the round
Of the wide Empyreum, where he walks
Among ten thoufand thoufand leffer lights,

                                Behold

Beholds no rival!—In like manner, reigns
Jove over gods; and, over mortals, Cæsar—
But, not with lawlefs fway.—Rome, CYMBELINE,
Whofe empire gathers in the fcatter'd realms
Of our remoteft world, fpreads forth her wings,
Even as a parent-bird, to fhield her young,
And fofters while fhe rules—nor would leave out
Your diftant Britain from the wide protection.

  CYMB. Protection! have we fought it?—Say
        to Cæfar,
That Britain is a world within herfelf,
Imperial, independent; from the birth
Of nature, fet apart, fair, full, and free,
And all-fufficient ever.   Britain is
Another fea-born Venus, girt around
With her cerulean ceftus, her chafte zone,
Which Rome fhall not untie.—Protection! where,
Where was this proud difplay of Rome's protection,
When every petty ftate of petty Latium,
Gave her to tremble for herfelf?—No, Roman!
Britain is likelier, o'er a fubject world,
To ftretch her own domain, than from that world
To learn the leffon of a vile fubjection.
When Rome fhall afk our help, our will and power
May anfwer to her wants; we want not her's,
Nor will accept fuch Greek-like gifts—Protection!
Britain, we truft, fhall well protect herfelf
From fuch protectors.

  CLOD. Your uncle Caffibelan, CYMBELINE,
Would not have anfwer'd our firft Cæfar thus.

  CYMB. My uncle Caffibelan, CLODIO,
Did anfwer your firft Cæfar thus—that Julius,

O 3

Whofe

Whofe boaft of conqueft over mighty nations,
Was, that " he came and faw."—Was that his
     boaft
O'er Britain alfo?—No.—At firft, he fmiled
At our fmall fkill; but foon was taught to frown
At our great courage. Twice repuls'd, and driven
To hide his fhame in Gaul, at length he learn'd,
By force of faction, rather than of fteel,
With our own arms to win us.—If the gods
Shall ever doom us to a foreign yoke,
'Tis not the arms of Rome, or of the world,
We have to fear—Britain can only fall
By Britain !

    Clod. Your uncle, Caffibelan, in behalf
Of his fucceeders in the Britifh throne,
Did gage to Julius, his acknowledg'd lord,
A yearly rent of feventy golden talents.

    Cymb. Let Julius claim!—He laid his coun-
     try, too,
Under like contribution.—Tell me, Roman,
Did Brutus well, when, by one godlike ftroke,
He gave her freedom ?

    Clod. We have nought with this.—
We come to claim the tribute—What's your an-
     fwer ?

    Cymb. That ye have ta'en us fomewhat un-
     provided—
Of money ?—no, but marfhal'd men—with fuch
We mean to pay you.—Tribute! wherefore tri-
     bute ?
When Cæfar can obfcure the golden fun,
Or hold the winds from breathing upon Britain,

He may demand a tax for light and air—
Till then, no tribute, Clodio.

Clod. Yet, bethink you.
Loth am I to pronounce the world's wide lord
An enemy to Britain; to call forth
Rome's thunder yet reftrain'd, confufion, wrath,
And ruin, not to be refifted.—Cæfar,
Who numbers more of monarchs in his train,
Than Cymbeline of menial-fervitors,
Yet tenders peace and amity.

Cymb. On terms
Of equal amity, we would embrace him.
But, why, with prefent menace, do we deem
Of future iffues, which the gods, alone,
Have in their keeping?—
Let us be brief, and fum our laft refolves.

Clod. War, or fubmiffion?

Cymb. Liberty, or death!—
Lords, give our guefts fuch tendence, as befits
Their high condition—A good night to all.
      [Exeunt feverally, Cymbeline and his Attendants—
          Clodio and his train.

Queen. Cloten, I do bethink me, that the
          gods,
If there are gods, or dæmons, or whate'er,
That may obtrude their influence, unafk'd,
On mortal counfels, or concerns—I think,
We have no caufe to thank them—Leonatus
Is now beyond our reach; and Cymbeline
Muft not be laid to fleep, until the known
Events of war fhall tell us when to ftrike.

O 4

His daughter, too!—but for thy foolifh lufts,
That bar had been away, by this.
    CLOT. My mother,
I afk you not to give her to my love—
Yet, fpare her to my vengeance, to the chaftening
That's due to her contempts!—By all the gods,
Should fhe efcape inviolate, your CLOTEN
Muft pine upon the throne.
    QUEEN. Well then, be fpeedy.
    CLOT. The KING has put me into large com-
        miffion.
    QUEEN. The KING, my child?—no matter for
        the KING;
He's ours already.   'Tis the Roman power
That's yet in doubt—Both fides muft be fecured,
That fate may find no further way to crofs us.
    CLOT. And how may that——
    QUEEN. No more—but be attentive.—
With the firft dawn, take this difpatch to CLODIO,
It is addreft to LUCIUS, Rome's elect
For this high expedition; and imports
A tender, on our part, to great Auguftus,
Of double tribute, and our Pictifh bands,
In aid of Rome's thin legions—thus condition'd,
That Britain's crown fhould be confirm'd to us.
Be clofe and dark as night—Away, my fon,
To bed, and dream of honours!
                            [Exeunt feverally.

                                    SCENE

S C E N E   VII.

A BEDCHAMBER.

IMOGEN enters, with a Book and Taper.

A large Coffer in a Corner.

IMOG. The night's far gone—It is a ſleepy tale,
                              [Lays by the Book.
And I'll to bed—Thou ever wakeful Fancy,
Who makeſt new worlds, and peopleſt them with
        beings
At thine own will—O, take my LEONATUS
Into thy kind creation; give him to me
In all his love and lovelineſs; a ſhade
Paſſing all waking ſubſtance !—ſo ſhall night
Atone my griefs by day; and, what is not,
Be prized o'er all that is—   [Lies down.
From every power of darkneſs, guard me, gods!
And ope your Heaven within !   [Sleeps.

CLODIO riſes cautiouſly out of the Coffer.

CLOD. Soft—All is ſtill—except the cricket's
        chirp;
And the death-worm, that ticks its midnight
        watch
To ſilence—Tarquin, thus, with ſtealthy pace
Came o'er the ſleeping Lucrece, ere he waked

                                        The

The chaftity he wounded—Firft, to mark
The tales impannell'd on the pictured boards,
And needled in the arras.
The fifteenth Danaide—Hero, from the tower,
And, from the beach, Alcione, juft fprung
To join their loves below.—Panthea, arm'd
Againft her life, hangs o'er her mangled lord !
Strike, woman,
Put the beholder out of pain !—By Proferpine,
All that is fabled, yet, of female worth,
Is call'd together here, to be affirm'd
By yonder fole perfection !—Now, for marks
Of nearer, dearer annotation—fuch
As may, with jealous frenzy, rend the foul
Of that loved, envied, curs'd, detefted favage!—
Gently—as moufers tread by night—Kind fleep,
Image of death, lie thou upon her fenfe,
As monumental marble on a tomb
In fome ftill chapel.—'Tis her breathing, fure,
That thus perfumes the chamber—Cytherea,
How thou doft fanctify thy fhrine !—fair lilly,
Queen of the vale—more fpotlefs, yet, within,
Than all external purity—Soft, foft,
Come off, thou precious bond, come off—'Tis
     mine—   ['Takes off her bracelet.
A witnefs againft truth, more ftrong, than all
Our Roman batteries !—O, the gods ! what's
     here ?—
On the left fide, beneath the beauteous pap,
A mole cinque-fpotted, like the crimfon drops
Ith' bottom of a cowflip—Here's a voucher,

                       Beyond

Beyond|what law can make!—She stirs!—enough—
I'll to my trunk again—
Ye dragons, who draw on the team of night,
Ply faft your leathern wings, that chearful morn
May rife to win my freedom!

[Goes into the coffer.—The fcene clofes.

END OF THE SECOND ACT.

ACT

A C T   III.

S C E N E   I.

The COUNTRY.   A Wood and Cavern at a
diſtance.

LEONATUS and FAUSTUS enter.

LEON. FAUSTUS, look out—they cannot
          yet have paſt—
This way returns them to the camp.
    FAUST. They come—
'Tis CLODIO's trumpet—
    LEON. Get thee, then, apart,   [Exit FAUSTUS.
Till we have cloſed our conference—If LUCIUS
Has juſtly ſtiled him brave, he will not take
The vantage of his numbers, to de bate
Againſt a ſingle arm——

S C E N E   II.

CLODIO and his Retinue.

CLODIO, thrice welcome.
A word, with your good pleaſure ; and that word,
As you are a valiant Roman, aſks no witneſs.—
Might not your train proceed ?—

                              . CLOD.

Clod. Yes—forward—on !

[To his Retinue, who go out.

I'll follow—Now, your will.—

Leon. You bear, in mind,
Your insult, and late offer'd enterprize
Against my wife.

Clod. You named her not as such.
I hold my friend's connubial couch for sacred,
Although his spouse should place the pillow for me,
And wooe me to the parley.

Leon. Well—pass that—
And say, what rich returns thou hast brought home
From thy bold venture to the coast of beauty.
Is there no worth, save what is masculine?
Or, does the weather-gage of thine opinion
Turn from that restive point ?

Clod. Your pardon, sir.
You menaced me at parting.   I hold not
My life so cheap to risque it for a woman.
Grant a safe course and latitude of converse,
Or here my tale is ended.

Leon. I do swear it.
Give me fair facts. I quarrel not with truth,
Though it should blast me—Thou hast seen a
          princess—

Clod. Unparagon'd—a wonder, even to eyes
That have seen all things else !

Leon. And her chaste name,
Still unimpeach'd.

Clod. It is my soul's firm faith—
No woman chaster, or more fondly bound
To the memorial of an absent husband.

Leon.

LEON. O, I did know my IMOGEN was chaste,
As fnow new-fallen upon the mountain top;
And conftant as the vine that clafps its elm,
And dies upon divifion—Say, good CLODIO,
Waft thou not welcomed?

CLOD. Yes—at once—moft warmly.
In that I was a debtor to her love
For LEONATUS—At the kindly clofe
Of our firft interview, I did advife her
Of fome rare matters that I brought from Rome,
And begg'd permiffion at her fhrine to lay
Great Cæfar's offering—with a gracious nod,
The goddefs gave affent.

LEON. On—what enfued?

CLOD. Our audience at the Britifh court—'twas
     long—
The night was then advanced—'twas late—time
     prefs'd.
I urged, and was admitted to her chamber.

LEON. Her chamber!—was it her's?—art thou
     affured?—
But, fay it were—and fo thou might'ft have been
To that of Lucrece——

CLOD. True.—I laid before her
Rich robings, gems of curious fet, and pearls
That left the Orient poor—no futile nets
For feminine affections.

LEON. Well—the procefs.

CLOD. While fhe retired, in fafety to difpofe
Her precious lading, I did mark the chamber—
The tale-recording tapeftry and paintings,
Storied, I doubt, with more of nuptial truth

Than

Than quondam hufbands met with.—Soon re-
    turn'd, .
She held me to difcourfe, with pleafant queftions
Touching our Roman gallantries and cuftoms.
  LEON. Was thy ftay long ?
  CLOD. Long ?—no—our prefent nights
Serve but as prologue to an early dawning.
  LEON. Plague and perdition !—   [Afide.
How were ye employ'd ?
  CLOD. Nay, take your colour to you—No
    harm done ;
Nothing but chat, and inoffenfive dalliance.
  LEON. Slave, villain, lyar !—by the gods, 'tis
    falfe—
Dalliance !
  CLOD. Your oath is forfeit—fare you well—
                        [Going.
  LEON. Come back, thou fcap'ft not fo—Pro-
    duce me, here,
Some token, but the lighteft feather, won
From her high-plumed virtue—or, by hell,
Whereto thou goeft, thy lateft glafs is run !
  CLOD. You fhall be fatisfied—But will you,
    then,
Be peaceful ?
  LEON. I do fwear it—though the proof,
Like the Tarantula's envenom'd touch,
Should fting me into madnefs.
  CLOD. Know you this ?—   [Shews the bracelet.
  LEON. Gape hell, and fwallow all affiance up !
All faith and truft, and fabled truth, in woman !|
Know it ?—too well !—it was our band of nuptials,

With thefe confiding fingers fondly tied,
Even on the marriage night.—How gott'ft thou
       this?
Tempter acccurs'd!—the means—the circum-
       ftance—
   Clod. Half by confent—and half, by fweet
       conftraint—
I loofed, and toy'd it from her.
   Leon. O, I fee
It is enough!—thy triumph is accomplifh'd
Over our peace and honour.—Get thee hence!—
It muft, yet cannot be—Hold, Clodio—anfwer!
Haft thou not practifed on her cooler blood,
With fome infernal drug?—or, by thyfelf,
Or fome confederate villainy, purloin'd
That fpecious trophy?—Have I found thee, Cacus?
Traced thy fteps backward to thy den?
   Clod. So leave it.—
Why, what have I affirm'd to touch you, thus,
With jealous frenzy?—
Have I yet told you of the crimfon gem,
That fweetly neftles under the left fwell
Of her defcending bofom?
   Leon. O, I am choak'd!—
She's wreck'd—the world's bright pinnace funk
      for ever!
Should thoufands of concurring witneffes
Rife to her honour now, I'd not believe them.—
Is there no hook to hold me from the brink,
Where the brain turns?—Yet—arm me with a reed,
And I will fight for her departed truth,
Though demonftration fhould be fheath'd in fteel,

                         And

And weapon'd right and left—Fiend! damn'd
    magician!   [Seizes CLODIO.
How haft thou wrought impoffibilities?
Soft—I have fworn—your pardon, gods!—All's
    well—
Depart in peace—Quick—hence—left fudden
    wrath
Grind out thy foul, and fcatter thee as duft!
              [Exit CLODIO.
Down, climbing paffions! whither would ye mount—
To fpurn at Heaven and fate, who made things fo,
As cannot now be mended?—Ruin! ruin!
Worfe than the wreck of nature!—Is it thus?—
Or is it a negation—all, a whirl,
Of things that are but dreamt of?—Hold, hold faft
The feat of reafon, gods! a little fpace—
For fomewhat is to do—Racks, dying pangs,
What are ye, to the fall of Heaven's own houfe,
The human mind o'erthrown?—I muft be fpeedy.
FAUSTUS!——

        Enter FAUSTUS.

  FAUST. My lord.——
  LEON. Come hither, my good FAUSTUS—
Thou feeft thy mafter at the heavieft plunge
That ever call'd for help.—Thou haft loft thy
    mafter!
  FAUST. Alas!——
  LEON. His name and honours laid, all, low in
    earth,
No fofterer, friend, or mournful ftep attending!—

I thank thy tears—mine cannot chufe but follow.
————————FAUSTUS !

 FAUST. What would my heart's belov'd mafter?

 LEON. I fnatch'd thee, once, from twenty circling deaths,
At peril of my life.——

 FAUST. You did, you did.

 LEON. And thou art fworn, on any quick ex-
   treme
Of life or death, to do my fearful bidding,
No queftion afk'd.

 FAUST. I live, but till you fay,
Die, FAUSTUS !

 LEON. Didft thou hear aught that paft ?

 FAUST. Too much !—What's to be done ?

 LEON. I had a wife !

 FAUST. Difpatch her !

 LEON. And, fo, quench the kindling fires
Of luft and foul difhonour, that muft, elfe,
Blaze to a pointing world !——

 FAUST. Right.

 LEON. Wilt thou ?——

 FAUST. Yes.
It fhall be done.

 LEON. Not butcher-like, my FAUSTUS—
But gently, as the nurfe would lay to fleep
Her querulous babe—
O, give her not the twenty thoufandth pang
Such as now grapple at my foul !—Be fpeedy—
And, when the deed is done, thou mayft expect me
Near the great oak, that neighbours to the temple.

FAUST

FAUST. Farewell, farewell!—be happy, as you can,
My beft, my nobleft mafter!   [Exit FAUSTUS.
    LEON. This CLODIO, too, muft be provided for,
At the next turn—Why, this is gallant!—foon,
I fhall be deep in blood.
Thefe buffettings of fortune, how they harden
A heart, ônce, not inhuman!—
The fources of my living fhame once ftopt,
What follows?—what is to be reap'd from feeds,
Sown thus, or thus?—Eternity, to me,
Can yield no future harveft!—If I look
For peace in Heaven, or o'er the travell'd earth,
Through life, or time, or aught beyond, ftill, ftill,
I meet it fo bound up in IMOGEN,
As never to be funder'd!—O, my love!
O, my loft love!—O wretched, paft refource!
Undone, undone, loft, ruin'd LEONATUS!   [Exit,

S C E N E   III.

Near the CAVERN.

BELLARIUS enters from it.

BELL. Hail, Power! whoe'er thou art, who fitt'ft fupreme
O'er good and evil, o'er this fair immenfe
Of manifold exiftence, worlds replete
With works of varied grace!—I will not afk
How partial Ill hath fallen into the ways
Of wifdom infinite. The time may come,

When

When Thou ſhalt reign unqueſtioned, unoppoſed—
When guilt and pain ſhall ceaſe—when to be good
And happy, muſt be one—and all ſhall grow
Conſummate, and renew'd, within the will
Of their great maker !—
There reſts my laſt of hope ; and, thence, I learn,
To bear ſuch ills as ſeem to paſs all ſufferance—
Heaven, what a glorious form !—Some viſion, ſure,
[Looks out.
So far excelling all of mortal ſeeming !—
Alas, it wrings at ſome diſtreſs ! Can aught
Of Empyrean temper, thus, extort
Pity from poor humanity ?

S C E N E IV.

LEONATUS enters.

Bright being !——
How may the native of an upper ſphere
Appear partaker of the general woe,
That makes the lot of man ?
   LEON. O ſire revered !
You ſee a man, of miſerable men
The loweſt, and moſt loſt.
   BELL. Son of my age,
Son of my ſorrows alſo—if ſage counſel,
Or kind companionſhip in grief, may ſerve
To ſooth calamity ; then art thou come
Into the land of balms.
   LEON. No balm for wounds,
Deep as exiſtence !

1

BELL.

BELL. That's a depth, beyond
What death himfelf can ftrike! The caufe was,
          fure,
Moft capital.
    LEON. It was, it was—the fame
That fack'd the feven-fold walls of aged Priam,
Butcher'd his race, and laid his Afia wafte—
A woman's want of truth!
    BELL. O, I could pour
Into a friendly hearing, fuch a tale
Of a loft woman, as fhould foon exile
All woe, fave that alone, which is comprized
In her fad ftory!
    LEON. Once, I had a tear
For griefs that were not mine—Proceed, good
          father!
    BELL. The prefent King of Britain had a fifter.
Who faw her not, could form no femblance of her
From aught that he had feen —I woo'd, and won,
And wedded her in fecret.—
But, O, the richnefs of the bright poffeffion!
The world wants wealth to rate it. Three bleft
          moons,
Three moons, the brighteft that had ever changed
Upon the changeful blifs of man, fcarce wain'd,
When I was fent ambaffador, by CYMBELINE,
To Julius, Rome's dictator—Woe the while!
My love, my bride, my ADELAIDE proved
          pregnant—
She was impleaded of incontinence,
Even by her cruel brother was impleaded,
And urged to name the fire—but, kindly fearing

P 3   What,

What, haply, might befall the haplefs man,
Whom more than life fhe loved, fhe, to the death,
Perfifted in her filence; and was offer'd,
On the curs'd altar of the dire Andate,
The richeft incenfe of the trueft love
That ever breathed to Heaven!

    LEON. Thrice happy hufband!
Death may foon draw the veil that, from your arms,
Shuts your expecting ADELAIDE—but mine
No kind hereafter can reftore!—Your pardon—
Forward, I pray.

    BELL. Thine eyes, my fon, grow heavy—
Come to my friendly cave, and I will try,
With the fad tale of my remaining woes,
To charm thy griefs to flumber.

    LEON. O, for ever!—
That were to be moft happy.   [Exeunt.

SCENE V.

FAUSTUS and IMOGEN enter.

    FAUST. We have croft the public paths, and,
        now, are paft
All rifque of further queftion.
    IMOG. Stay thee, FAUSTUS.
This is a gloomy place—I feel my fenfes
Seiz'd with I know not what of fudden horror!—
Where is my lord, where is my LEONATUS?
Didft thou not fay?—Why pales thy colour, man?
Why doft thou look with that ftern pity on me?—
What doft thou fearch and feel for?

                        FAUST.

Faust. Nothing, miſtreſs—
Be not alarm'd!—Where left you that ſame
    bracelet,
Which my fond·maſter, on his nuptial hight,
Bound to you with his troth?
  Imog. Alas, good Faustus,
Even all the gems that light my father's crown,
I'd give for its redemption. Late, laſt night,
I pray'd, and thought upon my love, and wept;
And kiſs'd that holy relick of his faith,
And dreamt of him till morning—when awaking,
I found my arm was worthleſs!
  Faust. O, beware,
It be not gone to tell my lord ſtrange tales
Of woman's breach of faith!
  Imog. Hòw, Faustus! No—
My honour ſits above the blaſt of ſlander;
And, like the top of Atlas, bears a Heaven
Upon a mount of ſnow.—I do aſſure thee,
Had I been born in any age, ſave that
In which my Leonatus won my ſoul,
With graces all his own, I ſhould have died
The votary of Dian.
  Faust. Pardon, miſtreſs!—
Know you one Clodio?
  Imog. A Roman, is he not?—He brought me
    letters
From my heart's maſter.
  Faust. That ſame Clodio, lady—
Did you admit him to your chamber?
  Imog. How!——
Thou doſt amaze me, Faustus. Save the time

P 4 H:

He told his meffage in, before, nor fince,
I never met, nor mark'd him.

    FAUST. By the gods,
Within this hour, thefe eyes—the amazed eyes
Even of your LEONATUS—faw that bracelet
In CLODIO's boaftful hand! Nay, he did quote
Each fure memorial of your bedchamber—
Defcribed your midnight fcene of wanton dalliance,
With fuch leud deeds, as would have turn'd to
        fhame
A face of folid bronze.—He ftript you, lady ;
And gave to record fuch peculiar notes,
Found on your precious body, as a chafte one
Would not deliver to the fettled gaze
Of a loved confort.

    IMOG. Oh——   [Faints,
    FAUST. The fwoon of death is on her !—O fole
        flower,
Of Britain's fummer ! haft thou vanifh'd, then,
So fudden ?—Tongue accurs'd !—No need of fteel
For murder, here—the very touch of fhame
Hath cut her thread of life !—O IMOGEN—
Awake, fweet miftrefs !—beggar not the world
With lofs of all its worth.—I will maintain it,
Againft ten thoufand villains, fuch as CLODIO,
Tho' champion'd to the teeth, that thou art
        wrong'd.
What proofs can front that purity of face—
The book, where Heaven, in characters divine,
Hath writ down truth and honour ?—She recovers.

    IMOG. Away, and let me die.

                        FAUST.

Faust. Cheer you, my royal lady; cheer, sweet
    mistress!—
You are injured—by the gods, you are—I know it.
Some traitorous machination, deep as hell—
And there I'll dive, but I will bottom it!
Look up, transcendent Imogen, nor cloud
The face of Heaven with grief!—
Tell me, my spotless, my thrice honour'd lady,
Did you not take some presents, at the hand
Of that damn'd Clodio?

    Imog. No.

    Faust. Rich robes, and gems
Of oriental lustre?—

    Imog. Nothing of them.——
He spoke indeed of matters sent, by Cæsar,
To me and to my lord; and pray'd I'd take
The coffer that contain'd them, for one night,
Into safe custody.

    Faust. A coffer, mistress?—
A coffer!—was it large?

    Imog. The men, who bore it,
Bent at the burden.

    Faust. Certain—it is so!—
I have found him, deep as Erebus—the fiend!—
Curs'd Clodio, ruthless, ravening hound of hell!
There shall be blood for this—a number'd pang
For every pang that we have felt.
O, my deceived, distracted, happy master!
O injured innocence, sweet Imogen,
Blest, precious mistress!—O the gods, the gods,
Blest be the gods for this!

Imog.

Imog. Why doft thou weep,
Good Faustus?

Faust. O! for joy, for joy, to find
That you are fafe, and fpotlefs—
Even as a chryftal vafe, intire, and clear,
No flaw nor ftain throughout.—Come, deareft lady.
I will entruft you to revering hands,
The prieftefs of Andate's neighbouring temple.—
Then, to my lord, with the moft rapturous tidings
That ever bleft his ear!   [Exeunt.

S C E N E VI.

The PALACE.

Enter King, Queen, Cloten, &c.

Cymb. Spread feveral ways—break open all the
      locks—
Search clofe!—She can't be far—Malicious fortune
Takes the worft time to crofs us!

Queen. Good, my liege,
Faustus, the flave of banifh'd Leonatus,
Was feen, fome few hours fince. Put we to this,
That Leonatus, moft affuredly,
Hath join'd his arm to that of Rome—what
      follows?
But that the princefs is, with Faustus, fled;
And, with her paramour, will fhortly come·
To claim your kingdom.

Cymb. My kingdom, madam?—
I want my child, my Imogen—my kingdom

Is not of my begetting—O, my QUEEN,
You have a child!—I would to Heaven, that mine,
From my fond arms, may not have been diſlodg'd
By uſage too ungentle.—CLOTEN, fly!—
Take with thee a ſwift band of our light-arm'd—
Purſue, and ſave her for me.   [Exit CLOTEN.
The Roman, as we hear, intends, this day,
To offer battle.—Patroneſs of Britain
Inſpire, and then diſpoſe us, as thou wilt!
Victorious goddeſs, great Andate, give
Death—or that good for which we wiſh to live!
                                        [Exeunt,

END OF THE THIRD ACT.

ACT

A C T IV.

S C E N E I.

The WOOD and CAVERN.

LEONATUS and BELLARIUS enter.

BELL. WHERE did I leave?—but age is narrative,
And tirefome to your ear.
    LEON. No, father, no—
Could griefs, like mine, admit of confolation,
'Tis in your lenient converfe.
    BELL. I have told you,
Of the dark horror that involved my foul
On my return to Britain, when I heard
My ADELAIDE was loft—yet, how, with fmiles
I veil'd my depth of woe, till, on a day,
I feiz'd the bloody hour of ftudied vengeance,
And left the barbarous CYMBELINE for dead.
Thereon, I vainly fought a flight from forrow,
Through regions moft remote—ftill the barb'd grief
Stuck faft, and rankled inward. Sick, at length,
Sick of the world, and all the bufy ways

Of

Of empty anxious man, I wish'd to mix
My mortal ashes with the native duft,
From whence they firft arofe.   Ten toilfome years
I fpent in travel ; and ten lonely years
Have found me here, fecluded from the face
Of aught fave Heaven, in wifhful expectation
Of the laft, painful, happy hour, that fhall
Strike off the fhackles of mortality,
And wing me to my love !

 Leon. But, is there not
A fhorter way to peace ?

 Bell. O no, my fon. ·
The Power, who gave exiftence, can, alone,
Have right to take it hence—And who fhall warrant
Peace to impatience ?

 Leon. Father, about this time, a faithful flave
Attends me, near at hand—a little fpace
Returns me to you.

 Bell. May the Power I worfhip,
Reftore your hopes, and run before your wifhes !
[Exit Leonatus.

S C E N E II.

Bellarius retires towards the Cavern.   Cloten
enters attended.

 Clot. Our fcent is warm ; fhe can't be far from
  hence.
Fly feveral ways, fearch well the facred wood—
Who finds, and hales her to yon cave, I fwear

Is

Is mafter of my purfe—Away, and profper!

[Exeunt Attendants.

Pan, and Priapus, aid me in the hour
Of rape, and rapturous vengeance, on the charms
Of fcorning, ftruggling beauty—Hark, old fellow!
Didft fee a man and maiden this way?

BELL. No.

CLOT. Is yon den appertinent
To thee and to thine heirs?

BELL. It is.

CLOT. Not quite
Unfurnifh'd, holy father, as we hope,
Of female confolation.

BELL. Out upon thee!

CLOT. Canft thou not play the pandar, for a
friend?

BELL. Hence, abandon'd ruffian!

CLOT. Come—fhew me to thy rufhes.

BELL. Stop—low wretch!
Take caution of thine health—thou com'ft no
further.

CLOT. Now, by Andate, I do much fufpect
Thou holdeft, in thy faintly tutelage,
The very wench I look for—Give me way.

BELL. Beware——   [Lifts his ftaff.

CLOT. Nay, then, thy fhrivell'd autumn, thus
Drops at my blaft.   [Draws.

BELL. An arm, that was not wont
To need the fecond lifting, greets thee, thus—

[Kills CLOTEN.

Come,

Come, to the public pafs, and, there, make trial
If thou art worth the owning.—

                     [Exit dragging out CLOTEN.

S C E N E   III.

LEONATUS enters.

LEON. FAUSTUS is gone—or not yet come—
      I met
A man, who, paffing in his hafte, declared
The princefs miffing, and the court in uproar.
'Tis fo—the deed is done—or doing!—Hold,
Hold, FAUSTUS, or I execrate thy duty,
Worfe than thy breach of faith—Why fhould fhe
      die ?—
Who could furvive, if all were to be doom'd
For one defect in nature ?—That fhe loved me,
The proofs are mighty, as the mighty proofs
Of her incontinence—Was not her heart
Sufficient, then, to mine—tho' her fweet perfon
Were common as the kiffing air ?—Yes, IMOGEN,
Give me thy heart, in life or death, all mine,
I afk no other Heaven—but, no intrufion,
No footy thought, no curs'd contamination !
O that eternal robber, who hath foul'd
The veffel of my peace ! Though fhe were purged
By fire tenfold intenfe, though fteep'd an age
In the Lethean furge, the deed obfcene
Would never from her thought—O, fhe muft
      die !—
That fpeaks the doom of LEONATUS too,
Who cannot live divided—No, I feel

                     A force,

A force, more ſtrong than nature, draw me after,
Though never more to join her—Imogen,
My deareſt Imogen, why, why was this ?—
If paſſion, boundleſs as the claſping air,
And warm as the meridian, might ſuffice,
It was not well, my love !—Is there no cure,
No hope, no help for this—to right or left,
Or forward thro' the length of time, tho' ſtretch'd
Far as exiſtence ?—O, ſole miſery !—
Your pardon, Heaven !—I aſk you not for bliſs;
I aſk but for oblivion.—

S C E N E IV.

To Leonatus enter Bellarius.

Bell. Welcome, my ſon !—The country's all
        in motion—
Some flying from, and ſome to arms ! But, here,
Within our cavern's maze, we reſt ſecure,
And ſmile at war and tumult.
    Leon. No—when life
Was prodigal of every promiſed bliſs
That youth could look for, honourable danger
Ne'er ſaw my ſhoulder-blade—and ſhall I now
Turn from the death I wiſh to earn ?—No, father !
An hour, and I am nothing, ſave a name—
But it may be a loud one.   A ſhort joy
Reanimates my boſom—Gods, I thank ye !—
Loſt to myſelf, I ſhall be found to others,
Found in the fixing of my country's rights ;

                                And,

And, by my my death, affirm that liberty,
Which makes the life of Britain.

    BELL. Be it so.
Since we can't live, why, let us die together.—
Hear me, thou son of my electing soul!
Among the noble youth that graced our isle,
I, once, stood obvious to the public eye,
For thou wast not in being then ; and when
Discourse ran high on soldiership, my name
Was not far off—If thou dost think me, yet,
Worthy thy fellowship in arms, then, help
To buckle on my ancient mail.   O, Thou,
Whose will disposeth what thy wisdom form'd,
Make our last hour a great one!—be our day
Of glorious dissolution, here on earth,
Our natal-day in Heaven !

    LEON. My father, come!
I long to emulate your high example ;
In your loved fight to have my prowess tried,
And fall, applauded, by your honour'd side.
                                  [Exeunt.

S C E N E V.

Drums and Trumpets.   Romans march over the
    Stage.   CLODIO enters, his sword drawn.

    CLOD. Close—and with measured motion, as
        put on
By one informing spirit, march, and join
The ranging phalanx.

As the Soldiers pafs off the Stage, FAUSTUS enters.

FAUST. If the loud din of war hath reach'd
        his ear,
The field of honour is the likelieft place
Wherein to find him.—CLODIO!—O, ye powers
Of juftice and of vengeance, nerve my arm,
And ride upon my weapon!—Good, my lord,
Your ear—I bear a meffage to you.
    CLOD. Whence?
    FAUST. From my kind miftrefs.
    CLOD. Speak—
    FAUST. In thunder—thus!   [Draws.
    CLOD. Prefumptuous flave!—Then take this
        anfwer back,
To thy detefted mafter.
        [They fight, and FAUSTUS falls—Exit CLODIO.

    FAUST. Curfe on my feeble arm—that, thus,
        hath foil'd
The caufe it fought for—O, I fee, I fee,
This world is not the foil where Heaven e'er meant
To plant or profper truth: it is the field
Where the flagitious triumph!—If there be
In ftore for worth, or where wrong'd innocence
May look for retribution—that bleft region
Is far removed from hence.

SCENE

SCENE VI.

LIONATUS and BELLARIUS enter.

LEON. My FAUSTUS here—
And bleeding!

FAUST. Bleſt gods—mine eyes, mine eyes
Have ſeen him, ere they cloſe for ever!—O,
Your hand—'twill footh me in my dying pangs—
My kindeſt, ſweeteſt, deareſt, nobleſt maſter!

LEON. Alas—how happen'd this?

FAUST. I vainly hoped
To vindicate your quarrel—CLODIO is.
A——Oh——my time is ſcanty—IMOGEN—
Be happy, for your IMOGEN is——Oh——   [Dies.

LEON. As thou art, my beſt FAUSTUS,—O, my
        friend,
My follower thro' all fortunes!—had I time
To pay the tribute due,
I would embalm thee with my daily tears,
And tomb thee in my boſom.—Help me, father,
Help to bear this kindeſt of Heaven's creatures
Out of the public path, where trampling hoofs
Might ſpurn his loved remains.
                [Exeunt bearing the Body.

Q 2   SCENE

S C E N E VII.

CYMBELINE and Britons enter.

CYMB. Bid our fcythed chariots wheel to either
        hand,
And flank our wings—myfelf will point the wedge,
With which we truft to pierce their boafted
        phalanx.
Pe not deceived, my friends—ye are brave men,
And have brave men to cope with!—victory
Muft here be fweated for, even till the drops
Do turn to crimfon.

A ROMAN OFFICER enters.

OFFICER. To CYMBELINE I bear important
        greeting,
From the proconful, LUCIUS.
    CYMB. Speak his purpofe.
    OFFICER. He bade me fay, that Rome difdains
        to conquer
By means that honour cannot warrant—Read.
                                [Gives a pacquet.
    CYMB. What's here?—Our confort and her fon
        confpired
Againft our ftate and perfon?—Treafon, treafon!
This was a bofom'd fting—Alas, my children!
Then ye were wrong'd—O, my loft IMOGEN!
My fon, my fhield, my banifh'd LEONATUS!—
                                        Tell

Tell me, brave foldier, as thou art a Roman,
Does Leonatus draw his fword for Cæfar?

Officer. No. He refufed to lend his arm to
  Rome,
And, with averted action, thruft away
The proffer'd crown of Britain.

Cymb. That he were here! that I might wafh
  his truth
With tears of kind contrition—Tell your general
We would embrace his worth, on any terms,
Save of our country's freedom—but, for that,
For that we grapple, to our laft of life,
With arms of rival honour—Follow friends,
I lead you to the onfet.   [Exeunt.

S C E N E   VIII.

Drums and Trumpets. Noife of Battle without. Britifh
  Soldiers and Officers pafs over the Stage.

1ft Offi. The King's engaged already—up, for
  fhame!
Up to your fellows.
2d Offi. Forward, countrymen,
To death, or conqueft, hafte!—   [Exeunt.

Noife of Battle continues. Several Britons return as in
  flight, with Officers.

Offic. All's loft—the King is taken—All is
  over,
And Britain is no more!—Shift for your lives—

SCENE IX.

Enter LEONATUS and BELLARIUS.

LEON. Stay, Britons, turn—Shame, fhame!—
      By great Andate,
Who comes upon me, rufhes on a death
More fure than Rome can give—Stay, ftay, I
      charge ye.
Ye ftand amazed—behold, 'tis I—your general,
Your LEONATUS!—Turn—for fhame—for ho-
      nour—
Your wives, your infants—for pofterity,
To lateft times—for Liberty—for Britain!
'Tis I, your LEONATUS leads you on,
Againft the power and infolence of Rome—
Againft the world—for Liberty, for Britain!—
Follow me, friends!—

   ALL. A LEONATUS, a LEONATUS!
Liberty, and LEONATUS!—   [Exeunt fhouting.

SCENE X.

Noife of Battle continues. Several Romans return, as
retreating from the Britons; CLODIO following.

   CLOD. How the day is turn'd!
And conqueft, in an inftant, ftrangely wrung
Out of our very grafp—Stand, Romans, ftand.

For honour, for your ancient name, return!
Let me prevail——
                    [Exit with them, endeavouring to ftop them.

S C E N E XI.

LEONATUS enters.

LEON. In vain I feek for death, among the
        thickeft,
Where the field burns—the fpectre flies me ftill,
As tho' he held me for his foe——

CLODIO re-enters.

How, CLODIO!
By the gods, welcome—Nay, no fhrinking,
        CLODIO—
The time of reckoning's come !—

CLOD. I fought thee not.
But fince thou croffeft me—altho' thou wert
The genuine fon of Mars and dread Bellona,
I front thee—thus.

LEON. And, with my weapon's wind,
Thus do I win thee.   [CLODIO falls.

CLOD. Curfes blaft thine arm,
Triumphant favage ! for it has awaked me
From a long dream of greatnefs—Tell me, Briton,
How haft thou dealt with IMOGEN ?

LEON. Difpatch'd her.

CLOD. Then I'm reveng'd!—and I will wring
      thy foul,
With tortures worfe than death—Thy IMOGEN
Was guiltlefs.

LEON. How?—

CLOD. The heavenly light, lefs chafte!
I got myfelf convey'd into her chamber
In a gay coffer, fent, as I pretended,
With precious ware from Cæfar; and, at mid-
      night,
Even, while the fimple, fleeping innocent,
Dreamt of her LEONATUS, I did mark
The chamber; and, in ftealing that fame bracelet,
Spied the rich mole that ftung thee into madnefs.
Fool, ideot, dolt—
Who had the jewel of the univerfe,
Yet caft it from thee!—

LEON. O fiend, without a fellow!—damn'd,
      damn'd CLODIO;
A depth, below all bottom, damn'd!—Hope not
That death fhall fnatch thee from my vengeance—
      No—
Even, in mid plunge, I'll feize thy fhrinking foul,
And it fhall be my endlefs Heaven, to tear,
And torture thee for ever.—Thou hell-tyger,
Thy pangs are not half ftrong enough!—Thus,
      thus,
And thus——   [Stabbing him.

CLOD. Hold, hold—Oh—Curfes—curfes catch
Thee, and the fiends that gave thee force—Oh—
            [Dies.

            LEON.

LEON. And now, to follow!—

[Turns the sword to his breast,

Soft—If death should be
To cease from thought, and, therein, from the rack
On which my soul is stretch'd; how then is
    IMOGEN
Avenged?—or how may my own wrath be wreak'd
Against myself, on whom I swear to wage
War without truce, for ever? Fool, fool, fool!
To credit even these eyes, where, against proof,
Her truth was demonstration.—O, my love,
Were my guilt greater than e'er call'd for justice,
The loss of thee were penal, beyond all
That justice could inflict!—and have I caus'd
That loss?—Avenge her, Heaven and hell!—rehd,
    rack me!
Multiply pains on pains!—O, rose of beauty,
How art thou cropt—how faded from amidst
The garden of the world, now waste!
And shall I never, never, never more
Behold thee, IMOGEN!—nor hear the voice,
That spoke soft tunings to my soul—nor see
That aspect, which arose upon the morning
In a new day of comforts, shedding peace
And joy around?——

[Exit,

SCENE

S C E N E XII.

Drums and Trumpets. Enter CYMBELINE, BEL-
LARIUS, &c.

CYMB. A Briton, art thou ?

BELL. Yes, so please my liege ;
A Cambro-Briton, and my name BELLARIUS—
Unworthy further note.

CYMB. Whoe'er thou art,
Henceforth, my friend and brother, share my
power,
And bosom confidence.

BELL. You far o'er rate
My scantiness of merit.

CYMB. No—thy works
Proclaim thy worth aloud—and I have found
Thy friendship in the rescue which thou brought'st
me
From the strong gripe of Rome. A friend as
thou art,
Is the best gift of Heaven, a second self !—
Receive me, then—I fly into thine arms
From bosom'd treasons, which I fondly cherish'd
In the curs'd venture of a second bed.   [Embrace.
Did ye not say, that my victorious son,
My LEONATUS was at hand ?

1st LORD. We did.
Even now, we all beheld, when, in the instant
That conquest was assured, he vanish'd.

CYMB. Yes—I knew, I knew,
It was some god—'twas Victory, herself,

That

That took his glorious likeness—I beheld him
As lightning from the east—he shot upon them—
I saw their firmest phalanx shake, throughout,
And wither at his presence.

    BELL. Some few hours
Before the battle, he became my guest.
I held him, first, for somewhat more than mortal;
And, as he spoke, I felt, I know not what
Of force and fond emotion, stir me inward,
And knit my soul to his.

    CYMB. Prepare we, then,
One hundred of the noblest Roman captives
To be, with grateful incense, offer'd up
On the triumphant altar of Andate—
So shall her force our future arms await;
And, with like favour, guard the British state.

                          [Exeunt.

END OF THE FOURTH ACT.

A C T V.

S C E N E I.

The PALACE.

QUEEN and Attendants.

QUEEN. ARE there no tidings of the princeſs,
          yet?
WOM. No, madam, not the leaſt.
QUEEN. Nor of my ſon?
WOM. Not any.
QUEEN. That is ſtrange!

MESSENGER in haſte.

How now!—whence come you, with that deadly
          look
Of pale and breathleſs terror?
  MESS. From the battle.—
The KING is captive to the arms of Rome,
With our two chiefs, Cingetorix and Cadwal.
All's done—all on the rout—and Britain flies,

                              Scatter'd,

Scatter'd, and driven along the field, like duft
Before the raging wind.
    Queen. That's fomewhat worfe
Than we did wifh for.   [Dead march witho*t.*
Ha! what found is that?
That, with an heart-alarming fuddennefs,
Brings death upon us?

     Messenger enters.

  2d Mess. O, my royal miftrefs!—
  Queen. Speak, man—and yet—I dare not
       afk—
  2d Mess. Nor dare
Your wretched fervant anfwer—O—your fon—
Your Cloten is——
    Queen. Dead?—Oh—   [Faints.
  Wom. Help, here, fupport—
Her fit is ftrong upon her—
    Queen. What have ye waked me to!—O hor-
      ror, horror!
This was not among all my dreams—And, had I,
Had I no friend, in Heaven, or hell, to fnatch
From ruin that yet wants a name?—What's here?

[A Bier carried acrofs the Stage, with Soldiers attending.

A bier!—Ah—tell me not my child is there—
Or I will give a curfe fhall blaft the world,
And root exiftence up—Fates!—hoftile powers!—
Slaves, cowards, who forfook him—thus I fpread
Deftruction, death, among ye all!—[Draws a dagger.

SOLD. Shift—fly!
Fly from her fury, all!

    [*Exeunt, the* QUEEN *purfuing and ftriking at them.*

SCENE II.

Drums and Trumpets. CYMBELINE and BELLA-
RIUS, &c. enter in Triumph.

    CYMB. Welcome, my brave deliverer, to your
      own—
To the poffeffions of a lavifh friendfhip,
That will not know partition!—Seek we, now,
To purge our palace of domeftic evils,

      OFFICER *enters.*

And traitors, late moft loved.—Where is your
      QUEEN ?—
    OFFIC. O, my dread lord, the winds, in all
      their whirl,
Are not fo wild—madder than twenty Maniacs.—
When fhe beheld her fon, brought home, a corpfe,
She fwoon'd ; but, waking into fudden frenzy,
She drew a poniard, flew on all fhe met ;
And, though, with difficulty, now difarm'd,
None dare approach.
    CYMB. Is CLOTEN dead ?
    OFFIC. He is.
    CYMB. Then, Heaven has faved a labour—Here
      fhe comes—
Mark her.

                      SCENE

S C E N E III.

Qu*een* enters, with a cup of poifon in one hand,
and a dagger in the other.

Queen. Pfha, filly boy!—the crown is thine—
but I
Muft wield the fcepter.—
Sayft thou?—afleep?—foft then—we'll grope our
way.
Is it not midnight?—lie thou there awhile—
[Lays down the cup.
We'll find a fpeedier medicine—here—I have it—
Keen as a launcet.—Hufh—where life is feated—
[Strikes.
He has it, at his heart—Lights, lights here—
lights!
This is not Leonatus—Murder—murder!
Thefe are the groans of Cloten! ot my child!—
No—look—'tis Imogen—our old King's daugh-
ter.—
Soft—draw the curtain—not a word.—
Cymb. Unhappy, guilty mifcreant—how her
dreams
Exprefs her waking purpofes of horror!
Queen. Return'd, you fay, from battle, faint,
and thirfty?
'Tis well—here's that will quench him.
[Takes the cup.
Which is he?
Which of you is my royal, loving hufband?—
No—this is not the cup—I have miftook—

This

This is Nepenthe.   'Tis the drink of gods,
The balm for cares, deep canker'd—for a foul
Parch'd like a blafted fummer !   [Drinks.
    CYMB. Hold—ftop—prevent her, quick !—Nay,
        then, I doubt,
She has, herfelf, imbibed the very bane
She meant for others.

    QUEEN. Who, who are ye all ?—
My hufband here !—fave, fave me, keep him from
        me !—

He was not wont to wear that head of fnakes,
Nor point thofe fcorpions at me—Oh, fick, fick !
If ye have charity—a little covering—
It is the top of Zembla—and the winds
Blow—the keen launcet atoms—thro' my vitals !—
More cloaths—heap, heap !—your fires around
        me—quick—

Plunge me in Phlegeton, the burning gulph !
Hell is not hot enough—Hold, hold me—where,
Where am I hurried round and round?—ftop—fix—
Impale me—for I cannot bear this fpin—
This whirlwind of the brain—

    CYMB. She faints—fupport,
And bear her in.—   [To her women.
    QUEEN. Oh———
Pull not fo hard—the joints—the panting cords,
Rack'd to a fibre !—Nature cannot bear
This fundering from herfelf—this horrid rending !
There—take my limbs—my vitals—
To the four winds, difpers'd—Oh—   [Dies.
    CYMB. With what a fuddennefs, the flaming red
Is turn'd to livid !—Bear her to her chamber—

                            O, my

O, my fole friend, how poor a thing is kingfhip,
When fhorn of every focial name that gives
Domeftic feeling or fupport ! —thou art, now,
The only good that's left—I'll to the temple,
And afk the gods, for which of my miftreadings,
·Thefe ills are come upon me.   [Exeunt.

S C E N E IV.

The Infide of the TEMPLE of ANDATE.

PRIESTESS and IMOGEN enter.

PRIEST. And fent his man to murder thee ?—
IMOG. What could he lefs ?—Had I an hundred
          lives,
They were too little for the bare fufpicion
Of fuch a naughtinels !—I fear, I fear.—
     PRIEST. Fear not, my daughter, my fweet
          IMOGEN !
All fhall be well—thy lord, thy LEONATUS,
Shall be new plighted, in a double bond
Of frefh endearment, to thee.
     IMOG. Never, madam !
He never can forgive—never expel
The rooted jealoufy—What, in my chamber—
A ruffian, and at midnight !—then, to quote
Each circumftance of time and place—confirm'd
Even by my nuptial bracelet—and fuch marks,
As ought to have been lock'd from every eye,
With bolts of triple fteel !
     VOL. III.   R   PRIEST.

PRIEST. But when he hears
The subtle means devised—

    IMOG. Ah, sacred lady!
Against such proofs, what witness can avail?
Not the confession of the lurking fiend,
Who plotted my undoing. O, I am
Distracted too to think of what he suffers,
For such a falling off!—for, though he is brave
As the bay'd lion; yet he is gentle, too,
As is the turtle, lately fledg'd, and peeping
Into a new-found world. I feel—and to
Your ear I will confide it—had I but
The twentieth part the cause to think he had
            given
My rights in his loved person to another—
I feel, I could not bear it.

    PRIEST. Kindest, truest,
Lovelieft, and best beloved, my child, my
            IMOGEN—
Mine by fond ties, that must not, yet, be told!
Peace to thy gentle heart—all shall be whole;
Trust me, it shall.

            A PRIEST enters.

    PRIEST. Bright emblem of our goddess, sacred
            lady!
The rites are all prepared; a hundred victims,
With fillets and fresh garlands, duely bound,
Wait to be offer'd, in their holy trim,
To the great power of Victory.   [Exit PRIEST.

                        · · PRIEST.

PRIESTESS. I come—
Ill would such scenes, as those, my daughter, suit
Thy gentleness of nature—I, who am
Bound, by my duty, to the horrid vision,
Still shudder at the sight of human blood.
Retire, my IMOGEN.   [Exit IMOGEN.

S C E N E V.

Opens and discovers the inside of the Temple; the Altar
   of Incense, with the sacred fire, and the Altar of Sacrifice.   The Choir and sacred Music at the upper end.
   The Priests ranged on either hand; a Roman Victim
   standing behind each Priest, with his hands bound, and
   adorned with ribbons and garlands.

PRIESTESS. Begin your dread solemnities.

Symphony of Music, and the Hymn sung by Priests and
                    Priestesses.

H Y M N.

I.

Goddess of conflicting arms,
Of the field and of the fight,
   Brazen sounds, and dread alarms,
Conquest, slaughter, fear, and flight!

II.

To thee, triumphant, potent maid,
Be our vows and offerings paid !
Should domeſtic guilt difpleafe,
Hoftile blood ſhall beſt appeafe.

PRIESTESS. Lift now—Thus ſaith our ancient
oracle :

When a victim, free to live,
Shall his life for others give—
Human offerings ſhall, no more,
Stain the land with human gore.

So fays the fentence of two thoufand years—
But, no fuch victim comes !
Ye know your duty.
      [To the Prieſts—each of whom feizes his Captive,
      and draws a poniard, ready to ſtrike.

S C E N E   V

LEONATUS enters.

LEON. Hold—ſtop your horrid rites !—Refrain
    your hands,
Ye bloody fervants of a barbarous godhead—
Behold, I give thofe valiant Romans freedom !
Come, bring your fire and ſteel, your racks, and
    engines—

On

On me, alone, be emptied all your stores,
All your artillery of death—I claim,
And scorn your utmost efforts.

PRIEST. Ay, this, indeed,
This is a victim which the gods might take,
In lieu of twenty thousand, and be gainers!—
Art thou come, noble youth, to stay the shedding
Of human blood in Britain?—

LEON. Therefore come.

PRIEST. A voluntary victim?—

LEON. Free as air,—
Not so invulnerable.

PRIEST. Yet retire.
Fearful is death—

LEON. To those who wish it not.

PRIEST. Aye, but the pangs—

LEON. I have, already, felt
More than you can inflict.

PRIEST. And hast thou, then,
No nature in thee?—no compunction for
Thy friends, thy kin—perhaps, a raving father,
Or mother woe-begone?—less pity than
Thine executioner, whose eye, their loss
Compels to weep compassion.

LEON. I claim the sentence of your Oracle—
I have no words to waste.

PRIEST. Unfeeling boy!—
Thy will, then, be accomplish'd.—Bind him,
virgins,
And dress him for his death!

While

While fome of the Prieftefles bind and adorn Leonatus, others join the Priefts in the following verfes, part in recitative, and part in fong.

> Not in malice, but in love,
> Drefs him as a feaft for Jove.

> Let the melting ftanders by,
> Want of weeping kin fupply ;

> And with tears, and fighs profound,
> Fill all the fadden'd air, and wet the mourn-
> ing ground.

[Leonatus is laid on the Altar.

A Prieft ftands over Leonatus with a poniard, while another gives the bowl to Adelaide.

Priest. My hand denies its office—Here, Bonduca,
Take thou the bowl of death—
   Bond. We are ready—When you like,
Give the folemn mandate—
   Leon. Strike!——

Thunder and Lightning. The Stage is darkened, and the facred Fire extinguifhed.

Priest. Hold your rafh hand!—the powers are in difpleafure—
The Heavens are moved—the holy fire extin-
guifh'd !

Unbind

Unbind your victim—this is not the one
Our goddefs will accept.—He looks diffatisfied—
Withdraw, and leave him to my further queftion.
[Exeunt Priefts, &c.
I do adjure thee, by the power thou worfhipp'ft,
Art thou of earth, or Heaven, or whence ?—In-
   form me.
   Leon. I know not.
   Priest. No?
   Leon. Not whence—but, what I am,
I know—in nature's work, of no account,
And hateful to myfelf!
   Priest. Whoe'er thou art,
To have thee, thus, alive, and fafe, I joy,
As though thou wer't new come into the world,
My only, and firft born.. Thy parents—fay—
   Leon. I never knew them—
   Priest. O, my foreboding bofom!—No, that
   were
To be too bleft!—With whom brought up ?—O,
   anfwer—
Quick, I adjure thee—
   Leon. With King Cymbeline,
A beggar'd foundling !
   Priest. And thy name, thy name is—
   Leon. Leonatus.—
   Priest. Mighty goddefs!—Yes—thou art—
   thou art
My fon—my Leonatus—O, my child,
Child of the tears of twenty mourning years !
Till late, I knew not that I had a fon—

 The

The faireſt, braveſt theme of every tongue—
The hero of our age!—My Leonatus,
My ſon, my ſon, my ſon!   [Embraces.
    Leon. Great nature, powerful goddeſs—for a
        moment,
I yield me to thy feelings—thus, while, thus,
I bow beneath the feet of her, who gives me,
Firſt, to pronounce the ſacred name of mother !—
                                    [Kneels.
O, mother fair !
Thou art the parent of the wretched'ſt offspring,
That ever ſtain'd mortality with guilt,
And made perdition ſure !
    Priest. Fall bleſſings on thee,
Till Heaven can heap no more—
And bleſſed thou ſhalt be.
    Leon. No—never, never—
I have murder'd bliſs, have quench'd the light of
        Britain!—
O, Imogen, my love, my life, my wife,
My Imogen—O Imogen !
    Priest. But was ſhe not unchaſte ?
    Leon. Pure as the fleece of Heaven, ere yet it
        falls,
And neighbours to corruption.
    Priest. Peace—and thou ſhalt behold her—
                            [Waves her wand.
        Beauty, brighter than the morn,
        Queen of all that's Britain-born,
        Daughter fair, and daughter dear,
        Peerleſs Imogen, appear !

SCENE
5

S C E N E   VII.

Imogen enters veiled.

She throws up her veil. Leonatus stands in silent
amazement.

Leon. If the grave teems to life—
If univerfal nature, through her works,
Could yield another form like that—
All might not be illufion!—
Vifion of harmony and light, yet, ere
Thou fleetelt—thus I fix thee—O, 'tis warm!—
It lives, to fenfe, to rapture!

   Imog. My love, my lord, my life, my Leo-
       natus!
Do I, then, hold thee?—Doft thou think me true—
The feat of memory fo fill'd with thee,
As leaves no room befide?

   Leon. If I dwell not
Within the regions of creative fancy,
It is too much of blifs!—Methinks, I ftand
Upon a pinnacle, fo high in happinefs,
My eye can fee no bottom, whereunto
A doubt of this would plunge me.

   Priest. Hence with doubts
And fears, for ever!—Yes, ye are the two,
In whom I triumph; my bleft, happy pair
Of pricelefs pearls, fo match'd!—fo matchlefs, too,
Save by each other!—

Priest.

PRIEST enters.

PRIEST. Madam, the KING approaches—
PRIESTESS. It is well.
Renew the facred fire.—My precious children,

[Exit Prieſt.

You may withdraw, awhile—not far—the time
Will give a fpeedy fummons.

[IMOGEN and LEONATUS retire.

S C E N E   VIII.

CYMBELINE and BELLARIUS enter attended.

The PRIESTESS drops her Veil.

PRIEST. What would our CYMBELINE with
     great Andate ?
CYMB. O, facred dame, by whom the Heavens
     pronounce
Their paft and future purpofes ! you fee
A man, amid the pride of royalty,
Moft wretched—fhorn of children, and of kin—
Of all the joys and amities that could
Endear exiftence—as a lonely oak,
Lopp'd of his branches !—Tell me, facred dame,
For which of my miftreadings, have thefe ills
Fallen thick and heavy on me ?
     PRIEST. For a fifter !
     CYMB. The laws did warrant me.

PRIEST.

PRIEST. What law can warrant
Againſt the law of Heaven—great nature's law,
Writ in the boſom, ſtamp'd in characters
Of mercy on the human ſenſe divine,
That binds the feeling brotherhood of man,
And 'fines him into godhead?

CYMB. O pardon! I have greatly ſinn'd—the
          pride
Of novel kingſhip, and the ſcorn of ſhame,
So near our throne, thro' her incontinence,
Enforced the inhuman act.

PRIEST. Thus ſaith Andate:
Never ſhalt thou behold the chearing face
Of ſympathizing friendſhip, never feel
The bleſt embracements of a daughter's fondneſs;
Till that the melting eye of ADELAIDE
Shall weep, in kind compaſſion, o'er thy griefs,
And waſh thy ſtains away.

CYMB. That were too much—
Too much to hope from her forgiving goodneſs,
If that the gods, by means miraculous,
Had yet preſerv'd her to me—Never ſhall
Theſe eyes, in mortal ſockettings, be bleſt
With ſuch a ſpeculation!

PRIEST. O, behold!   [Throws up her veil.

CYMB. My ſiſter! my loſt ſiſter!—

BELL. O, the gods!—   [Fainting.

CYMB. Help here!—my friend is dying.—
                              [Supporting BELLARIUS.

                                   PRIEST.

PRIEST. Blefs'd powers!
Through all his guife—I think—'tis he—'tis he!—
My lord, my ever loved, my long lamented,
Loft LEONTIUS!   [Embraces.

BELL. O, ADELAIDE—thine arm—my Heaven
Has come too fudden on me!—

CYMB. Now, indeed,
I fee it is LEONTIUS—'tis the man
Who, long fince, fought the life he faved fo
          lately.

BELL. Not with a traiterous poniard, CYM-
          BELINE—
At noon, and hand to hand.

CYMB. True, true, my brother!
I fee the reafon, now—it was refiftlefs.
Had you but told me, ere you went to Rome—
Or had our ADELAIDE confeft her fpoufals
With my heart's chofen—what a mafs of guilt,
And grief, had then been fpared?

PRIEST. And would you, then,
Would you have pardon'd?

CYMB. Yes, with that full bounty,
That now I claim from both.

BELL. My KING, my mafter!—   [Kneels.

PRIEST. O, now, indeed, my fond, my new
          found brother!   [Kneels.

CYMB. Rife to my arms, my heart!—there
          reign, united,
And make up all my treafure!—   [Embrace.
Say, my fifter,
How came this ftrange event, this bleft reverfion

Of joys, the laft to look for ?—Saw I not
The flames afcend thy funeral pyre ?
    PRIEST. You did;
But then, a little charitable art,
Conveyed me, inward, by clandeftine ftairs,
Juft as the flames afcended.—Many a victim,
Our pious prieftefs, in like manner, faved,
For the dear meeting, and enraptured clafp,
Of fathers, fons, and brothers.
    BELL. But the pledge,
The pledge of our connubial loves, my ADE-
        LAIDE—
What hath befallen ?
    PRIEST. Our late good prieftefs, Etheline,
Some few nights fince, upon her dying couch
Confeft, fhe had my new-born babe convey'd,
Wrapp'd in rich veftments, to my royal brother,
With a fair fcroll, expreffive of thefe words—
" Andate fends a fon to CYMBELINE."
    CYMB. And was our LEONATUS, then, the fon
Of my fole fifter ?—Let mine eyes, but once
Behold my IMOGEN and him united,
Then, clofe them, gods, in peace!
    PRIEST. Approach, my children,
And take the bleffing of your KING and father.

SCENE·

S C E N E   IX.

Leonatus and Imogen enter and kneel to
Cymbeline.

Cymb. My child, my Imogen!—It is too
  much—
My son, my injured Leonatus too!—
Rise, rise—I cannot speak—this flood of blef-
   fings !—
Enter my bofom, both.—   [Embracing.
  Priest. See, my Leontius,
Behold your glorious fon !
  Bell. Heavens!—I do think,
The very fame—Soft, Adelaide—and note
If he takes knowledge of me.
  Leon. What, my hoft,
My holy father here ! O, valiant fire,
We have had a change, to which Omnipotence
Was deem'd unequal—There you fee the Heaven,
Whofe lofs I mourn'd !—had but your Adelaide,
Been added to the blefling !
  Bell. Art thou, then,
That god, to whom we have been paying vows
For victory ? My fon, my child, indeed—
My heart foreknew thee mine !—There ftands our
   Adelaide,
Even thine exulting mother.
  Leon. O, my father !   [Both kneel.
  Imog. Here, too, my duty bids me bend.

         Bell.

Bell. Great power!
Grant them, with equal tranfport, thus to blefs
The children of their children!

An Officer enters.

Offic. My liege, Rome's great proconful, mak-
          ing head
To favour his retreating legions, was
Befet and taken prifoner.
    Cymb. Bring him to us—
We owe him many honours.

S C E N E   X.

Lucius brought in bound, attended by Roman
            and Britifh Chiefs.

    Leon. What, my friend
In bondage?—O, indignity to honour,
To virtue!—Trueft noblenefs, thus let me
Unbind my country's fhame!—Thou art free, my
            Lucius,
Free, as at Rome, and full as well affected.
Command in Britain,, tafk us to thy will
In all things—fave, fuch bonds as thefe!
                        [Cafting away the fhackles.'
    Lucius. O, great
In goodnefs, as in glory!—I rejoice
In the high fortunes of my Leonatus,
Though at the coft of Rome.

                                    Cymb.

CYMB. Lucius, in eſtimation of thy virtues,
We give, to every Roman captive, freedom ;
With truce and entertainment to thy legions,
While they remain in Britain.—Next, to Cæſar
We ſhall appoint a ſpecial embaſſy,
With twice the value of his late demand—
But, not as tribute, Lucius !

     LEON. No, my friend !—
Wherefore ſhould Rome from others wreſt that Li-
        berty,
Which, for herſelf, ſhe prizes more than life ?
From us ſhe muſt not—No—the gods have given
To Britain, independence on all lands
By her enfolding waters, her wide field
Of future empire !—O, my mother's ſpirit
Swells my prophetic breaſt—I ſee the ſails
Of Britain ſpread, from eaſt to weſt, their wings
Of wide protection !—How the nations flock
Beneath them !—This, indeed, is true dominion—
To humble pride, and to ſubdue oppreſſion ;
To lift the fallen, and to ſuſtain the weak ;
To bind a willing world with her beneficence ;
And wide, as rolling waves, or wafting wind,
Reign, the requeſted miſtreſs of mankind !

MONTEZUMA:

A

TRAGEDY.

PERSONS.

INDIANS.

MONTEZUMA, Emperor of MEXICO.

ODMAR, his eldest son.

GUYOMAR, his younger Son.

ORBELLAN, } Son of the late deposed INDIAN QUEEN by TRAXALLA, and Brother of ALMERIA and ALIBECH.

SPANIARDS.

CORTEZ, the SPANISH General

VASQUEZ, } PIZARRO, } Commanders under him.

INDIAN WOMEN.

CYDERIA, Daughter of MONTEZUMA.

ALMERIA, } ALIBECH, } Sisters, and Daughters of the late deposed INDIAN QUEEN, by TRAXALLA.

SCENE, MEXICO, and the adjacent Country.

PRIESTS, INDIAN GUIDES, GUARDS, ATTENDANTS, &c.

MONTEZUMA.

ACT I.

SCENE I.

The COUNTRY near MEXICO.

Enter CORTEZ, VASQUEZ, PIZARRO, *with Spani-*
ards, and Indians of their Party.

CORT. ON what new happy climate are we
     thrown!
It looks as if old nature, purged by fire,
Had paſt the general doom, and here aroſe
A new-created world.
 VASQ. By ſcience unrefined, this world is laid
In nature's ſimple lap. Mechanic arts
Hold no republic here; but all is wild
And ſavage, as the ſoil.
 CORT. Savage and wild,
Are terms we give to faſhions not our own.
Better, perhaps, that man had yet been left,
To the rude dictates of his native virtue;

S 2

Than

Than to be wrought and polished into vice,
By arts too much refined.

    Piz. The soil, though savage, yields spontane-
        ous plenty,
Beyond what toil and culture can produce
In our o'erlabour'd world.   This country is
The fabled Danae, sure, in whose fair lap
The glittering Jove descended : mountain floods
Here pour a golden torrent ; here again,
The lucid stream, with rich vicissitude,
Flows o'er a bed of silver.

    Vasq. Ay, this is worth
A soldier's fighting for—the great reward,
The prize beyond compare; which Heaven reserves
For unexampled valour; since we dare,
With scarce one squadron, and a few brave foot,
To war upon a new-found world.

    Cort. Pizarro,
Valour is not sustain'd by vanity.
Far, far unequal were our power to that
Of mighty Montezuma, did not faction
Divide these savages against themselves :
The spacious empire of the late Traxalla,
Groaning beneath the yoke of Mexico,
Crouds our thin ranks, and sues to us for freedom.
We will not yet proceed, by close deceit,
Or lawless rapine; we shall first propose
The sword, or branch of peace, to their election.
Say, guide, how far to Mexico ?

    1st Ind. A league
Brings you within the prospect of the city,

That

That rifes from the lake, as newly bathed,
And fhines to either fhore.
   2d IND. This morning's fun
Rofe on the day that gave their monarch birth;
And folemn rites, fuch as may fuit his pride
And their fervility, are now preparing.
   CORT. Forward—March, friends!—I gladly
        would be prefent
At this imperial feftival—But, mark me;
Let not an Indian raife his arm in anger,
Not, for his life, till juftice, and the word,
Shall give his weapon weight. Proceed, brave
        friends!
Honour's the road that beft leads on to conqueft.
                 [Exeunt.

S C E N E II.

An INDIAN TEMPLE.

HIGH PRIEST, and other PRIESTS—To them a
MESSENGER.

   MESS. Difpatch, ye holy priefts—the King ap-
      proaches.
   PRIEST. We for his royal prefence only wait,
To end our folemn rites. Five hundred captives
Beheld the morning fun, whofe eyes no more
Shall open to the light—Your incenfe now
On this fair altar, facred to the Power
Of Love, heap largely; till the clouds afcend
In fragrance to his godhead.
        S 3   SCENE

SCENE III.

Enter MONTEZUMA, ODMAR, CYDERIA, ALMERIA,
ALIBECH, ORBELLAN, and Train.

They place themselves.

H. PRIEST. All hail to MONTEZUMA, to our
    KING,
Son of the Sun, and father of his people!
May he behold his subjects celebrate
This happy natal day, from year to year,
Till time shall be no more——

Other PRIESTS. { Hail!
          { Hail!
          { Hail!

H. PRIEST. Sound instruments! and let the
    vocal choir
Perform the hymn to Beauty.

HYMN.

I.

Tell us, ye gods, what power is this,
    That rules with such resistless sway;
To whom the mightiest bow submiss,
    Whom crouds adore, whom kings obey?

II.

It is the power of Beauty's charm,
    That can all other powers subdue,
The savage tame, the fierce disarm,
    And teach subjected pride to sue.

III.

Great monarch! if you haply find
    The force of her enchantment here,
Her temples with your garland bind,
    And crown her empress of the year.

[MONTEZUMA rises, goes to ALMERIA, bows, and
offers the Garland, which she rejects.

MONT. Since my Orazia's death, I have not
    seen
A beauty so deserving of a crown,
As fair ALMERIA.
    ALM. Me, my lord, to me—
The daughter of those dear and royal parents,
Who fell the victims of your dire ambition;
Whose crown you have usurp'd, whose wretched
    subjects
Still bend beneath the weight of your oppression!
What may your mightiness demand, in lieu
Of such beneficence?
    MONT. Your pardon, first;
And next, your pity.

ALM. Such as you conferr'd
On great Taxalla, my unhappy father,
Receive the like from me.

MONT. Think, fair ALMERIA,
If I deprived thy father of a crown,
I lay a brighter at his daughter's feet;
And yeild myself and my dominions up,
The conqueft of her charms.

ALM. Yes, MONTEZUMA,
It is a conqueft I do glory in,
That I, with tyranny and pride, like thine,
May exercife my power.

MONT. The gods, themfelves,
Require but our fubmiffion for our faults,
And then delight to pardon.   Heaven is thus
Beft worfhip'd and appeafed.   [Kneels.

ORBEL. Behold, ALMERIA,   [Kneels.
Your brother alfo bends, and joins the fuit
Of fupplicating majefty!

ALIB. Your fifter,   [Kneels.
Low at your feet, with like proftration, bows,
And fues for favour to our royal mafter.

ORBEL. Think, with what joy, our late dif-
          aftrous parents,
Will look from Heaven to fee their crown reftored,
And placed, with double luftre, on the head
Of their ALMERIA.

ALM. Well—I do accept
Your garland; not as any inftance, meant,
Of grace or favour in return; but merely,

As the submissive mark of homage, due
To the supremacy and rights of Beauty.
      [MONTEZUMA places the Garland on her Head.

S C E N E   IV.

GUYOMAR enters.

ODM. My brother GUYOMAR !—his steps are
      hasty;
And his amazed countenance foretells
Uncommon tidings.

MONT. What, my GUYOMAR,
So soon return'd ?—I sent thee to the frontiers.

GUY. I went, dread sir, by your command, to
      view
The utmost limits of our land; that shore,
Beyond whose beaten verge no world is found,
Save a wild waste of waters and of air,
Illimitable.   There I stood, awhile,
And ponder'd on the vast expanse, stretch'd out,
Perhaps, to infinite: when, as I look'd,
As far as my capacious ken could take
The wide horizon in, even to the line
Where the low bending vault of Heaven appear'd
To rest on ocean—somewhat thence arose
Like clouds, at first unshapely; large, and larger,
As near, and nearer they approach'd, they grew
In bulk and figures, of amazing form,
And terrible distinction !

                        MONT.

Mont. Say, my fon,
To what known figures may you beft compare
Their wonderful appearance?

Guy. Firft, they feem'd
A moving foreft; but, inftead of leaves
And fpreading branches, they affumed fuch wings,
As left it doubtful if they fwam in air,
Or fkim'd the furface of the feas—Anon,
As near and nearer they approach'd, they grew
Of wondrous bulk beneath; and now they feem'd
A floating city, with afpiring tops
Of fheeted towers, and pinnacles that gave
Their ftreamers to the wind.

Mont. Ye mighty gods!
What may thefe monfters bode?—Did they ap-
      pear
As things inanimate?

Guy. If voice and motion
Give evidence of life, they lived too furely.
To right and left I faw them turn, with eafe,
Their vaft enormity: I heard their word;
They breathed deftructive fires, and fpoke in
      thunders.
They are, furely, of the race of thofe above,
Who whirl the rapid tempeft from on high,
And launch the dreaded lightnings. Mortal
      courage
No longer could fuftain the horrid vifion—
I do confefs, I fled—for the firft time,
My feet avowed my fears.

H. Priest.

H, Priest. A prophecy of ancient date imports
The failure of our ſtate, when bearded men
Shall land in floating palaces.

Mont. Go ſtraight—
Solicit, and enquire of all our gods,
What theſe portents foreſhew, that we may learn
To ſtand the fate that cannot be avoided.—

[Exeunt Prieſts.

In the mean ſeaſon, let our rites proceed.
Odmar, our kingdom's heir, our eldeſt born,
Let thine electing wreath, in public here,
Avow the ſecret miſtreſs of thine heart.
Within this ſtarry round of dazzling beauties,
All daughters of the Sun, all fair and bright
As the refulgent ſire from whom they ſprung,
Thou canſt not chuſe amiſs.

Odm. Alas, my father,
I have no choice to make—long ſince determin'd
By fond and irreſiſtible attractions,
My movements center here.—

[Places his Wreath on the Head of Alibech.

Mont. Well placed, my ſon!—
Next to the beauties of divine Almeria,
The world could yield no choice like Alibech,
The ſiſter of Perfection.

Alib. Pray you, pardon.
My humble ſtate permits me not to ſcorn
The grace you mean me—I accept your garland,
But muſt reſerve my heart.

Mont. Now, Guyomar,
Our kingdom's ſecond hope!—to what fair ſhrine
Does thy devotion bend?

Guy.

Guy. I have no garland,
No fading fweets, no tranfitory pledge
Of paffion to confer.   My wreath is form'd
By links of plighted love, and truth that breathes
A never dying fragrance!—Pardon, brother!
I fpeak my approbation of your choice,
By humbly bending here.—

[Bends on one knee to Alibech.

Odm. How, Guyomar!—
Does thy prefumption overleap the bounds,
That guard my rights of elderfhip?

Guy. No, Odmar—
The kingdom, by priority of birth,
Is thine, unenvied: elderfhip, my brother,
Though a good plea in empire, never yet
Was held a plea in love.

Mont. 'Tis true, my children.
Since you, unhappily, have fix'd your hearts
On the fame object, let her choice decide
Your rights of rivalfhip.

Alib. My heart, my lord,
Is that of a cold virgin; though long woo'd,
Not lightly won.   Who ferves his country beft;
Who e'er in council, or the field of danger,
Shall veft his name with a peculiar luftre;
To him I yield my perfon and my heart—
Not as a gift, but the reward of virtue.

Mont. Greatly determin'd. Honourable maiden,
Happy, as glorious, be thy fair election!—
Orbellan, has thy garland been compofed
To wither in thine hand?

Orbel.

ORBEL. Not fo, my liege,
Might I affume the boldnefs to approach,
Where the afpiring ardour of my love
Would breath its incenfe!

MONT. Love, ORBELLAN, is
An arbitrary lord ; nor will fubmit
His rule to our direction. 'Tis enough,
However high and dignified the object,
To fue with reverence, and to hope with honour.

ORBEL. Suppofe the daughter of my fovereign?—

MONT. How!—
O, I do fee—the gods, in fpight of victory,
In fpight of death, are bent to vindicate
The empire of Traxalla; while his progeny,
With galling retribution, caft their chains
O'er me and mine!

ALM. Proud monarch!—Yet reflect,
Who fcorns the fuit or perfon of my brother,
Makes light of the difpleafure of ALMERIA!

MONT. I ftrive in vain—the lion's ftruggling
     heart
Is wound about with toils!—CYDERIA, take
Thy lover's wreath; and, if thou doft efteem
Thy father's welfare, treat him not unkindly.

CYDER. Obedient to your pleafure, royal fir,
Though much repugnant to my own, I take
A pledge of love I never can return—
Nature and deep difguft would therein prove,
Too ftrong for your commands.

OFFICER

Officer enters haftily.

Offic. Break up your rites !—
A hoft of foes, who lurk'd within the wood,
Burft from their ambufh, and enclofe the temple.
    Mont. Make to the city, by the poftern gate.
Freedom, and conqueft, or a glorious death,
Beft fits a foldier and a king !   [Exeunt

Alarm without. They all re-enter as driven back by the
                    enemy.

    Mont. Confufion !—on all fides befet !—Here,
        ftand,
And let us make this paffage good—If not
For victory, why, let us fight for vengeance !
So fhall our valour raife one trophy more,
Even in the gate of death !

CORTEZ without.

    Cort. Slaves, villains, cowards !—Stay, reftrain
        your outrage.

S C E N E V.

Enter CORTEZ, VASQUEZ, PIZARRO, Spaniards,
        and Traxallans.

    Cort. Did I not charge ye not to fight, on
        pain
Of capital difpleafure ?
                                        TRAXAL.

TRAXAL. Dread commander !
You know not whom you would protect—Thefe are
Your firft, your greateft foes ; the very life
Of Mexico, the vital heart and head
Of twenty millions—mighty MONTEZUMA,
Caught in our toils, with all his royal race!
Permit us but to ftrike, and the wide world,
Like fruit o'er-ripen'd, falls into your hand,
Without the pain of plucking.

   CORT. Stay, I charge ye !—
They fhall not die—my clemency defends them.
VASQUEZ, draw up our Spaniards, and give fire
On all who dare to difobey.

   TRAXAL. O, mercy !—   [Traxallans kneel.
Mercy, dread fovereign—at your feet we fall
For mercy! — Silence, then, your thundering
          gods !—
If they but fpeak, we die !—

   CORT. Upon the inftant,
Withdraw—and hence be taught a due fubmiffion.
                              [Traxallans retire.

   MONT. The fierce Traxallans lay their weapons
          down,
And fearfully retire.—Some god prefides,
And fhields us from deftruction.—
Patron of Mexico, great power of battles !
                              [To CORTEZ.
If you are he, whofe noftrils take delight
In carnage, and the fcent of human blood
Hot fuming from the heart, ten daily victims
Shall gafp within your fhrine.—But, if you are,
As rather it fhould feem, that deity,

                              Whofe

Whofe fweeteft incenfe is an act of goodnefs ;
The widow and the orphan, through our land,
Shall tune their hearts to gladnefs ; and our pri-
            foners
Spring from a thoufand dungeons, to exult
And gambol in your prefence !

    CORT. Generous prince,
Imperial MONTEZUMA !—I am a man,
To you, and many others, much inferior;
Unlefs exalted by a foldier's worth,
That to the fword of honour ties humanity.
To you I come, ambaffador of peace
And friendfhip, from the world's moft potent king,
The mighty Charles of Spain.

        MONT. We know him not.—
Yet, if we know ourfelf, we alfo know
The world contains not one fo great—not him,
Our brother of Peru, the fecond throne
That rifes o'er the earth !—The reft are, all,
Of order fubaltern, or petty lords,
And tributary vaffals ; as the Heavens
Contain but two great lights, with leffer ftars
That form their regal train.

      CORT. Miftaken monarch !
The world contains a multitude of empires ;
Within whofe fpacious tracts, thy Mexico
Would fhew but as a province.   Full four moons
Have watch'd our nightly courfes, fince we
            launch'd
And left the neareft fhore : all elfe, between,
Is ocean ; o'er whofe bofom we have ply'd

                                    Both

Both fail and oar, with unremitted fpeed,
Through light and darknefs.
      Mont. Wondrous are the things
Thou telleft, as if Heaven had lately form'd
A new invented world!—In all events,
If he, whofe potent delegate thou art,
Be great, and good, and gracious, as thyfelf;
There's nothing more to fear.   Say, firft of mortals,
What would thy monarch with a king and ftranger?
      Cort. Vasquez, do thou unfold our high com-
            miffion.   [Addreffes the Ladies.
      Vasq. Charles, by the gift of all-difpofing
            Heaven,
Chief monarch of the world, and king of kings,
Firft wills that you refign your crown and fcepter,
To be return'd, and held, from him and his,
By you and yours, in regal deputation,
Even to the end of time.
      Mont. 'Tis in my hand—
What if I hold it?
      Vasq. War and violence
Shall wreft it from you.
      Mont. By what right?
      Vasq. The grant
Of our great Pontiff; who, in Heaven and earth,
Gives kingdoms, and refumes them.
      Mont. If he grants
In Heaven, as now on earth, what is not his,
We pity his expectants—Would your king
Aught further?
      Vasq. Yes—your golden ore.

Vol. III.   T   Mont.

Mont. 'Tis his.
Though we refuſe our kingdom to his pride,
We yet beſtow upon his poverty
The treaſures we deſpiſe!—Is there aught elſe,
In which our new-found maſter would command
         us?
   Vasq. He, laſtly, wills you to forſake your
        idols,
Your worſhip of the works of human hands,
And ſpirits reprobate; and to adore,
With him, One Power Supreme.
   Mont. If he can ſhew us
A god of juſt pre-eminence, whoſe power
Wiſdom directs, and goodneſs miniſters,
Our choice ſhall follow reaſon—our own reaſon,
Not that of others.
   Vasq. Pardon, royal ſir!
Herein you muſt be govern'd.   We have brought
        you
Inſtructors, deeply learn'd; all holy men,
Commiſſion'd, by infallibility,
To root out error, and to plant the truth
Of our unerring doctrine.
   Mont. Men, you ſay;
And yet infallible?—O, I do ſee
The threefold motives of your journey now!
You, firſt, would plunder us of our poſſeſſions;
You, next, would bend our bodies to your
        burdens;
And, laſtly, ſtretch the ſcope of your dominion
Over our free-born minds—It is too much!
You cannot hold us worthy of your friendſhip,

Should

Should we accept it upon terms fo bafe,
So utterly degrading!
    CORT. What's the conteft?——
VASQUEZ, I fear thou did'ft exaggerate.
What fays the imperial power of Mexico?
What fays our royal friend?
    MONT. Firft, as a man,
By your protecting virtue fnatch'd fo late
From imminent deftruction, much is due,
And more would I return.—But, as a king,
Bound to defend an independent crown,
And a free people, I reject all terms
That favour of fubmiffion!
    CORT. Know, great fir,
A new and powerful motive binds me, now,
To court your friendfhip; and, howe'er compell'd,
By the ftern duties of my high commiffion,
To ftand in arms againft your Mexicans,
I cannot be the foe of MONTEZUMA.

    MONT. Hear me, ye guardian gods of Mexico!
If that, in Heaven or earth, a power is found
To your's and mine fuperior—If fome fate,
Unknown, fhall yet intrude upon our world,
And caft us from dominion—may that fate,
With my friend's hand my ravifh'd fceptre grace,
And rule thefe realms in juftice!
      [Exeunt all feverally, except CORTEZ and CYDERIA,
        who feems going, yet lingers behind.

    CYD. 'My duty bids me go—and yet fome power,
More ftrong than duty, holds me!
    CORT. Faireft creature!
Will you vouchfafe your prefence, for a moment,

T 2

That

That my fond eyes may gaze upon your beauties,
Like to bewilder'd travellers on fnow,
Till they grow blinded with excefs of brightnefs.
    Cyd. Fair ftranger!—why I would ftay here, I
       know not.
Yet, fomewhat keeps me—fome unknown emotion
Stirs all my foul, and makes me figh, and figh,
Altho' I feel no forrow!—Tell me, fir,
What holds you, alfo, from your late affociates?
    Cort. You do, bright excellence!—I am your
       captive;
And you have bound me with a chain more ftrong
Than links of triple fteel.   All other flaves
May chance to break their fetters—I, alone,
Can ne'er be free; for I am in love with bondage.
    Cyd. I would—I would, indeed, you were my
       prifoner!
For I would bind you with a gentle thread;
Nor ever put you into harder fervice,
Than thus to look, and talk, and walk before me—
And yet I fear me, it is you have caufed
This new difturbance in my peaceful bofom,
That thrills my blood, and heaves within my heart,
And pains me, fadly, when I think of parting!
    Cort. O, native honour, heavenly purity!
That needs no veil, but fhames the courtly mafk
Of practifed guile, and ftudied affectation!

To them Orbellan.

    Orb. Princefs, your royal father fends for you,
And wonders much at your delay.
Cyd.

Cyd. Alas,
So great a wonder for fo fhort an abfence!
    Orb. It is his ftrict commandment, that you
        come
Upon the inftant—
    Cyd. Has he alfo fent
To bring the ftranger?
    Orb. No—his high placed love
Rather demands correction.
    Cort. O, thou haft,
Within the facred prefence of thy princefs,
A charter, wide as air, for infolence!
Make ufe of her protection—but beware,
When next we meet!—
    Cyd. Ah, I do feel, in parting,
That I muft leave my former joys behind;
And carry nothing, in exchange, from hence,
Save new found wretchednefs.
    Cort. Where e'er you go,
My fighs, my foul, and every faculty,
Attend upon your fteps.   [Exeunt feverally.

END OF THE FIRST ACT.

A C T   II.

S C E N E   I.

A Cave.

To the High Priest Montezuma enters.

Mont. HAIL, holy pontiff!—It is not the fate.
Of doubtful war, the froward turns of fortune,
The fall of kingdoms, or the change of ftates,
I would alone explore—I feek to know,
What haply fcarce the gods can tell, the fprings,
The fecret turns and movements of the foul,
A woman's foul!—O, give me to unfold
The myftic volume of ALMERIA's mind,
And let me read my fate!

 H. PRIEST. My powerful charms not dæmons
   fhall withftand,
And gods fhall anfwer to my king's command.

INCAN-

INCANTATION.

I.

Moon, pale regent of the night,
Goddefs of each magic rite—
In this dread and dreary hour,
Aid us with thy light and power!

II.

O, ye ftars, ye feeds of light,
Radiant gems of gloomy night,
In whofe ever-varying round
Prefent, paft, and future's found;
Who, in characters, comprize
Falls of kingdoms, ere they rife,
To our favour'd fight reveal,
Whate'er, from vulgar eyes, with caution ye
        conceal!

III.

Ye fpirits infernal, dark partners of woe!
Ye dæmons who wield ebon fceptres below!
Ye goblins and fairies, or dufky or fair,
Who mine in the earth, or who dance in the air!

          IV. My

IV.

My wand demands ye, from hell, earth,
  and fkies—
    Arife, arife, arife!

A TERRESTRIAL SPIRIT afcends.

SPIR. Prince, mourn your fearch—your gods are
  all controul'd;
Silent, and bow'd before fuperior power!
    I dare no more.   [Defcends.
H. PRIEST. Hence, dark and daftard fpright!—
  Calib, my ever fmiling friend!
  Circled with radiant light, defcend;
  Our bofoms with thy wonted tidings cheer,
  Speak comfort to our heart, and mufic to
    our ear!

CALIB defcends in white, and fings.

I.

CALIB. Mighty emperor, attend;
    Heavy, heavy things impend!
      Many a conflict, many a fight,
    Defolation, fear, and flight,
    Lofs of empire, life, and light,
      All rufh upon my fight!

II.

Yet, thro' the horrors of this threatening sky,
One radiant beam I spy.
It comes, the singly smiling hour,
That puts our Indian world again into thy
power!

III.

They stand, they stand,
Within thine hand,
This horrid, hostile, ruthless band—
Strike, strike, and save the land!   [*Ascends.*

Mont. Thanks, shining monitor!—If I reject
Thy counsel, let me perish!
Empire is now assured: but what of love,
What of Almeria?

H. Priest. Ye spirits, o'er subtlest effluvia re-
fined,
Who feed upon thought, and reside within mind;
Who mark, with a pleased unevadable eye,
The swiftness of feminine whims, as they fly—
Be your Almeria's purpose shewn,
Altho' to reason, rule, and right, and to herself
unknown!

The Indian Queen rises with a Dagger in her
Breast.

H. Priest. Ha!—we call'd not for thee—
Hence, bloody spectre, visionary victim,
I   Avaunt!

Avaunt !——She will not ; and a sudden winter
Freezes my blood !

    Mont. The gods, amidst the living and the
        dead,
Could not have found another form, like that,
To shake my soul !

    Ind. Queen. Ungrateful prince, your empty
        hopes resign ;
Almeria's charms will soon be cold as mine.
Your course of empire, fame, and life, is run ;
And all shall set, before a second sun—
I wait you on the ghastly brink of death,
To catch your spirit, and to drink your breath.
For your dear love, I did my life forego ;
And thence I claim you in the realms below.
The morning dawns—I sicken at the view :
A sudden meeting fits a short adieu !

                    [Descends.

    Mont. Give me a narrower date !—ye adverse
        powers,
Finish your purposes ! Why this dread knowledge
Of what we cannot shun ?—worse, than the
        worst
That death can threaten, are the living pangs
Of curs'd anticipation !—

                    [Exeunt.

                        SCENE

SCENE II.

A GROVE between MEXICO and the
SPANISH Army.

CYDERIA and ALIBECH.

CYDER. Think you he'll come?

ALIB. Come, child?—how young you are!
How deep you under-rate your own perfections!
You know not what a strength of pinion wings
The lover to his love.   Your message is
As sure as fate had summon'd him—as happy
As he were call'd to Heaven!

CYDER. I would to Heaven
It may be so—His stay is wondrous long.

ALIB. Thou hasty innocent! although he rode
The corner'd winds, they could not post him
          sooner.
But, mark—upon that rubied lip, CYDERIA,
The fate of Mexico depends! Do thou,
Perfuafive orator, with firmnefs plead
Thy country's caufe; and love shall soon subscribe
The terms that beauty dictates.—Soft, he comes,

SCENE

S C E N E III.

To them CORTEZ and VASQUEZ attended.

CORT. CYDERIA here, dread powers! upon the
    brink
Of danger and of death?—Hafte, precious maid,
Back to thy father's palace!—Soon this fpot
Shall all be cover'd, or be clofed about
With clafhing armies, and with gafping fquadrons,
The dying and the dead!—Hafte, royal maid!
When kites and ravening hawks are on the wing,
The white dove takes to cover!
[VASQUEZ addreffes ALIBECH in dumb fhew.

CYDER. CORTEZ, I think, they call thee.
CORT. True, my miftrefs.
CYDER. I love thee, man—I fhame not to con-
    fefs it;
For I do think that thou art brave and honourable.
  CORT. Celeftial purity!—where no fpot is,
No veil is wanting.—Goddefs of my vows,
Thus let me offer up a grateful heart,
[Kiffes her hand.

Even on this holy altar!—Come, my love,
I will myfelf convey thee to fome place
Of more affured protection.
  CYDER. Tell me, Spaniard,
Is it, indeed, for me that thou art alarm'd?—
Is it my danger that thou feareft?
  CORT. Heavens!—
Is that a queftion?—Take this fignet, foldier,
Hafte,

Haſte, bear my order through the ranks, that not
A Spaniard, or Traxallan, move to action,
Till this dear truſt ſhall be diſpoſed in ſafety!
    CYDER. CORTEZ, think not I bear theſe feather-
        ed ſhafts,
And ebon bow, for ornament.—'Tis true,
That when ambition, when the fire of blood,
And martial ardour lead the ſoldier forth
Upon ſome deſperate enterprize; war, then,
Is man's peculiar province.—Learn, however,
That when we are aſſail'd, when hoſtile force
Knocks at our gates, and overlooks our ramparts;
Weakneſs gets ſtrength, and cowards catch at
        valour—
Women and infants cluſter to defend
Our houſehold fires, and guard our common
        country!
    CORT. Immortal powers! would my CYDERIA
        foil
Thoſe virgin ſhafts with human blood?
    CYDER. Yes, Spaniard!
In ſuch a cauſe, even with thy blood—then,
        think not,
I fear to ſhed my own!—By yonder Sun,
My radiant fire, I ſwear, if thou, this day,
Shalt dare to offer battle, I will front thee;
Nor ceaſe to point my quiver at thy breaſt,
Till ſome bleſt dart find entrance!
    CORT. You diſtract me!
Are there no means, by which I may preſerve
Your precious life from danger, and myſelf
From terrors worſe than death?

                    CYDER.

CYDER. Yes, generous CORTEZ!
Bid thy bold troops draw off—then, as a friend,
Enter the gates of Mexico; and, next,
Enter the heart and arms of thy CYDERIA!

   CORT. Confummate virgin, moft divine CY-
      DERIA!
Daughter of truth and order, brighter far
Than yonder Sun, whom you have deign'd to ftile
The father of your race!—would you, indeed,
Would you difgrace the leader whom you ftoop
To honour with your favour?

   CYDER. No, my foldier!
Thou fhalt be worfhip'd as a guardian god,
Throughout our Indian world.

   CORT. Ah no, CYDERIA—
Did I ftop here, I fhould alike be fpurn'd,
On either part, by Mexicans and Spaniards,
For fhrinking from the bright and kindling courfe
Of never dying glory!

   CYDER. Glory? Spaniard—
What is this glory, which you would prefer
To the falvation of a grateful world,
And your CYDERIA's love?

   CORT. Glory, my princefs,
Is that which kindles fouls to great atchievments.
It is the price of danger, toil, and bloodfhed;
It warms the winter's camp, and turns the flint
To a down pillow for a foldier's head.
It is a being in the breaft of others—
'Tis the high prize, for which we die with pleafure;
Since glory gives us to furvive our fate,
And rife to immortality!

CYDER.

CYDER. Is glory then and immortality
The price of evil actions—the reward
Of rapes and maffacres, of blood and burnings?—
O glorious famine, glorious peftilence!
You, like the Spaniard, can make grafs to grow
In cities, and give wafted kingdoms up
To birds and beafts of prey!
    CORT. O, you have conquer'd—blafted be the
        laurels, .
That ever fhall be planted on the woes
And wafte of humankind!—Yet, think, my
        miftrefs;
I act but by commiffion from my prince,
And, though the deed fhould prove a crime in
        him,
In me 'tis duty.
    CYDER. Duty, to do wrong!
Who has a right to give it?—No, my CORTEZ,
Then, when you dropt like a defcending god,
And faved the royal houfe of MONTEZUMA,
Then you were truely glorious.—O, be ftill
Our guardian deity!—My grateful father
Has regions of unknown extent; fair realms,
Where you, my foldier, with your bleft CYDERIA,
May reign in your own right.
    CORT. Refiftlefs tempter!
The caufe is yours—Retire, but for this day;
Retire, my love!—To-morrow, I do fwear it,
And all the morrows of my future life,
Shall rife at your difpofal.
    CYDER. Spaniard, no.

                              This .

This day—I fwear it too—fhall end my life,
Or free my country !

    Cort. Vasquez, go ; our wars
Are ended !—bid our men draw off.

S C E N E IV.

Pizarro enters.

    Pizar. Hafte, general !
Our troops call out, impatient for their leader,
And claim the infpiring prefence of their Cortez.
Already is the fight begun.—Orbellan,
Follow'd by hofts of fhouting Mexicans,
Falls like a tempeft on our ranks, and all
Is blood and uproar.

    Cort. Now, divine Cyderia,
Would you now wifh me to ftand idle ?

    Cyder. No.
Thus charged, and by a rival, I refign
This day to honour—but, remember, Spaniard,
Your future life belongs to love.

    Cort. To love,
And to Cyderia, be all my days devoted,
Till time can count no more

        [Exeunt Cortez and Vasquez, &c. oné way,
        Cyderia another.

SCENE

SCENE V.

To ALIBECH enter ODMAR and GUYOMAR.

ODM. Now faireſt daughter of the day, bright
    ALIBECH,
Now, ere I ruſh into the thickeſt battle,
Give me to know my doom!—Thoſe lips can
    ſpeak it,
Surer than all yon armed hoſt.
  GUY. I alſo,
Trembling attend my ſentence; as the criminal,
At ſome tribunal, waits the doubtful word
That ſhall decide on life or death.
  ALIB. Brave princes!
One of you is much dearer to his ALIBECH,
Than light to ſome benighted traveller;
Or life to him, who ſhivers on the brink
Of mortal diſſolution.   Who he is,
The dear one, that ſits ſcepter'd at my heart,
And lords it o'er my wiſhes—neither looks
Nor words, that I am miſtreſs of, ſhall utter!
For once it ſhall be ſaid, that worth alone
Controul'd a woman's fancy—The fond love
Of one of ye, by all due right, is mine;
Your country, by a dearer claim, demands
The life of both—who ſerves that country beſt,
Becomes my maſter—Princes, ye are ſummon'd!
                    [Trumpets.
  GUY. My merit, death or conqueſt ſhall approve.
Fall on!

Odm. Fall on!

Guy. For liberty!

Odm. For love!

[Exeunt Odmar and Guyomar one way,
Alibech another.

S C E N E   VI.

Alarm to the Battle. Montezuma, Orbellan,
and Mexicans enter.

Mont. They fly, the apostate rebels, the
Traxallans;
Bold in base ambush, but, in open fight,
Fearful as dear that scud along the lawn
Before their hunter!—Charge, charge home, my
friends;
Confirm your conquest, Mexicans! I ask
The bravest and the youngest but to follow,
Where your old King shall lead!   [Exeunt.

S C E. N E   VII.

Cortez, Vasquez, Pizarro, and Spaniards enter.

Cort. May curses catch them in their flight.—
May death,
And wounds of foul dishonour, from behind,
O'ertake the servile herd, these vile Traxallans!
Is this their vaunted prowess, this the fruit
Of their confederacy, their hate of Mexico,
And promised efforts for atchieving freedom?

, Let

Let them all perish!—Breathe awhile, my friends,
My firm, tho' little band of faithful followers—
Thank Heaven, we are yet entire!
    VAS. See where, wide scatter'd o'er yon distant
        hill,
The panting dastards run.
    PIZAR. Great MONTEZUMA;
Active as youth, and eager as the hound
That bears and breathes upon his prey, pursues
And mixes with their flight.
    CORT. Haste, VASQUEZ, seize
The fair occasion—take our generous horse,
Few as they are, and, while our numerous foes
Are in confusion, charge them in the rear—
Pursue the fierce pursuers!   [Exit VASQUEZ.
PIZARRO, let us range our little band
Of brave Castilians in yon copse; and thence,
While these triumphant Mexicans return
Assured of fickle victory, we'll flank
And pour our thunder on them!—   [Exeunt.

SCENE VIII.

ODMAR and GUYOMAR, from different sides.

GUYOMAR and his few followers bleeding.

    ODM. Where hast thou been, young dastard?—
        In a day
Of such wide triumph, wherefore has my eye
In vain sought GUYOMAR, amid our host
Of conquering Mexicans?

Guy. Forbear, my brother,
Forbear to load a man already burden'd,
With heavier imputation.—We confefs,
Our powers inferior to thefe men, or dæmons,
With whom we dared the conteft.—Thefe wounds
  fhew
The few that, of my generous friends, yet live,
Were not quite idle.—Say, where is the King,
Where is our father, Odmar?

Odm. Flufh'd with conqueft,
He drives the routed hoft of the Traxallans
Over the plains of Mexico.

Guy. Traxallans!
Why fpend his bootlefs fury on Traxallans?
Our braver women were enough to quell
Two armies of Traxallans.

S C E N E IX.

Guns go off within. Montezuma, Orbellan,
  and Mexicans enter as retreating.

Mont. All, all is loft—the gods have arm'd
  our foes
With their own thunders!—What the utmoft
  force
Of man can do, we fear not——but when earth
And Heaven combine againft us—to retire,
Is due fubmiffion!

Orbel. We but hear a found,
And fink in death, for ever!

           Guy.

Guy. Hark, they come!—
Hafte fir, and gain the town, while I remain
To guard your rear, and chearfully return
That life you gave me. [All retreat, except Guyomar.

S C E N E X.

Enter Cortez, Vasquez, Pizarro, and Spaniards.

Cort. Prefs forward, fellow foldiers, take ad-
          vantage
Of their new panic! Spare, yet fpare the blood
Of Montezuma's royal houfe!—Succefs
And glory crown our arms—Come on!   [Exeunt.

As Cortez is going out, Guyomar advances and meets
          him.

Guy. Hold, fir—you pafs no further—I propofe
To win a feather from you; or to grace
My fall, ennobled by your hand.
          [Strikes at the helmet of Cortez, his fword breaks.
Cort. Thou art my prifoner, Indian!—Had
          thy fword
Been equal to thine arm, I had not lived
To tell thee fo—Ha!—let me look again—
Art thou not he, that defperate Mexican,
Who fingly dared, this day, to prefs upon us,
Even in the face of thunder?
Guy. Cortez, as I hope—
Art thou?
Cort. Yes, valiant youth.
U 3

Guy.

Guy. Bring me my chains—from any other
          hand
I fhould have blufh'd beneath them.
     Cort. Whoe'er thou art, my foul claims kindred
          with thee!—
May'ft thou ne'er put ignobler fetters on,
Than thofe that bind thee now!—
                                        [Embrace.
     Guy. My heart's great mafter!—
Your bounty, generous leader, muft not rob you
Of the large ranfom which you ought to claim
Know, that the captive of your arms is fon
Of Montezuma.
     Cort. What, Cyderia's brother?
     Guy. Cyderia's fecond brother.
     Cort. Bleft event!
My dear, dear brother!—may I dare to tell you
I am the captive of your fifter's beauties?
Never, again, O, never may my Guyomar
Come thus expofed to battle!—Be this helm
The guardian of that precious head—this corfelet,
                    [Dreffes Guyomar in his Armour.
Be it henceforth a fence of triple fteel
Before thy valiant heart—and may this fword,
In that ftrong hand, be ftill affured of conqueft!—
     Guy. More eftimable are your gifts, my con-
          queror,
Than all things, fave the giver!—Eafe my heart,
And teach me how to thank you!
     Cort. With your friendfhip!
Let that o'erpay me.—Go, my Guyomar;
Thus glorious in the fpoils of Spain, return,

                                        And

And fpare the many tears, that now, in Mexico,
Bewail your death or bondage.
   Guy. O, my friend,
My beft loved brother, till we meet again,
My heart is ftill your captive.——
   Cort. O, farewell!
                [Embrace, and go out feverally.

END OF THE SECOND ACT.

A C T III.

S C E N E I.

The PALACE.

ALIBECH and CYDERIA enter in tears, ODMAR
following.

ALIB. AWAY, away!—
ODM. You wrong me, by the gods!—
What mortal force, or mortal courage could,
I did, and dared.—
Could I ſtand up againſt my brother's fate,
Or, what is more, againſt his folly?—No.
He caſt life from him, as it were a cup
Of ſomewhat baneful—in a frenzy, ruſh'd
Amid a hoſt of his ſteel-coated foes,
And periſh'd.

    ALIB. Yes, all glorious, peerleſs youth!
His promiſe is accompliſh'd—" Death, or con-
       " queſt!"
It was his parting ſentence.—Hence, thou vile
      one!
Is it becauſe the eyes of men, alone,

Have

Have feen thy back, that yet thou dareft to face
A woman? and, half breathlefs from thy flight,
To wooe a daughter of the Sun?
  Odm. Yet, hear me.
That very Sun, thine all-difcerning fire,
Will witnefs that I fled not—As a tyger,
Baited by hunters, I retired reluctant,
My face ftill toward my foes—the guardian fhield
Of routed Mexico, the very laft
Who entered at her gates!
    Alib. No more, no more.
Thou never hadft a portion of my heart;
Now, thou haft all my hatred!—Where, where
            is he,
My Guyomar, my loft, loft love?—Ha, Odmar!
Has not thine envy of fuperior worth,
Leagued with thefe curs'd invaders, to unprop
Thy tottering country?
    Odm. No, injurious princefs!
Your brother, had he look'd behind, had feen
Odmar, the guardian of his rear.—Yet, look
To do me right!—You are mine by compact,
            lady—
Nay, more, by fure neceffity; the world
Affords you, now, no other choice!—In fpight
Of froward affectation, you are mine;
Nor is there power in earth, or higher Heaven,
To wreft you from me, but with life!
    Alib. Thine, Odmar?
Thine, fayft thou, and by compact?—No, fond
            man!
I was affianced to the braveft—not

To him who fled—but, to my Guyomar,
Who ftood, and fought, and fell, to fave his
    country.

   Odm. Proud and infulting as you are, you
    fhall not,
You fhall not hope to rob me of your beauties.
That hoft, for whom I fought and bled this day,
Shall yeild you to my arms, howe'er reluctant;
The bride or victim of my love, I reck not!

   Alib. While there are daggers, poifons, lakes,
    or flames,
I cannot fear to 'fcape the arms of Odmar !—
Stay, prince, and mark my final refolution.
I am the wedded of thy brother's fpirit;
And, to my Guyomar, 'fore thee and Heaven,
I plight my faith for ever!—Here I kneel,
Vowing to keep my body from the ftain
Of mortal touch, fave that of death ;
Till, born in brightnefs, on my father's beams,
I fhall be wafted to the bleft abodes,
Where love, and Guyomar, fhall give new life,
And fill up immortality !

   Odm. Proud maid !
Then be it fo—a hafty death, this day,
Shall make thee Guyomar's ; or life, to-morrow,
Shall give thee all to Odmar !   [Exit.

   Cyder. Ah, my fifter !
Why, with the ftings of fcorn, would you provoke
A mind, by nature prone to gufts of paffion ?
Alas, he is my only brother, now;
Confider that, my Alibech ; reflect

                      He

He is the only brother that is left
To your CYDERIA!

ALIB. Save me—fee, CYDERIA!
He comes, all hero as he died!—he comes,
Sheath'd in celeftial arms, to take me hence!—
Nor waits the vifit, which I had refolv'd
To Heaven and GUYOMAR!

S C E N E II,

GUYOMAR enters.

GUY. My love, my ALIBECH!—
Doft thou then fade, thou flower of Mexico?
I catch thee, thus, e'er thou declineft!

ALIB. There——
Take me—together—foul and body, both—
For both are thine!—Bear me beyond the hills—
To fome ftrange world, where we may find,
          perhaps,
A freer air—for here are mifts—too thick
For breath—all dark and ftifling—Oh!   [Faints.

GUY. CYDERIA, help!—Alas, fhe faints, fhe
          dies—
And I am fcarce alive!

CYDER. Do you live, indeed?

ALIB. Where am I now?—how far upon our
          journey?

GUY. You are in the arms of GUYOMAR, my
          love,
Your own bleft bower!

ALIB. Am I all fpirit, now?

GUY.

Guy Spirit and flesh, as I am, Alibech;
But your's the faireft, pureft, heavenlieft, fure,
That ever cafed a mind !

    Alib. You, alfo, feel as though you had not,
        yet,
Attain'd to immortality.

    Cyder. My brother !
Shall not Cyderia, alfo, fhare the joy
Of your return to life ?

    Guy. My deareft fifter !   [Embraces.

    Alib. We heard, my Guyomar, that you
        were hewn
To pieces, and that every Spaniard took
A portion of the precious fpoil.

    Cyder. Say, brother,
What fword is this, that glitters at your fide ?
This plumey helmet, and this blazing corfelet ?
Are they the gift of fome protecting god ?
Or are they, rather, fome confummate work-
        manfhip
Of this new world of Spaniards ?

    Guy. Thefe were, late,
The armour of that boafted chief of Spain,
The mighty Cortez—Hand to hand, we ftood
Oppofed in mortal duel—
And, on his cafque I hew'd, while my good fword
Could hold its temper.—Ha!—why pales the
        cheek
Of my Cyderia?—Soft—I did but feign—
I did but feign—He lives, my fweeteft fifter,
Your Cortez lives, my girl! as true in love,
As he in war is valiant !

SCENE

SCENE III.

ODMAR enters.

ODM. What, GUYOMAR return'd?
GUY. My brother ODMAR!
          [Offers to embrace ODMAR, who turns away.
Why thus cold, my brother?
Although in war, as love, you are my rival,
You are yet a rival moſt beloved—I know
You ſcorn'd to take advantage of my abſence.
I come, the faithful witneſs of your valour;
And plead no better merit to our princeſs,
Than that I dared, from ODMAR's deeds, this day,
To take my great example!
    ODM. Free, alive,
Unhurt?—O'er-ruling powers, 'tis wondrous, all!

SCENE IV.

MONTEZUMA, and ORBELLAN, attended by Mexi-
          can Chiefs.

    MONT. See that our walls be doubly lined
          around!
And let our boats bear off the ſick and maim'd,
Infirm old age, and helpleſs infancy,
Safe to the ſouthern ſhore, that fronts the coaſt
Where now our foes entrench. Sambello, Malech,
See this perform'd!—
          [They proſtrate themſelves, riſe, and go out.

                              GUY.

Guy. My father, and my King !—
[Bends his knee.
Mont. My Guyomar ?—by my great fire, the
    Sun,
The nobleft gift that he could fend !—My child,
[Embraces.
Champion of Mexico, thy country's pride,
Thy father's boaft, his younger Montezuma !
The gods, the gods be praifed !—
    Guy. O, royal fir !
O'erwhelm me not with honours much unmerited.
I blufh to fay a fon of Montezuma
Was, this hour, captive to the arms of Spain,
Even of that Cortez, whofe protecting word
Late faved the royal houfe of Mexico,
From the infulting arms of falfe Traxallans.
I am the fecond offering of his bounty ;
And, from his fide, and head, and generous breaft,
He pluck'd thefe arms, and put them on his flave,
To make the glory of your Guyomar
Look bigger than his fhame !

S C E N E V.

Melmar enters, and falls proftrate.

Mont. Your bufinefs ?—Rife.
Melm. 'Tis for the private ear
Of Montezuma, and the prince Orbellan.
    Mont. All elfe retire !—   [The reft withdraw.
Now fpeak.

Melm.

Melm. Moſt mighty ſire,
Let not miſdeeming hate, or pride imperial,
Rejeât the ſervice which I come to olfer.
Bold be my words, but honeſt!
      Mont. Forward—boldly.
      Melm. When the wide empire of the great
            Traxalla,
Bow'd to the arms of greater Montezuma,
Had he not ruled us with too ſtraight a rein,
We had not caſt for freedom.
      Mont. Your full purpoſe—
Speak it.
      Melm. To·quit the galling yoke of Mexico,
We put on that of Spain—to ſcape the flood,
We plunged into the flame!
      Orbel. If I miſtake not,
My friend, and kinſman, Melmar!—art thou
            not?
      Melm. Yes, my loved prince.
      Orbel. A valiant man, my liege!
And chief of our Traxallans.
      Mont. He is welcome.
Tell me, brave Melmar! I would gladly hear
Somewhat of theſe new lords, our Spaniſh inmates.
      Melm. Cruſh them, ye falling Heavens! Earth,
            ſink beneath them!
Plague, famine, fire, conſume them to their en-
            trails,
And hell hounds gnaw their bones!—They are,
            they are,
In luſt, more rampant than a ſummer's fly ;
Lawleſs as winds,· remorſeleſs as the rocks,

                                    And,

And, as the gulph of Mexico, devouring!—
Then they are fcornful, cruel, and infulting;
As though our Indians were but pifmires, placed
For their proud foot to tread on!

Mont. Wifh ye not
To change your mafters?

Melm. Therefore I am come.
Say, fire, what terms Traxallans are to hope for,
When they have joined their powers to thofe of
        Mexico,
And fcourged thefe pefts back to the noifome fens,
From whence they firft arofe?

Mont. Be witnefs, Sun and Moon, and all ye
        lights
That fhed your comforts on our Indian world!
The day that frees us from thefe Spanifh dæmons,
Who roll infernal thunders o'er our heads,
Shall fee Almeria on the throne of Mexico;
And this, your native prince, your loved Or-
        bellan,
Upon the throne of his imperial parents,
Traxalla and Acacis!

Melm. 'Tis enough.
Now mark me—Near the tent of their great
        Cortez,
My fquadrons quarter—fince our laft engagement,
He did me fomewhat of difgrace——Suppofe,
Within this hour, I bring him to your prefence,
Indignant as a tyger in the toils,
And tearing at his chains?

Orbel. Your leave, my liege,

                                I pray,

I pray, to make a party in this enterprize,
With a few gallant friends!
　　Mont. The night's far spent,
And casts a favouring cloak upon your daring.
Glory, and all the gifts of Montezuma,
Attend on your achievement!　　　　　[Exeunt.

S C E N E　VI.

The Camp of the Spaniards.

Cortez enters unarm'd, except his sword.

　　Cort. Heavens, what a glorious canopy is
　　　　　spread,
O'er unobserving silence!—how the moon
And wakeful planets dance their glittering maze,
In ceaselefs evolutions!—Earth is no more,
From the creation to the last of things,
The tomb of all its offspring!—What a scope
Is here for human thought?—

A Mexican enters.

　　Mex. From Guyomar—
In haste, and breathless!—Treason is at hand—
I dare no more—take warning!—　　　　[Exit.
　　Cort. Treason!—whence?
All are at quiet in their nightly death
Of sleep and silence.—Hark—what ruftling's that?
Stand!—Come no nearer.

ORBELLAN enters fuddenly, his fword drawn, and followed
 by Mexicans.—He lays hold on CORTEZ.—CORTEZ
 fprings back, draws, and kills ORBELLAN at the firft pafs.

 ORBEL. You are my prifoner.
Silence; not a word!

 CORT. Deeds were, perhaps, as well!

MELMAR and Traxallans enter behind, and feize and bind
      CORTEZ.

 MELM. Bind, bind him, fure.

 CORT. Guards!—Vafquez!

 MELM. But another word—and this
Shall filence you for ever!—

       [Offers a dagger to his breaft.

O, he is flain,
Our prince is flain!—Soft—take the body up—
Lead off your prifoner!   [Exeunt.

S C E N E VII.

THE PALACE.

ALMERIA and ALIBECH.

 ALM. 'Tis fure, my fifter,
Some fecret purpofe is in agitation,
Dark as the night!—The found of cluftring feet
Is all we hear; while crouds, fucceeding crouds,
Throng toward the weftern gate.

 ALIB. Our brother too
Is miffing. O, the gods, the gods preferve

          The

The laſt male pillar of the ancient houſe
Of great Traxalla!

ALM. Liſten!—Hear you not
The fife and golden ringer?

ALIB. Diſmal ſound—
It is the knell of death!

[A Bier born by Traxallans, others follow trailing
their Enſigns.

ALM. Ah, friends! whom bear ye,
With ſuch a pomp of woe?

TRAX. Our prince, ORBELLAN—
Yet warm, and bleeding from the hand of CORTEZ.

ALIB. Unhappy brother!—

ALM. O, the light,
The light of our great father's royal houſe,
Is now extinct for ever!

ALIB. Would to Heaven,
Would I had died for thee, my brother!—I
Had been well ſpared; or, haply, well away
From bonds and foul diſhonour!

ALM. Fatal Mexico!
Ill omen'd race of hoſtile MONTEZUMA!
Father and mother, and both brothers now,
By you have fallen—Hear me, gods and dæmons!
[Kneels.
This MONTEZUMA, blaſt him!—Let him ſtand
On the bleak heath, quite lopp'd of every branch
That now adorns him!—Sudden death engulph
His offspring! that no future name may riſe,

To tell, by whom, our father's high built houfe
Was dafh'd to ruin !   [Rifes and follows the bier.

S C E N E   VIII.

Enter on one fide Montezuma, Odmar, Nobles
    and Guards; on the other fide Cortez in
    Chains, with Melmar, Mexicans, and Trax-
    allans.

Mont. Whence are thofe fhouts ?—Hafte, fol-
        dier, learn the tidings.
What, the redoubted thunderer in the toils ?
He, whofe almighty breath, to our low world,
Can dictate bonds or freedom, life or death,
And change our gods and cuftoms at his pleafure ?
Spaniard, thy power, like lightning from the weft,
Hath fpent a fudden blaze, and now is vanifh'd !
    Cort. Indian, there's not a link in thefe vile
        chains,
But what fhall be a mountain's weight, to whelm
Thee, and thy Mexico !
    Mont. Thy voice ftill founds
As that of thunder—but, we heed it not,
'Tis emptied of its bolt.—Yet, noble Cortez,
We do not yet forget we are thy debtors;
And, as the man we love, thou fhalt command us
Much more than as the god we fear'd.—Speak,
        Cortez;
And, if the terms, thou wouldft enjoin, are fuch

As

As may not sink us to a servile depth,
Below the friendship of the man we honour ;
We ratify thy will.

   CORT. O, 'tis beneath the mighty MONTEZUMA
To chaffer with his slave.

   MONT. Yet, to that slave
We give, with honour, more than we would yield
To ten such iron-harnessed hosts, as those
Which thou hast led against us.

   CORT. Off with thy crown; and prostrate at my
        feet,
Sue thou for peace!—My answer, haply, then,
May not displease.

   MONT. Hence, with him, to the dungeon !—
Ere morn, we may determine of his fate

S C E N E   IX.

GUYOMAR enters in haste.

   GUY. The friend of MONTEZUMA's house in
       bondage ?
Shame, shame eternal!—O, my royal father !
              [Bends his knee.
In haste, permit me to unbind the chains
That hang so heavy on our honours !

   MONT. Hold,
Rash boy !—thou know'st not with what insolence
He spurns our condescensions.

   GUY. O, my father !
He is noble; and great minds are known to rise,

X 3

Propor-

Proportion'd to the weight that preffes them.
Think, how he refcued you, your fons, and
   daughters,
From death, or inftant bondage and pollution—
And me, a fecond time, his recent captive,
The recent object of his grace and bounty!
Perifh all conqueft that difhonour gains,
That infamy muft follow!

 Mont. Well, fet him going—let him do his
   fpight!
We weigh our own reproach above his power,
And that of his licentious band.

S C E N E   X.

As Guyomar unbinds Cortez, Almeria enters.

 Alm. Stay—what are ye about?—He is my
   prifoner.
Bind him, yet fafter!—Know you, Montezuma,
This wretch is warm in my dear brother's blood,
The laft ill-fated fon of great Traxalla?

 Mont. I know, fair princefs, he was late the
   guardian,
Even of Orbellan, and his beauteous fifters,
When fudden ambufh had foredoom'd us all
To fure perdition.

 Alm. O, it is not that
Which makes his merit in the baleful eye
Of Montezuma.
He is the butcher of Almeria's brother,

Of

Of the laſt rival of the line of Mexico—
And thence derives his freedom.

    Guy. No, Almeria!
He is enfranchiſed by the voice of benefits,
That ſpeak as loud as thunder—benefits
Conferr'd on us, on you! He ſtands protected
By every Indian virtue, that takes ſanction
From faith or gratitude!—Your brother found
The fate he look'd for.

    Alm. Hence, audacious boy!
Or fear for thine own ſafety—Thus I offer him
To juſtice, to revenge!   [Draws a dagger.

    Mont. Hold yet, Almeria!—
Why wouldſt thou ſink me underneath a heap
Of foul ingratitude?—Obſerve me, Cortez!
The world ſhan't ſway me to ordain thy death;
And love forbids me to appoint thy freedom.
Odmar, take thou the charge, and hold him ſafe,
Alike from friend and foe, from Guyomar
And from Almeria—Gods, conduct our ways!
And honour light us through this puzzling maze!
        [Exeunt.

END OF THE THIRD ACT.

A C T   IV.

S C E N E   I.

ALMERIA and MELMAR enter.

ALM. YES, MELMAR, I deteſt them both
          alike,
Spaniards and Mexicans—I would to Heaven,
That neither ſide may ſheath the ruthleſs ſword;
That fire and famine may, with mutual death,
Conſume them both, till Mexico and Spain
Lie in one grave together!
    MELM. There ſpoke the godlike and impetuous
          ſpirit
Of your great ſire, Traxalla!—O, my miſtreſs,
That were a golden day!—to ſee you throned
On the high ſeat of your imperial anceſtors,
And the exulting remnant of your ſubjects
Bow'd down before you, pouring forth their thanks
To you and Heaven, for freedom!
    ALM. This ſame CORTEZ—
But that he has embrued his murderous hands
In my dear brother's blood—I would, in ſpight
To MONTEZUMA, and his hated progeny,
Give their great foe enlargement.

MELM.

MELM. O, beware,
Beware of that, my princefs!—CORTEZ is
Much more the friend of MONTEZUMA's houfe,
Than of Traxalla's—He traduces us
As cowards, fugitives, traitors alike
To Spain and Mexico.

    ALM. A poniard thank him!
He lives not to behold another fun,
If wiles, or threats, or golden promifes, ·
Can pafs me through his guards!—Mean fpace,
       good MELMAR,
Thou, and thy true Traxallans, at a diftance,
Watch well the avenues leading from the tower,
Left his young friend, induftrious GUYOMAR,
Should compafs his efcape.   [Exeunt feverally.

SCENE II.

A PRISON.

CORTEZ in Chains. GUYOMAR enters with a
    fheathed fword in his hand.

    GUARD. You pafs not here, my lord.
    GUY. Give me way, friend;
Behold your emperor's fignet!—Where's your
      prifoner?
My friend, my brother!—

        [Runs and embraces CORTEZ.
Thefe hands were made for fcepters, not for bonds—
Quick, let me loofe them!

              CORT.

Cort. Stay thee, Guyomar!
Thou art a fubject, and a fon, young man;
Thou muft not, in a fit of private friendfhip,
Cancel the duty of thofe dearer ties,
That ought to bind thee to thy king and country.
I prize not freedom at fo high a coft,
As the difhonour of my friend!

Guy. O great,
And glorious ever!—Yes, I know it, Cortez,
Well do I know, that, if the gods have doom'd
The final ruin of our ancient empire,
'Tis that right hand, alone, that has the power
To fhake it from its bafe.—But, O, the empire,
Even of the world, were joylefs, if obtain'd
By mean ingratitude—the chains of him,
Who granted life and freedom to his binders!

Cort. No more—thefe manacles and I are
   friends,
Till we can part on terms not quite inglorious.

Guy. Think not that I am come without com-
   miffion:
I bear the royal mandate, even the feal
Of grateful Montezuma, who confents
To the enlargement of the only foe,
Whom he has caufe to fear.

Cort. Then, let him come,
And with his proper hand ftrike off my fhackles.

Guy. My brother, ftand not, thus, upon
   punctilio.
Your precious life's in peril! You have flain
The laft male hope of the imperial houfe
Of fallen Traxalla; and the fierce Almeria

Thirfts

Thirſts for your blood, as gaping fields for rain
In ſummer's fervour. — Haſte — my fears and
        friendſhip
Concur to force you hence !—The night is dark,
And helps to ſkreen you from her darker purpoſe.]
                       [Unbinds him.

   CORT. Beware !—Remember,
I gage for no conditions, while I ſtand
On hoſtile ground.

   GUY. Even as you liſt, ſo be it !
If peace, when next we meet, I'll greet you thus—
                     [Embraces.
If war, I know where CORTEZ may be found—
Even in the front of battle I will face him,
And on his temper'd helmet prove the worth
Of this his late donation ! [Puts his hand on his ſword.

   CORT. When you are fallen,
I think I ſhall not fear another bar,
In my high road to conqueſt !

   GUY. Take your ſword.
Would that I were a tutor, fit to teach
That right arm in its manage !—Hither, ſoldier !
Here is the ſignet of our emperor—.
Conduct his friend, in ſecret, through the gate
That opens on the camp.—Be faithful, thou,
I ſhall not be forgetful !—

   CORT. Fare you well.   [Exit with the Soldier.

A Chief

A Chief of Mexico enters difguifed.

Mex. Where is my prince, where's Guyomar?
Guy. Who afks?—
What, Adramelech, fhrouded in the cloud
Of a flave's habit?—

Mex. Yes.. This hook and cord
Help'd me to fcale our wall, and let me down,
Where I furrender'd to the Spanifh watch,
As a deferter. I was ftraight convey'd
To the proud tent, wherein their captains fate
In midnight council.—Time cuts off my tale.—
I gain'd their confidence—they reft affured
Of fudden conqueft; and, in riot, fpend
The fhort remainder of the night.—Be fpeedy!
If we fucceed, and feize them at their banquet,
Yet, ere another hour fhall pafs, they enter
The northern gate in chains!—

  Guy. O, hero, patriot, Mexico's firft boaft!
                                [Embraces
I have, yet, a band of friends, who will not fail us.—
For glory let us hafte—for country, kindred,
For liberty, for virtue!—   [Exeunt,

SCENE

S C E N E   III.

The STREETS of the CITY.

ALMERIA enters attended, on one fide ; and MEL-
MAR with his Traxallans on the other.

ALM. He is not in the tower—Spread feveral
        ways !
He cannot yet be far—His guard inform'd me
He was this inftant freed, by the command
Of MONTEZUMA, our arch foe—Hafte, friends !
We meet at the fouth angle.   [Exeunt feverally,

S C E N E   IV.

CORTEZ and his Guide enter.

COR'T. Why doft thou fculk, like fome o'er-con-
        fcious felon,
And fhift me, meanly thus, from ftreet to ftreet ?—
Forward—where thou wer't order'd !
    GUIDE. O, my lord,
I doubt we are befet !—at every turn,
I meet the faces of Traxallans ; elfe,
This fignet had affured your fafety.
    CORT. On !—
Thou bear'ft the feal of Mexico—I bear
A fignal to Traxallans.   [Draws.

MELMAR

MELMAR and Traxallans enter.

MELM. He is here.
Surround and make him fure!
    CORT. MELMAR, again?
A fingle ftroke may punifh double treafon!
                                    [Kills him.
. MELM. Curs'd CORTEZ!—Quick perdition
        fwallow thee,
With the two tyrant worlds, of ruthlefs Spain
And Mexico!—   [Dies.

As CORTEZ kills MELMAR, ALMERIA enters with Trax-
    allans, who furround and feize CORTEZ.

    ALM. Secure him—there!—Take up your
        flaughter'd chief—
Shift for yourfelves; and leave him to my venge-
        ance!   [Exeunt Traxallans with MELMAR.
With what audacious dignity he looks,
What fteady confidence!—but I fhall fhake him.
                                    [Afide.
Thou muft die, Spaniard!
    CORT. I have heard no lefs—
They tell me I am mortal.
    ALM. Ay, but Now—
At this tremendous Now!—a fudden death,
Unlook'd for, fearful!—Think, exiftence loft
For ever!—Haply, worfe—to plunge, at once,
Amid ftrange beings, down unbottom'd fteeps,
Or gulph'd by fmould'ring fires!
    CORT. I take my venture.

                                    ALM.

ALM. This in an inftant, then, decides thy
          doom
For all futurity !   [Offers to ftab him.
     CORT. Strike !—
     ALM. Doft thou know,
Wherefore I kill thee ?
     CORT. Yes.   I flew thy brother.
     ALM. Ah cruel !—Why has Heaven, to that
          hard heart,
Granted an afpect not inhuman ?—Tell me,
What had my poor Traxallans done, to bring
The wrath of CORTEZ on them ? Were they not
Thine allies ? thy firft friends ? a haplefs people,
Who claim'd thy promifed refcue from the yoke
Of fell oppreffion ?
     CORT. Therefore I commenced
My war on MONTEZUMA.
     ALM. Therefore, traitor !
Why, then, affift to bring thefe evils on us ?—
Waft thou not told, how that inhuman tyrant
Laid wafte my country ; caus'd my royal parents
With their own hands, to free themfelves from
          bonds,
Ill-fuited to their birth ; in cold blood flew
Traxalla's eldeft hope, my valiant brother ;
And held three helplefs orphans, the remains
Of our loft houfe, as butchers cherifh lambs
Ordain'd to flaughter ?—And does CORTEZ, too,
Does their protector come, to crufh the fallen,
Who cried to him for fuccour ?—O, 'twas cruel !—
It was not foldierly—it was not like
The hero, or the man.—Alas, my brother,

How art thou quench'd, fole light of loft
		Traxallans,
Even by the ruthlefs hand that fhould have
		nourifh'd
And kept thy flame alive!

	CORT. Your dagger, hafte—
It cannot prove fo keen as your reproaches!
I fwear I knew him not—he came upon me,
Like an affaffin, in the night.—But this
Atones not my offence, or your affliction.
Unhappy, injured fair one! by the worth,
That weds a foldier's daring to humanity,
My heart weeps blood in your behalf!

	ALM. I fee it—
That ftarting tear has cancell'd half our quarrel!
Say, what remains?

	CORT. To expiate the reft
By my warm blood—or by fuch deeds of duty,
As call a foldier forth into the world,
To fuccour innocence, to right the wrong'd,
To be the champion of offended beauty,
And war upon oppreffion!

	ALM. Wilt thou, CORTEZ?

	CORT. By the true honour of a chriftian foldier,
If Heaven fucceed my purpofe, I will place
The wrong'd ALMERIA on the golden throne
Of her great anceftors.

	ALM. But wilt thou, CORTEZ,
Inftruct her how to govern?

	CORT. To my power,
She fhall command.

ALM.

ALM. A throne's a lonely feat—
And afks an abler hand than mine, to guide
The reftive reins of empire.
    CORT. Doubly bleft,
Beyond what empire can beftow, is he,
Whom the firft princefs of the world fhall ftile
The prince of her affections !
    ALM. Tell me, Spaniard—
Wouldft thou, indeed, believe him bleft ?,
    CORT. Moft happy,
Above the lot of man !
    ALM. Suppofe his name
Were CORTEZ ?
    CORT. O, you mock your fervant, fure—
He, whom ALMERIA honours with her hand,
Should have a heart to give !
    ALM. Ha, Spaniard!—Sayft thou ?—
Where is that maid, whofe more than mortal charms
            charms
Have triumph'd o'er ALMERIA ?
    CORT. Firft, and faireft !
If love, and truth, and fealty, were, alone,
To wait on the pre-eminence of beauty,
All hearts were, then, ALMERIA's.
    ALM. Yes, I fee it—
'Tis as I have heard—the tyrant's daughter, traitor !
'Tis with the hoftile houfe of MONTEZUMA,
That thou doft feek alliance—therefore fell
My royal brother, to make copious way
For his new rival in CYDERIA's love !
But mark me, CORTEZ—there, thy hopes, ere morning,
            morning,

Shall be for ever blaſted.—By the powers
That India worſhips, never ſhall the eyes
Of that young ſorcereſs open to behold
Another ſun!—

CORT. If that thou doſt but raze
The whiteneſs of her ſkin—I, alſo, ſwear,
Should fortune ever caſt theſe ſhackles from me,
To make a general tomb of thy dominions,
And in it bury all thy father's houſe,
And even the name and memory of Traxallans!—

ALM. Go, mighty leader, execute thy threats,
Upon the remnant of my wretched people!—
ALMERIA breaks thy preſent bonds in ſunder;

[Unbinds him.

And dares thee to the further breach of thoſe
Whereby thine honour binds thee!

CORT. O, ALMERIA!
Bright, royal, generous maid, excuſe the warmth
Of ſudden paſſion—Faireſt of all creatures,
Love is not in our will—but gratitude,
Friendſhip inviolate, and firm attachment,
Are ever thine!—Upon my knee, I bend,
To deprecate thy wrath!—O, ſpare her, ſpare
That innocent!   [Takes her hand.
Should'ſt thou, and for my ſake—I ſwear, AL-
            MERIA,
I'll not ſurvive her!

ALM. That were ſomewhat worſe,
Than the entombing of my father's houſe,
With the whole name and memory of Traxallans!
Well, I will think upon it.—Tell me, then—

Wilt

Wilt thou make trial, wilt thou do thy beſt,
And love me—if thou canſt ?
　CORT. Yes, fair ALMERIA—
Dear to my heart, and next to my CYDERIA,
I plight my duty here !　　　　　[Kiſſes her hand!

SCENE V.

CYDERIA enters.

　CYDER. CORTEZ !—and at the feet of proud
　　　　ALMERIA !—
Traitor, falſe Spaniard !
　CORT. Fly, thou lovely maid !
Haſte from this hoſtile ground—thy life's in
　　　　danger,
Thy precious life !—back to thy father's arms,
From death, and from ALMERIA !—
　CYDER. Yes, I ſee,
My coming was not in the ſeaſon, CORTEZ.
Faithleſs and baſe—apoſtate, as thou art,
To love and honour !—did I not behold thee,
Breathing thy vows upon the plighted hand
Of my triumphant rival ?
　CORT. O, 1 am true—
Truſt me CYDERIA, I do love thee more
Than cowards love their life.—Away, thou dear
　　　　one !
So thou art ſafe, ſuſpicion matters not—
Time will unfold my truth.
　ALM. Can I bear this ?

Y 2

CYDER.

CYDER. Yes, Spaniard, I will leave thee to
          the ties
Of thy new trothment—vowing, from this mo-
          ment,
Never to hear thee, but with ears of hatred ;
Never to fee thee, but with eyes of horror !
Falfeft and moft perfidious of mankind,
Adieu for ever !   [Going.
     CORT. O, my diftracted heart !—Yet ftay,
          CYDERIA !—
Cruel ALMERIA, thou couldft witnefs for me,
My truth, my faith inviolate !
     ALM. Yes, princefs !—
When thou didft fee thy CORTEZ at my feet,
He was a fuppliant for CYDERIA's life.—
Vain was his fuit—as vain as mine for love !
And thus I anfwer to his fcorn—
          [Draws the dagger fuddenly, and rufhes on CYDERIA,
            CORTEZ catches her hand and difarms her.
     CYDER. Ah, fhe will kill me !
     CORT. Hold thee—tyger-hearted,
Bloody ALMERIA !—Fly this fury, love,
Hafte to the fhelter of thy father's arms !
He comes—I can no more—Adieu !— [Exit CORTEZ.
     ALM. Princefs, another day muft end our
          ftrife—
Decifive of no lefs than love and life !   [Exit.

                                   SCENE

S C E N E VI.

To Cyderia enter Montezuma, Odmar, and Alibech, attended by Mexican Nobles and Guards.

Mont. He comes, the glory of our Indian world !—
My son, my Guyomar, my hero comes,
The champion, the deliverer of his country !

Shouts, and found of numerous inftruments. Guyomar enters in triumph, followed by Mexican Officers. To them fucceed the Spanifh Officers and Soldiers in chains. The Mexicans range themfelves on each fide, while the Spaniards are led off. Then enter the Chief Prieft, followed by a train of Priefts and Priefteffes.

Guy. My King, my father !   [Bends his knee.
Mont. O, ·my honour'd child !—
The weight of Heaven, in bleffings, fall upon thee ;
For thou art worthy of its glory !—Alibech !
Here, take thy foldier, recent from his toils—
Beauty, like thine, can beft reward them !—

H. Priest. Begin your song of triumph and
thankſgiving !

S O N G,

By Priests and Priestesses.

I.

Thunder ſleeps—the ſtorm is o'er;
War and terror are no more.
See their horrid hoſts retire—
Fainting worlds again reſpire!
By our conquering hero fell'd,
Spain is ſhackled, force is quell'd!
Peace reviſits India's ſhore—
Thunder ſleeps—the ſtorm is o'er!

C H O R U S.

Peace reviſits, &c.——

II.

Now, through every glen and glade,
In the ſunſhine, in the ſhade,
Vacant Innocence ſhall ſtray,
Fearing neither wile nor way!
Sons ſhall laugh within the ſhed,
By their ſires and grand-ſires ſpread;

Peace

Peace ſhall ſlumber, Toil ſhall ſnore—
Wars and terrors are no more.

CHORUS.

Peace ſhall, &c.

III.

In wedlock, again, loving pairs ſhall be tied,
And children ſhall run by their glad father's ſide;
Long poles ſhall be fix'd, where the minſtrel
  ſhall ſound,
And where holy-day crowds ſhall dance chearly
  around;
Birds ſhall chirp in the groves, and beaſts friſk
  in the plain,
Nor be ſcared by the thunders and lightnings
  of Spain.
Through our clime, Mirth ſhall carol, and
  Laughter ſhall roar;
For war, tumult, terror, and Spain are no more!

CHORUS.

Through our clime, &c.

[Prieſts and Prieſteſſes go off in order, followed by a
proceſſion of Mexicans, laden with the ſpoils of the
Spaniards and Traxallans. As they go off MONTE-
ZUMA ſpeaks.

MONT. Now to the temple lead our grand
  proceſſion,

       Where

Where to the gods, and GUYOMAR, be paid
Our vows for fafety !—then, in lafting bands
Of happy rites, and nuptial fanctitude,
Be Valour join'd to Beauty—Nor thou, ODMAR,
Grudge, to the worth of thy triumphant brother,
This fmall, tho' lovely portion of the world,
Which he hath faved for thee, my eldeft born,
Now thy fure heirfhip!—Sound your inftruments—
Let feftal clarions rouze the flumbering night,
And the long triumph hail the coming light!
                                        [Exeunt.

END OF THE FOURTH ACT.

ACT

A C T V.

S C E N E I.

The DUNGEON of MEXICO.

ODMAR enters.

ODM. THEY, yet, are scarce retired to rest, and ALIBECH
May still be brought, a virgin, to the arms
Of late despairing ODMAR.—Ha! what's this
That checks my faltering steps—and tells my
    soul,
It is not right to loose these dogs of war
Again to slaughter, ravishment, and burnings?—
Why—let my favour'd brother look to that,
The darling, the adopted of mankind
For every blessing!—What's the world to ODMAR,
But a dark inauspicious foe, alike
Detesting and detested?—Hence, compunction!
I will repay the wrong.   [Knocks.
  KEEPER. I ask not who you are—You get no
    entrance.

ODM.

Odm. 'Tis I, 'tis Odmar—on a hafty errand,
Exprefs from Montezuma.—Here's his fignet.
    Keep. Where, my good lord ?—

                                [Opens the door.
    Odm. There, flave—   [Stabs him.
Credentials for eternity !

S C E N E II.

Opens and difcovers the Spaniards chained
to the Floor.

    Odm. Ha, Spaniards, ye lie low indeed !
    Vasq. I think,
The imperial prince of Mexico ?
    Odm. Yes, Vasquez—
I come, the meffenger of inftant fate,
For death or liberty !
    Vasq. Unfold your purpofe.
    Odm. You are the foes of Mexico ; but Mexico
Is not the friend of Odmar.
    Vasq. Can it be ?
    Odm. Yes—my brother, the redoubted Guyo-
        mar,
The boy, whofe nightly treafon caught ye all,
As in one covey—he is, now, the fole
Renown'd of Mexico, the one ordain'd
To love and empire ?—Odmar is an outcaft !—
And, hark !—for you, the victims of his glory,
Even now the bloody priefthood whet their knives,
And deck their morning altars.
            [The Spaniards break out in deep lamentations.
                                Shame

Shame on your daftard groans!—What would
     ye do
For him, who fhould ftrike off your groveling
     chains,
Snatch ye from fudden death, and give ye up
To light and life, to worlds of endlefs gold,
And everlafting glory?

     VASQ. Speak, command—
We execute!—

     ODM. I claim no harfh conditions.
Firft, for the imperial crowns of Mexico
And of Traxalla, they are mine by right
Of heritage and conqueft—thefe ye fwear
To confirm to me.

     ALL. We fwear.

     ODM. Laftly, to fave my aged father's life,
And my young fifter's honour.

     ALL. We fwear!

     ODM. Thefe terms, upon your parts obferved,
     I gage
To freight, and fill your copious veffels up,
With Indian gold and pearl, and gems of price,
Till ye cry, Hold, they fink!

     VASQ. O, bounteous prince!—
All hail to royal ODMAR, mighty emperor
Of the new world!

     SPAN. Mighty emperor of the new world,
All hail!

     ODM. Thanks, valiant friends!—I loofe ye
     now,

                              To

To war, to conqueft—to the wafte of nations,
To the rich fpoil of Mexico.—Away!
        [As he unbinds fome, they help to unbind the reft.
                    [Exeunt.

S C E N E III.

A CHAMBER.

GUYOMAR and ALIBECH.

GUY. And art thou mine, at laft—and mine,
    indeed?
Is the blifs real—does it mount to certainty?
I fwear it is too much, this height of happinefs—
Higher than hope has ever dared to foar!
But, whence, my love, this tremor of thy limbs?
And, from thy cheek, why fhrinks the backward
    rofe
Of fummer's beauty?
  ALIB. Ah, I know not, fweet!—
A fecret dread of fome reverfe at hand—
A doubt that ALIBECH has not been born
To be fo bleft!—While thus I touch, and fee,
And hold, and would believe thee all my own;
Methinks fome fudden arm arrefts thine image,
And leaves me defolate!
  GUY. Away, my angel,
With this cold diffidence—   [Knocking at the door.
Ha, profane wretch!—
Whoe'er thou art, that dares this rude intrufion,
Thy life is forfeit!—

     I   SERV.

Serv. O, it matters not—
Open, my lord, quick—open!

    [Guyomar opens the door.—Attendants enter.

Guy. What's the buftle?

Serv. O, my dear lord, the Spaniard's loofe
    again—
Unfhakled and halloo'd upon the world;
Even by that traitor to his houfe and country,
Unnatural Odmar!

Guy. Hark—what diftant fhouts,
Mingled with horrid groanings!

Serv. From this window
You may behold where Mexico in flames,
Prevents the coming day.—All is blood and up-
    roar,
Rapine and ravifhment!

Guy. Hafte, Azim, gather my few faithful
    followers—
Hafte, my loved Azim!   [Exit Azim.
Bring me my arms!—

    [Attendants bring Helmet, Corfelet, &c. and lay
      his Sword down while he arms himfelf.

This Odmar—give me, but to meet him, gods!
And from his treacherous heart I'll wring that
    blood
Which has undone his race!—

Alib. Ah, Guyomar,
This is a fearful bridal!

Guy. Chear thee, my love!
All, yet, may be recover'd.

SCENE

S C E N E IV.

As Guyomar is juft armed, Odmar and Spanifh
Soldiers rufh in fuddenly, feize, and bind him.

Odm. He's caught, in happy feafon—Bind him
　　　fure,
And fear no other arm!—'Tis well, my friends—
Withdraw a while, and fhare the general plunder;
I have a bufinefs to tranfact in private.

[Exit Spaniards.

Guy. Accurfed Odmar!—O, infernal fire-
　　　brand,
Made to confume thy country!—thou fell dragon,
Born to devour the inaufpicious entrails,
That brought thee to the world!

Odm. Thou prating boy!
I fpare no breath to thy defpifed reproaches—
Come, Alibech, thy private chamber, love—

[Pulling her away.

Alib. Help, help, Heaven!—
Ah, Odmar, would'ft thou violate the wife
Of thine own brother?

Guy. Stay, fiend, and meet my vengeance!—
　　　Wouldft thou live,
Difpatch me, firft, from horrors worfe than hell!
For, after fuch a deed of deep damnation,
One world can never hold us!

Odm. With my firft leifure,
I'll rid thee of thy pains—Come, come along!

SCENE

S C E N E V.

VASQUEZ enters.

VASQ. Hold, ODMAR—Gracious Heaven, 'tis
        she, herself,
The goddefs of my vows!—Ruffian, forbear!
  ODM. How, Spaniard!—is thy tongue apostate,
        then,
To its late language, that, with bended knee,
All hail'd me India's monarch ?—Is not this
The fingle prize, for which I barter'd to thee
King, country, kindred ?
  VASQ. O, fhe is the prize,
Which fingly, in my mind, I held excepted
From all the wealth of thy rich world.
  ODM. Avaunt!—
And dread the fwift-wing'd judgments that de-
        fcend
On perjury and treafon!
  VASQ. Ha! on treafon?
Thou traitor manifold!—to father, friends,
King, country, falfe—to every fenfe, that puts
Its feal on human nature!—and doft thou,
Doft thou appeal to Heaven?
  ODM. If not to Heaven,
I call up hell to vindicate!—No more.
'Tis thus a monarch fhould chaftife rebellion.
  VASQ. Thou haft thy merits!
     [They fight; and while they engage ALIBECH un-
       binds GUYOMAR.—ODMAR falls.

                       ODM.

Odm. Perfidious Spain!—Blood thrifting dogs
  of hell!—
Open, thou gulph, and rid the world, at once,
Of them and me—down—down—for ever—Oh!—
           [Dies.
 Vasq. Now, daughter of the Sun, but brighter
  far,
Than thy all-chearing fire!—thou art my pur-
  chafe.
 Guy. Stay, Vasquez!—thou haft yet a mightier
  arm,
To mate with—and yet, mightier than that arm,
A caufe—I am her hufband.
 Vasq. I diffolve
The union.—This is thy divorce!— [Advancing.
 Guy. Breathe, Spaniard—
I would not take thee at advantage.
 Vasq. Now,
I do begin to fear—for thou art honourable!
In any other caufe, I fhould prefer
Thy friendfhip to thy fword!—Come on!
 Guy. If thou art lefs than thy great leader—
  this,
Alone, may ferve to fell thee [Vasquez falls.
 Vasq. O—thy hand!—
If, as I deem, 'tis that of Guyomar,
I fall with honour!—art thou?
 Guy. Yes.——
 Vasq. Thy pardon!
 Guy. I would to Heaven I could, with equal
  willingnefs,
Give life, and length of days!
           Vasq.

VASQ. O, no, no, no!
That dream is over—of immenſe deſires,
That ſwallow earth and main—of minim man,
Who truſts, within his graſp, to hold a world,
And finds it, nothing—O, farewell!—   [Dies.

GUY. Farewell, brave Spaniard!—Take their
      bodies hence.
                         [Servants carry out the bodies.
My faithful Mexicans approach—Come, love,
                         [Azim and Mexicans appear.
Let me beſtow thee in ſome place of ſafety—
Then fly, to ſhield my father's reverend head;
To ſave the living, or to join the dead!— [Exeunt.

S C E N E   VI.

The Inſide of the PALACE.

A Throne far back. Two Chairs of State brought
                  forward.

ALMERIA enters with a dart in her breaſt, and a
    dagger in her hand, ſupported by her women.
    CYDERIA follows, weeping, brought in by two
    Traxallans.

WOM. Send for phyſicians.
ALM. No, 'tis paſt the power
Of mortal medicine—the envenom'd ſhaft
Has reach'd my vitals; and my laſt of life

Muſt follow its extraction!—There—Oh—
    gently—
Set me down gently—So—
  Wom. Alas, my miſtreſs!
What bloody hand has done this deed?
  Alm. I know not whence it came, from friend
    or foe—
For, as I fled acroſs the palace court,
This random arrow ſtruck me.—Where's my
    victim?
Here—bring her forward—nearer!—
  Cyder. O, Almeria!   [Kneels.
Bright, royal, generous maid, have pity on me—
Pity my youth, my innocence, and weakneſs!
Pity is native to our gentler ſex;
And gentleneſs, with every ſoft perfection,
Shew lovelieſt in Almeria!
  Alm. Peace, thou ſorcereſs!—
Yet cloſer—bring her.—
  Cyder. Ah, if all my blood
Could ſtop the flow of thine—truſt me, Almeria,
I ſhould the readier yield it—What's my treſpaſs?
  Alm. Not one—but two, and both unpar-
    donable—
Thy beauty, and thy blood!—Thou art of the
    race
That robb'd me of my kingdom—thou, thyſelf,
Haſt robb'd me of my love!—And ſhall the houſe
Of Montezuma triumph, and grow ſtrong
Upon the ruins of Traxalla's?—No.
Die, thou—and let the living of thy race,
Learn, in their turn, to weep!— [Lifts the dagger.
                    Cyder.

Cyder. Stay, yet, a moment!—
I have wept for them, Heaven doth know I have;
Night after night, with tears, have mourn'd the
   fate
Of your unhappy royal houfe!
 Alm. But, then,
To live and revel in Almeria's fpoils,
While I am loft, alike, to love and empire—
It muft not be'!
Now, while I yet have ftrength to ftrike!—Nay,
   fhrink not—
Wherever dark futurity ordains,
We go together.!
 Cyder. O, the gods, he comes!—
He's here—and fhall I perifh in his fight?
Sink in the harbour—and without a ftruggle
For life—for love?

  [As Almeria attempts to ftrike, Cyderia rifes,
   catches at her arm, and, in the ftruggle, wrefts
   the dagger from her, and throws it away.

Alm. Alas—I am too faint!

SCENE VI.

Cortez enters attended.

The two Traxallans turn and fly.

Cort. My angel, my Cyderia!—
     [Runs and embraces.
 Cyder. Hold me, faft!
Say—do I live, do I yet breathe?

       Cort.

Cort. Yes, dearest!
I have thee, once again; nor shall the world
E'er part us more—Ha! what is here?—Almeria,
All pale and bleeding!

Alm. Yes, triumphant Spaniard!
Thou hast thy wish—and, thus, I pour my blood,
[Draws the arrow.
The last of an unhappy life,
To fate and Cortez!—

Cort. Ah, support—She's going!—
I wish thy death, Almeria?—Heaven is witness,
To save thy life, how gladly, grateful Cortez
Would risque his own!

Alm. Thine arm!—Cyderia's too!—
Fear not, I am past the power to hurt—Sweet
        maid,
Thou art safe—thank Heaven!—thy pity, and
        thy pardon!
I ask it with my dying breath!—Ah, Cortez,
Thou art with death familiar—dost thou know,
What 'tis to draw the blood—to drain the breath—
To shut out light, and dwell in chapless vaults,
Sister'd with night and everlasting silence?—
O fearful—not to be!—More fearful, yet—
To live to wretchedness—perhaps, for ever!—
I go—to try—if we may meet—again—
I shall be fraught with tidings—strange to—Oh—
[Dies.
Cort. She is at peace—Turn thee from death,
        Cyderia!
[Beckons to the Attendants who carry out Almeria.
Where is the King, my love, where is thy father?

Cyder.

Cyder. Alas, I know not.

Cort. Alvarez hafte—thou haft a human
heart!
Reftrain the fury of our favage countrymen,
Who range, like tygers, loofed from bonds; un-
fparing
Of fex, or infancy, or helplefs age—
Hafte, good Alvarez!   [Exit Alvarez.
Retire, Cyderia!—Ah, here comes a fight,
To make thee think, that blindnefs were a bleffing!

S C E N E   VII.

Enter Montezuma fupported behind by two
Mexicans, and by Guyomar and Alibech on
either hand.

Mont. O, my kind children!—'tis too much—
this goodnefs—
I fhall opprefs you with my weight—Alas!—
My limbs—all rent from their enfeebled burden—
Refufe to bear its bulk—There—feat me down—
Never to rife!—How bleft the dead—if death—
Is free from pangs, like thefe!—

Cyder. Alas, my father!

Cort. Doubly accurfed be the hands that did
This horrid deed!
            [Cyderia and Cortez kneel to Montezuma.
Mont. Away—nor blaft my fight
With the detefted afpect of a Spaniard!
                        [Cortez rifes.

Guy. O, Cortez, blame him not—there's
    caufe, there's caufe,
For hatred, never to be reconciled,
'Twixt Spain and Mexico!—I found him hemm'd,
Bound, and infulted, by a band of ruffians ;
His aged limbs, all ftrain'd upon the rack
Until they crack'd the cordage!

Cort. By the power
Whom the world ought to worfhip, they furvive
No longer, than my vengeful arm fhall reach
To hurl them to the fiends!—

Guy. Their doom is feal'd.
Pizzarro, as I think, they call'd their chief—
With the one ftroke of this thine honeft fword,
I gave his head to leap, three javelins length,
From off his fhoulders!

Mont. Do me juftice, boy!—
Say, did I, meanly, fue to them for mercy?
Did I degrade the majefty of kings—
Or bend, in vile compliance, to the terms
They wanted to extort?

Guy. O, no, my father!—
You bore yourfelf above mortality ;
And your fell torturers raged to find themfelves
Defeated of your groans!

Mont. O, my dear children!
Nature felt inward, ftill—and is the fame,
When circled by a crown, as in the cottage.—
O—they return—my pains—fure harbingers
Of final diffolution!—Now, again—
Now they extend me on the rack!—they ftretch
The leaping arteries, and the quivering members!—

I   Cort.

CORT. Support him—help!—his pangs are
     ſtrong upon him.
   [CORTEZ and GUYOMAR ſupport him, while CYDE-
    RIA and ALIBECH kneel weeping on either hand,

CYDER. O, my loſt father!

GUY. O, the falling pillar,
Of our now deſolated world!

MONT. My children—
Bear with me!—O—fain, fain would I ſupport—
As a king ought—theſe throes—this horrid
    cracking
Of the heart's cordage!—Nature ſinks beneath
The ruins of her pile.—O, for a ſoul
Of independence on this rending frame
Of mortal ſtructure!—'Twill not be—exiſtence—
Cannot bear up againſt the tumbling craſh—
Of its own being!—Oh—I am eaſier now—
What a ſweet Heaven this relaxation brings
From tortures inexpreſſible!—'Tis paſt—
The ſtorm of nature's laid—and all—to come—
Is calm—is quiet.—   [Dies.

ALIB. O, he is dead!

CYDER. He's gone—he's gone—for ever!
And I, moſt wretched, left to wear the night
With endleſs tears, and riſe, each cheerleſs morn,
A deſolated orphan!—

GUY. Down with thy towers, thou once exalted
    Mexico!
Crumble thy ſpires and palaces to duſt!
Never be muſic, or the voice of joy,
Heard in thee!—Through the waſte of thine high
    ways

Z 4

May

May all who meet, behold in either face
The feal of wretchednefs; and every ear
Hear founds of forrow, and the clank of bon-
    dage!
Fly, ye furviving innocents! to climes
Far diftant from invafion—leave your manfions,
Your once endearing homes, to the poffeffion
Of bats and birds of night, of Spanifh vultures,
And beafts of depredation!
    CORT. Thy wrongs are great, my friend, thy
    forrows juft—
I feel and fhare them all! Yet, cruelty
Is not the growth of Spain alone—Mexico,
Even thy own Mexico, produces ODMARS.
Chear you, my GUYOMAR!—chear, my CYDE-
    RIA!—
Youth muft fucceed to age, and life to death;
'Tis nature's procefs—Come, afcend the throne
Of your great anceftors, and rule a people
Bleft by your worth, and guarded by your valour!
    GUY. No, CORTEZ, generous chief, thou fole
    exception
To an inhuman race of men!—do thou
And thy CYDERIA grace the throne—I lift not
To rule o'er wretchednefs; nor to be verfed
In fciences that teach us to deftroy,
And arts that ferve to vitiate and corrupt
The honefty of nature.—Far from hence
I, with my willing exiles, will retire;
While my loved ALIBECH fhall light our way,
And blefs our fteps with beauty—there, nor
    gems,

                                    Nor

Nor gold, nor filver, fhall excite the luft
Of fell invafion; nor infatiate Spain
E'er come, in fearch of poverty!—Know, CORTEZ,
Where wants are few, a little will fuffice
To furnifh nature; and a light content
Shall make it luxury!—The fearlefs fports
Of focial Innocence fhall chear our heaths—
Beauty and Love fhall crown each peaceful night,
And morning wake to Liberty and Light!